The Present Conspires
Charlie's Promise Part 2
Book 5 of West's Ghost Ranch Series

A Novel by **Aidan Red**

To a great IP whose passion gave me the love of aviation and whose knowledge and patience taught me the skills necessary to fly and survive in an airplane. Thanks dad.

My many thanks to my editors.

Content Editing by Trenda London,
http://ItsYourStoryContentEditing.com

Copy Editing by Amy Jackson,
Copy Editing and Proof Reading, http://AmyJacksonEditing.com

Cover by
Aidan Red

.

The Present Conspires

With West shot by one of the South African Agents, and in the hospital, and the search for Howard intensifying, Charlie realized she had to be stronger than she had ever needed to be. She had to think of West and the ranch and those that lived there first, and trust the authorities would find Howard before he could do more harm.

Her fear was that Howard had always been extremely resourceful, deviously treacherous and darkly fiendish beyond any normal expectations. And now he was still lose and again hunting for her.

Chapters

Prologue
Saturday, September 30

Cecil Brown about jumped out of his skin when the man tapped on the driver side window. He turned to see the man leaning down and motioning for him to lower the window to talk. He could only think that a neighbor had seen him and come to inquire, but when the other man tapped on the passenger side window, sheer panic took over. He shifted the car into Drive and stomped on the accelerator. The car spun around the corner and raced for the next turn. In a matter of seconds, his heart pounding so hard it threatened to burst out of his chest, he turned onto Power Road and left the neighborhood.

At the corner of Ten Mile Road and Orchard Lake Road, he swung into the Shell station on the northeast corner and parked in front of the convenience shop. He forced himself to calm down, telling himself that no one had followed him. Then, after a number of deep breaths, he got out of the rental car, entered the store, and purchased a cup of their strongest coffee, black.

Back in the car, he decided that if Claude was crazy enough to break cover and go to the Williamsons' house to ask about Howard Collingsworth, then Claude would have to call him and ask him to come and get him. He was not going to go back into the neighborhood and wait like they had planned—not after being scared out of his wits by those two men.

Besides, it wouldn't take Claude very long since he was just going to ask a couple of questions. Claude was confident that no one would remember him from the hotel in Reno, since neither of the women nor their husbands had actually met them or had

1

reason to think they were being watched.

Cecil slowly calmed himself down and looked at his watch. It was just after nine, or just after five tomorrow morning in Pretoria. Three more hours before they could call deVon and tell him what little they knew about Howard's whereabouts. In the meantime, he would just have to wait and hope the two men that tapped on his car windows were gone when Claude called.

Tensely listening to the sounds of the night—a coyote somewhere across the mesa, the soft wind against the scrub trees and brush along the fingers of the ravines, the flutter of spooked birds—Mel urged her horse on until she finally saw the big trees, low-hung shadows to the left of the setting sun's brilliant orange disc.

She had been surprised when Robert, Mr. Ventura, had told her that she was the one that needed to go for help, even though she knew it had to be either her or Mike, her year-younger brother. She had just climbed up to a field of smallish boulders when he had turned to warn her to be careful and instead had tumbled head-first down the slope toward her. When he fell into the boulders and caught his leg, she nearly panicked, instantly afraid, concerned that they were alone, miles from the main house and the hangars; his yell when he stopped falling told her he was hurt and she quickly realized he was caught, his leg pinned in the wedge-shaped crevice between two large rocks halfway down the steep wall of the canyon.

She had felt sick to her stomach, suddenly feeling disoriented, but when Robert had lied, trying to tell her he was all right, something changed and she knew she could not succeed if she thought of herself as an almost-twelve-year-old.

She had to figure out how to get him free from the rocks.

As the sun slipped behind thin clouds, silhouetting the southern Rockies, she mistook them at first for another wide stand of junipers or piñons. But getting closer, she realized they were the tops of trees down in the *arroyo*, beyond the lip and not up on the grassy *llanura* like she had expected. Abruptly giddy, she kicked her horse into a gallop for the last half mile.

Robert had made sure she understood that finding the big trees meant saving nearly an hour and a half on her journey. He had marked her map and sent her up onto the rim of two-mile canyon to try to call Helen for help, but when she did not answer her phone and his phone died, Mel reluctantly followed his instructions and waved. Her brother Mike was only ten, but she knew he also felt the necessity and would take care of Robert as she started her race with sundown. She knew she had to find the big trees before the sun disappeared behind the distant mountains and the day's light succumbed to the coming darkness.

Reaching the lip beside the four big trees, she slowed to a walk to survey the typical dual parallel traces worn in the grass by jeeps and trucks. She exhaled and sighed with relief, kneeing her mount forward, down into the darkening gloom between the larger trees in the short forest of scrub brush, creosote, and juniper trees that filled the wash across the narrows and up onto the far lip. The sun was down, and in the deepening half-light she followed the trace the half mile through the main arm of the last finger. The road rose up to the *halgai* beyond—she smiled in surprise at thinking of the prairie in Navajo. Dani had taught her many words and phrases, but she did not expect them to just pop into her head by themselves. When she reached the lip, she stared in amazement: the headlights of three vehicles were coming toward her, coming fast enough to throw a dusty haze into the air behind them. Suddenly, she could not stop laughing, wondering if Robert had some other way to tell them they needed help.

Fumbling to get the bright flashlight out of her saddlebag, she finally caught it. Once in hand, she quickly shone the beam at the advancing lights, and in minutes Robert's familiar blue pickup truck stopped beside her. Dani opened the door and stood up on the doorsill.

"I'm so glad to see you!" Mel shouted. "So very glad."

"What happened?" Dani asked. "Is Mike all right?"

"Mike's fine," Mel said, forcing herself to calm her feelings and control her voice. She straightened her shoulders. "It's your dad. He fell down a rocky slope. I think he has a broken leg and a couple of broken ribs. Can't ride a horse."

"Okay, Mel. We saw where you were on Helen's map, but you lead. We'll stay with you and try to not run your horse too ragged. He still has to make it back to the barn after all of this."

"*Vámonos,*" Mel agreed, gesturing toward the trail, and reined her horse around to start back the way she had come.

When Mel stopped on the western lip of two-mile canyon, she suddenly felt giddy, seeing the light of a campfire below and a little south of straight across the gorge. Dani quickly got out of the truck and stopped beside her.

"Mike made a campfire," Mel blurted out loud, happy to see they were there and seemed to be okay. Then she pointed her flashlight at the wide trail that dropped off the lip of the mesa and quickly turned to the south. "It's wide enough for the truck and jeeps, but it's a bit rutted and bumpy. It has one sharp switchback near the bottom." She looked to the south, waving with her hand. "We have to go this way."

"Lead off, Mel," Dani said, and patted her leg as she turned back to her dad's truck. "We'll be right behind you."

Fifty

"Look there, Mike," Robert said with a chuckle that turned to a cough. He pointed to the dark western slope. "Your sister brought the whole *diné*."

Mike smiled when he turned and saw the small light switching around, flashing on different things as it led three sets of headlights down the cattle trail. "She sure did." He looked at his watch. "She got back quick."

"We'll find out how she did it in a few minutes," Robert encouraged as he stretched and tried to straighten up.

Mike quickly helped him scoot back against the boulder so he could sit more upright. Then Mike took the Winchester from where he had been sitting, and slid it back into the scabbard on his horse. "Don't need that now," he whispered happily to himself, thinking he would have to remember to tell Mel how he scared the small squadron of *javelinas* away.

It took Mel and her entourage more than a half an hour from the time Robert saw them until they reached Mike's impromptu campsite at the edge of the wash. When Dani stopped the truck, the three of them were quickly out and huddled around Robert.

"How are you doing?" Helen asked soberly as she started checking his scrapes and cuts.

"Better than I should expect," he retorted, smiling at Dani and Eddie's graven faces. "Mel cleaned me up and put gauze and ointment on my cuts before I sent her to get help. Mike wrapped a splint around my shin and watched for *maicohs* and chased

5

some hungry *javelinas* away while we waited."

"Looks like they did a good job taking care of you," Helen snipped, shaking her head. "Did you fall from up there?" She gestured to the rim above them.

"Only halfway." He looked at her with his twisted smile. "Mike made a crutch and I walked and slid the rest."

"Should've let the younguns do the climbing," she added as she started looking at the splint.

Mel watched until Helen and Robert started bantering and then, knowing he was going to be all right, she turned back to the others spilling out of the jeeps. She smiled at who all had come.

"June," she called softly. "Did anyone bring any oats?"

"Sure did," June answered, and grabbed a galvanized pail from the back of the jeep.

"And I have water," Ratchet added as he hefted the five-gallon jug out. In his other hand he carried three feed bags.

"The other two would probably like a treat," Mel began, and absently pointed to Mike and Robert's horses as she took a feed bag from Ratchet.

Without saying anything, Ratchet scooped some oats out of June's pail and poured them into Mel's feed bag. She nodded thanks and quickly turned to her horse, holding the bag for him. She knew he was tired, running and trotting more than he was used to. After he had eaten most of the oats, Mel found a small water bucket in the jeep and proceeded to water him, absently noticing that Mike was also watering his and Robert's horses.

Lost in thought, she was startled when Dani patted her shoulder. She realized it was completely dark except for the starry canopy above them.

"Ratchet organized the men and they have Dad loaded in his truck. Helen and Mom will ride in the bed with him and

Eddie will drive. And, we have the campfire doused and are ready to go," she explained with a wide smile. "We left in such a hurry, we didn't think to bring a horse trailer, so I'm going to ride back with you and Mike on Dad's horse, just to keep you company."

"Okay," Mel agreed, and glanced around to see everyone waiting. She started to ask what they were waiting for when Ratchet stepped up and took the water pail and the feed bag from her.

"You three take your time getting back. June and I'll follow you in our jeep while the others get Robert back to the house as quickly as they can," he added softly. "Please take the lead, Mel. Take us home."

Ratchet turned and walked back to June and the jeep as Bump climbed in over the rear bumper and settled crosswise in the back.

"Let's go," Dani urged, and patted Mike on the back as they turned to their horses.

Mel quickly mounted and directed her flashlight back down the wash. She kneed her horse into a fast walk and led the procession to the trail up out of the canyon. Dani and Mike fell in behind her, followed by Ratchet, the pickup truck, and the second jeep. She knew that something was different by the way everyone was acting, but she could not tell what had changed.

"Mom? Darn it, where are you?" Charlie asked herself, shaking her phone as she paced the corridor beside the Bradmont Hospital's surgical waiting room.

Cat had called 911 once they had assessed their situation—one dead and West was unconscious but breathing. The local Farmington Police had arrived with the ambulance, and while the EMTs loaded West for transport to the hospital, they had called for a second to tend to the body. Leaving Lloyd and Matt to answer the police's questions, Charlie had insisted on riding in the ambulance with West. Cat and Monte followed as quickly as they could secure the house and get away. But Charlie was doubly worried, knowing there had been two men in Reno and they had figured the second man probably also knew that both she and Cat were in Farmington.

Well, she thought, shaking her head, *there's only one left to bother us. Until, of course, new ones arrive.*

"Come and sit down," Cat said softly as she caught Charlie's arm. "You can call from a chair just as easy as you can while you're pacing."

Reluctantly, Charlie followed Cat to a chair and Cat sat down between her and Monte. Charlie tried to call again.

"I can't figure out why she isn't answering. It's what, ten forty-five back home?" Charlie asked absently, glancing at Cat's worried expression. "It's not really early for them, but it isn't all that late. What's going on? Why doesn't Mom have her phone with her?"

"I'm sure it's nothing," Monte added, trying to soothe the strong anxiety that Charlie was exuding. "Are they still hammering on the dining room?"

They both shook their heads. "They were painting yesterday," Cat explained.

Charlie withdrew into her thoughts, staring at her phone, knowing she would have to wait for Helen to see her missed call notifications.

An hour later, the surgeon stopped in front of her and Cat nudged her to get her attention. Charlie quickly stood and asked the obvious question, "How is he?"

"Mrs. Montgomery?"

Charlie nodded and squeezed her phone. Cat stopped beside her, caught her arm and held it tight.

"He's doing well, all considered. The bullet that hit him in his chest punctured his right lung and took a piece out of a rib. The bullet went through and we had to search a little to find

8

the rib fragment. Thankfully, we were able to find and remove the fragment without having to search too far, but it made two other punctures and damaged some of the veins in the lung. We removed the fragment and were able to rebuild the rib using a growth-stimulating fabric to bridge the gap. We closed the wounds in his lung and the external wounds with internal sutures. His chest is wrapped to help the rib heal."

Charlie nodded, thinking she understood enough so she could tell the others, or West, when he asked. "That sounds like a lot of damage in his lung."

"We will have to watch his progress over the next couple of days. He will most likely have some trouble breathing until his lung can heal, but once we have him up and walking, any fluid collection should clear up quickly." He waited as Charlie absorbed his explanation, then continued.

"His right femur was broken by the second bullet, but it missed the critical blood vessels and artery. That should heal normally with minor nerve damage, and he'll be in a cast for twelve weeks—"

"Twelve weeks?" Charlie's concern shifted from West's survival to how they would handle his recovery. "Shit, he'll be an absolute bear by then."

The doctor chuckled. "No weight bearing on that leg until the cast is removed." He consulted his notes and continued. "I see you're not from here, so you'll have to have your family doctor remove the cast when it's time."

"That'll be Mom. His mom, actually. She's our resident registered nurse and substitute doctor on the ranch."

"I see." The surgeon smiled. "Nice to have competent care close by. I think that is all I have, unless you have questions."

"I know this is too soon to ask, but how soon will he be able to travel?" Charlie inquired.

"I know you're anxious, but I will review his status on Tuesday. Then, depending on how he's doing and feeling, I may be able to release him from the hospital, but I will need to see him a week after that before I will know if he can travel any significant distance."

Charlie took a deep breath. "Okay." She looked up at the surgeon and then at Monte. "I'll have a plane come and pick him up when he can travel."

"A plane?" the surgeon asked before he thought.

"Yes," Charlie replied matter-of-factly. "We flew in yesterday and we have two planes here now, but only one pilot." She glanced at Cat and smiled sheepishly. "Well, one pilot and one in training." She looked back at the surgeon. "Monte's going to have his hands full with getting them ready to move, so I'll have someone come out to fly our second plane home, and when I leave I'll have someone stay here at the hospital with him."

"I assure you our staff is completely able—"

"I'm not questioning that, but I will have someone with him twenty-four seven until he's back home." Her tone was emphatic, though she tried to not be confrontational.

The surgeon squared his shoulders and smiled. "Yes, ma'am. If that's what you want, we will be sure they are comfortable as well."

"Thank you," Charlie added in a softer voice. "He's my whole life and he's going to get the best care you or I can give him."

The surgeon smiled again. "If you don't mind me asking, how did he get shot?"

"We were confronted by a gunman and he jumped in front of me, taking the hits to protect me and Felix—I mean Cat," Charlie answered vaguely in a soft voice, carefully evading the details of the deeper story and holding back her sudden urge to cry. "A private investigator friend of ours, he was with us when it happened, shot the gunman before he could shoot anyone else."

"I'm so very glad you two were as lucky as you were. We will do everything we can to make his recovery as fast as possible."

"Thank you," Charlie said again, and the surgeon shook her hand.

"He should be out of recovery in about an hour. The nurse will give you his room number a little before then and you can wait for him there."

Then, with a nod, he slowly turned and walked back to the operating rooms.

Sunday, October 1

After midnight

Charlie, Cat, and Monte arrived in West's private room and met the nurse filling out the whiteboard.

"Good morning," the nurse greeted, and did a double-take when Cat and Charlie entered side by side. "I'm...I'm Nurse Dean."

"Morning," Charlie greeted, catching the nurse's lightly veiled surprise. "I'll wait and see how good it is after they bring West in."

The nurse looked back at the board where she had printed "G. W. Montgomery" in the patient's name space. "West?"

"It's a nickname," Charlie admitted. "He's known as Glen West, and everyone that knows him simply calls him West."

"Aaah," Nurse Dean muttered as she changed the information on the board. "We'll just change this to West then." She glanced over her shoulder. "You must be his wife."

"I am. I'm Charlie, and these are our good friends Cathy and Monte."

"Good friends? Not sisters?" Nurse Dean extended her hand to Cat and then to Monte, still staring at her. "I swear, if you two had the same hair color..."

"No. Just good friends," Cat replied, and flicked her eyes sideways at Charlie.

"Well, nice to meet you, and you also, Charlie," Nurse Dean added. "I'll be his night nurse, nine to nine, and Nurse Greene will be his primary day nurse. I think you'll like her."

"Thanks," Charlie replied with a worried, tight smile.

"If you need anything, I'm just down at the nurses' station." Nurse Dean nodded and turned to the corridor and left.

Cat caught Monte's arm, whispered something to him, and scurried from the room.

"What's going on?" Charlie asked, suddenly feeling more alone with Cat's departure. Then she realized she had seen Cat abruptly leave them before, usually at breakfast.

Monte's expression melted into a gentle smile. "Just a little morning sickness. It really isn't bad this time around—not like it was with Mel. But after last night, her nerves are wound up more than usual."

"Will she be okay?"

"Yes, she will. She's actually doing a great job of keeping her emotions under control. It isn't easy and I feel pretty helpless, but she's doing really great."

"I'm glad."

Charlie was torn between watching the door for Cat's return and glancing at West's empty bed, feeling like her nerves could not take much more. When Cat returned, she blurted, "You okay?"

Cat smiled a tight smile and Charlie wondered if it was something wrong with the baby or just because of West's situation. Cat caught her hands and nodded. "The baby's fine. It's just an inconvenience I have to endure for a few weeks. Any word on West?"

Charlie shook her head and began pacing the room while Cat and Monte settled in the two straight-backed chairs.

When Charlie turned around at the door to start her third circuit across the room, her phone chimed.

She noted the ID and then put the phone to her ear. "Hey

Mom," she answered. "Thanks for calling back."

"Sorry, I didn't have my phone with me," Helen apologized. "Everything happened so fast, I just forgot to pick it up."

"What happened?" Charlie asked, suddenly anxious all over again.

Without thinking, Helen dove into the telling of Robert's plight and how the children had taken control of the situation. She praised them both for their maturity and explained how they had seen Mel's tracking button on the big screen and known something was wrong. Then she remembered that she was returning Charlie's call.

"I'm sorry, dear, but you tried to reach me—seven times, I think. I shouldn't be taking up your time talking about us. What's happened?"

Charlie dropped heavily into the overstuffed chair near the room's one window.

"I don't know how to make this easy, but West was shot tonight—last night," she gushed bluntly, and then recounted what had happened.

"The men from Reno?" Helen asked. "And West is okay?"

"We haven't seen him yet, but the surgeon spoke with us," Charlie replied. "He says they were able to fix everything, but he will have a recuperation period and there is a worry about possible complications. His leg will be in a cast for three months before he can put any weight on it, and he'll have to do breathing exercises. I'll get more details before we leave to come home."

"Leave? Stay as long as you need to."

"I really, really want to stay, but it isn't safe here for Cat or me, especially since those men found us so quickly. Someone needs to be here twenty-four seven to be sure West is taken care of. Like I said, Monte's private investigator friend shot the man that came to the house, but he told us the other one fled the neighborhood in their car before Lloyd got there. So there is still the other one, and he's probably looking for us now.

"So, what I need is another pilot to fly *Hell Raiser* back with us. Have Ratchet or Lenny come in the T206 and bring someone to fly *Hell Raiser*, then they could stay with Monte and bring West home as soon as the doctor releases him, probably in a week. He may be released from the hospital on Tuesday—or later depending on how he's doing—then he'll have a follow-up appointment, most likely a week later."

"Okay, dear. I'll talk to Ratchet and see what he wants to do." Helen sighed and it was a moment before she continued. "You're sure he's going to be all right?"

"As much as the doctor can say. Are you okay, Mom?"

"I'll be fine, dear. It's just so much to take in all at once. I'm glad you're there with him. It's a comfort to know that."

"Thanks, Mom. And it's good to hear your voice. Let me know who and when our reinforcements are coming."

"I will. Try to get some rest yourself and not worry too much."

"Thanks. I'll call when I know more."

With a deep sigh, Charlie suddenly felt their distance from home when the phone connection broke. She studied the room and smiled at Cat and Monte, thinking of a happier subject. "It seems your kids are celebrities. Mom told me that they had some excitement too last night."

"What about Mike and Mel? What have they done now?"

Charlie's smile widened and she retold them what Helen had told her. "I guess after Robert fell and got pinned in the rocks, Mel figured out how to get him unpinned, with Mike's help, using the horses and ropes. Then Robert sent her for help and Mike stood guard in case the wolves or other critters came looking for them. Mike even built a fire to keep Robert comfortable and even had to scare a bunch of *javelinas* away."

"And Mel went for help? Where were they?" Monte asked.

"Helen said two-mile canyon, which is on the eastern fence line," Charlie explained. "I'd have to look at a map, but I guess it was almost sundown when she left on horseback to go back to the hangars or the main house. She had to ride across the eastern mesa on the north side of the big wash, nearly seven miles to the hangars. Mom said they saw her on the tracking map when they hadn't gotten back for dinner. Seeing that she was alone and had left Mike and Robert in the canyon, Mom knew there was trouble, so Dani rounded up the militia, and everyone dropped everything and went to meet Mel.

"They just got back and got Robert situated in his bed. Mom says Mike did a good job fixing a splint and Mel had tended his cuts before she left to get help."

"His splint?"

"When Robert tumbled down the rocky canyon wall, the fall broke his leg and a couple of ribs. He told Mom that he watched Mel turn into a serious young woman when she knew he was hurt. Mike stopped their normal chiding and bantering and worked with Mel, following her suggestions without hesitation. He's very proud of your two children."

"Wow," Monte responded happily. "They really have changed."

"Probably not as much as you think," Charlie encouraged. "They were taught well, and it shows. Especially when their knowing was needed."

"Thanks, Charlie." Cat smiled and squeezed Monte's arm.

"Now, if they'd just bring West out," Charlie added softly, her worried tone returning.

Another hour had passed and Charlie was beyond concerned. She couldn't sit still and paced back and forth across the room. For the umpteenth time in ten minutes, she stepped into the corridor and looked for signs of Glen.

"I gotta find out what's taking so long," Charlie finally said, and turned for the door. "Something's not right."

"We're coming too." Cat was on her feet, pulling Monte behind her as she hurried to catch up with Charlie.

"I'm sorry, Charlie," Nurse Dean was saying when Cat and Monte stopped behind Charlie. "Sometimes it takes longer for a patient to wake up and get their bearings. The status says he's doing fine. It's just taking a little longer than normal."

"I want to see him," Charlie explained.

"I know," the nurse agreed, "but you'll have to wait until he's out of recovery and they bring him to his room."

"Why? He's my husband! I want to see him! I want to know he's all right!"

Cat quickly moved closer and hugged Charlie. "Charlie, stop. They know what they're doing. He's going to be all right."

"How? How do I know that, Cat?" Charlie was almost in tears as Cat pulled her away from the desk. "I have to know. It's taking too long."

"I'll have someone come and talk to you," Nurse Dean added, and picked up the phone.

"Thank you," Cat said to the nurse. "Come on, Charlie." Cat slowly turned Charlie back toward the room. "They'll bring him out as soon as they can."

Charlie let Cat lead her to the overstuffed chair by the window. She sat down to wait, but Cat had to keep reminding her to stay and relax. Charlie was not being cooperative.

After another fifteen minutes, a medium-height, slender man in scrubs stepped into the room. "Mrs. Montgomery?"

Charlie was up instantly, with Cat right behind her. "Yes. I'm Charlie," she offered in soft anticipation.

The man smiled and shook her hand and then hesitated, staring at Cat.

"What can you tell me? How is he?" Charlie continued, barely noticing the man's distraction.

"He's doing fine," the man admitted. "I'm his anesthesiologist. Like some patients, your husband took longer to come out from under the anesthetics than most. It isn't unusual for some patients to take somewhere between two to three hours to regain consciousness and to be able to recognize their surroundings and to remember things in their lives. I

understand your husband was shot without much warning"—
Charlie and Cat both nodded—"and that is probably why it took
longer for him to remember."

"He's going to be all right?"

"Everything indicates now that will be the case. His surgeon
will give you the details on what he will need for a full recovery,
but for now I can say he's doing fine under the circumstances."
He paused, then continued. "Do you have any questions?"

"Lots."

He waited another moment, but when Charlie did not
ask any, he continued. "It'll only take another twenty to thirty
minutes and we'll bring him out. He'll be groggy and not very
conversant most of the day. He'll sleep a lot, but should be pretty
well back to normal attentiveness by evening."

"Thank you," Charlie said softly.

"You're welcome, Mrs. Montgomery. I'm sorry no one
informed you sooner."

He nodded to Cat, Monte, and to Charlie, then turned and
quietly strode back up the corridor, toward the recovery rooms.

It was a half an hour later when Charlie looked up from
her conversation with Cat, hearing the sounds of people in the
corridor seconds before two orderlies guided a gurney into the
room.

She pushed her chair back into a corner to make room. Cat
and Monte stood and moved their chairs out of the way as the
orderlies parked the gurney beside the bed. Then one of the
orderlies asked them to wait in the hall while they settled West,
and Charlie followed Cat and Monte out.

Charlie paced back and forth in front of the nearly closed
door, listening to the soft murmurs of the orderlies as they
moved West from the gurney to the bed. She fidgeted, wringing
her hands even though he was out of recovery and now just
a few feet away. She inhaled and held her breath for a long
moment before releasing it; she had almost lost her composure
when she had gone to the nurses' station to confront Nurse

Dean. But thankfully Cat had stopped her, and she had forced herself to not explode and rant at the woman.

She knew without looking that Cat was watching her now, and releasing her deep breath, she again forced herself to patience.

Abruptly, the orderlies stepped out and told them they could go back in. Charlie grabbed a straight-backed chair, immediately pulled it up to the far side of West's bed, and sat down. She took his hand and gently began to rub his palm, barely noticing that Monte had settled in one chair on the other side of his bed and Cat in the overstuffed chair at the foot.

"West? Can you hear me?" Charlie whispered, then asked again a little louder.

Slowly he rolled his head toward her voice. His eyelids twitched and his eyes opened. He smiled. Then, softly, he asked, "Are...you okay?"

She stared at him and squeezed his hand. "Shit, West! You scared me out of my mind, and you ask how I am? What were you thinking? We're both okay, but you shouldn't have done that."

"Had...to." He smiled again, still focused on Charlie's face, holding her eyes. "I...couldn't let him...hurt you."

Helen had made her rounds to check on Robert early, setting his leg and securing it with a suitable cast. She had wrapped his rib cage and decided she would call their "family" doctor after breakfast. She was surprised at the number in the dining room when she entered, expecting to be more alone than she was.

"Good morning. Why aren't you all sleeping in?"

"We have things to do," Ratchet answered, and smiled as he helped June sit down.

Eddie quickly took her place, followed by Mel and Mike. Woody entered and took his place between Helen and Ratchet. Bump and Dani and Lenny and Jess settled in their places on their side of the table.

Helen smiled. "Mel, Mike. I want to thank you ever so much for everything you did for Robert last night. He is doing great this morning. Sorry, Mike, but I had to do away with your nice splint. I set his leg and put a cast on it, so he won't be riding fences for a while."

"That's okay," Mike agreed. "It wasn't good enough to be permanent. I'm glad he's doing okay."

"Mike and I want to ride back out and finish," Mel added, "if Becky can make us more meat rolls and tamales."

"Thank you, Mel," Helen commented in surprise, "but let's see where we are after breakfast." She nodded to Celina and the girls brought the breakfast platters in. "I have to thank all of you for dropping everything last night and assisting." She took a portion of eggs from the first platter and then some bacon and a slice of ham from the next. "But when I finally got back I realized I had left my phone here in the office when we hurried off to meet Mel and help Robert. When I looked at it, I saw that Charlie had been trying to reach me—many times, I'm afraid."

She looked around the table and realized that everyone had stopped serving themselves, waiting.

"Sorry, but the men we saw watching us in Reno showed up in Farmington." Helen inhaled deeply again. "Somehow, they figured out that they were there. Like Charlie told me, there is no easy way to say this, but to say it." She glanced at Mel and Mike. "One of those men came to your house and asked your dad about your grandfather, Howard." She looked back at everyone around the table. "When he was asked to leave, there was gunfire and West was shot. He protected Charlie and Felix, taking two shots that would've hit them."

"Is he all right?" Jess asked over the commotion of sudden questions and spoken concerns.

19

"How're Charlie and Felix, her baby?" June asked.

The cacophony of voices continued to ask simultaneous questions and conveyed the collective concerns until Ratchet raised his hand. "Hold your questions, please. Give Helen a minute to explain."

"Charlie," Helen continued in the nervous silence, "Felix and the baby, and Monte are all right. West was the only one that was hit, besides the man that started it all. Monte's friend, the private investigator, Lloyd—the one that helped in Broomfield, Gratiot, and in New Jersey—killed the man before he could shoot anyone else.

"Charlie said the surgeon was very optimistic. West was hit in the chest and in his upper leg. His leg is broken and will be in a cast for the next three months. No weight bearing until the cast is off, so he won't be flying."

"That's not going to fly well," Ratchet remarked softly, and Mel tried not to snicker at the unintended pun.

Helen gestured for them to continue with breakfast. "The dilemma now is that the other man from Reno fled the scene and is still likely nosing around. Charlie feels she has to get her and Felix back here to the ranch for their safety, but she's very torn over leaving West in the hospital."

"I would think so," Jess agreed. "Can one of us go and stay with West?"

"Well, that is what she asked for," Helen concluded. "She wants someone to fly the T206 out there and stay with West, and to bring someone to fly *Hell Raiser* back as their escort—"

"I'll fly escort," Dani said, her hand quickly in the air. "Probably should have Ratchet or Lenny stay with him. The hospital staff won't cross either of them if they think something is wrong. When do we leave?"

Helen chuckled and looked at Ratchet and Lenny. She smiled at Woody and then Bump. "Woody, Charlie thought you should stay since you have more going on than just restorations." She looked at Ratchet. "She knows you and June got the estimate done for Mr. Miles, but still have a lot on your plate. She asked for you or Lenny to come and stay with West. If one of you feel like you can."

Ratchet looked at June and she nudged him with a smile.

Helen glanced at Lenny as he hugged Jess.

"I'll go," Lenny announced before Ratchet said anything. "Sorry, Ratchet, but I think Charlie will need your help when she gets back. She'll be running things here and you're the most qualified to help her." Then he smiled at Helen. "I can have the 206 ready in half an hour and I can start right after breakfast. How long before West can travel?"

"A week from Tuesday at the earliest." She sighed and shook her head before she looked back at Lenny. "Charlie says she will stay at the hospital tonight, but Felix and Monte might go back to their house.

"She said the surgeon says they could release him from the hospital as early as Tuesday, so he'll have to stay at Monte's until his follow-up appointment, roughly a week later." She tried to smile. "Then it's agreed: we'll get the 206 ready and leave after breakfast."

Then she looked at Mel. "I will see if Peter or Philip can go with you two to look at fences, and then we'll talk to Cappie and decide when you can leave and how long you can be away." She smiled. "We'll work the details after we finish eating."

"Where have you been?" Bobby asked from the breakfast nook when Mary entered through the back door of her maternal grandmother's old house. "I've been worried sick. You shouldn't go off with no one here to watch him." Bobby nodded toward the downstairs back bedroom. He cocked his head and stared at her.

"I just had to run an errand," she deferred, and closed the

kitchen door behind her. "You don't need to worry. I made sure he was sedated—"

"He wasn't," Bobby said sharply, and leaned back in his chair, folding his arms across his chest. "Did you check the video before you left? He was thrashing in his bed and hollering for you when I got here."

Mary's mouth dropped open and she turned toward the bedroom, as if she could see through the walls. "He's quiet now?"

"Yeah," Bobby replied with a sigh. "I drained his bag while I listened to his very unkind tirade, then I fed him and hung a new drip."

"Sorry. I didn't mean to be gone long. I had planned on doing all of that when I got back."

Bobby's expression softened and he slowly resigned himself to the way things were. "I didn't mean to smack you with it. I was just surprised he was awake and on a rant when I got here, and I didn't know where you'd gone. Nowhere is safe that I know of and he's getting very irritated."

"I know," Mary agreed. "And he hasn't said anything that I can use to show I wasn't a partner in what he was doing."

"You still have the emails."

"Yeah. But they may not be enough. Each of the partners and investors with sons or daughters might well be considered accomplices by the court. They may not agree to testify on my behalf, but we'll see."

"We'll see? What did you do?"

"I contacted my mother's old personal attorney and gave him the names of those that replied to my question."

Bobby sat back in his chair and drained his coffee cup. "You think that was wise?"

"I have to go with what I have. Sooner or later, I have to do something with Howard, and he hasn't said anything that will help me." Mary got up and poured herself a cup of coffee.

"Have you eaten? I need to fix me something."

"Yeah. I ate at home before I came." He looked at his watch. "And I have to be at work in twenty minutes."

"Does your father know you're helping me?"

"Of course not. I doubt he would approve, but I decided to not involve him or the rest of his family in any of this."

"Probably a good idea." She hesitated and leaned back against the counter beside the sink. "I was surprised that you offered. Circumstances wouldn't let me be in your life much, and you have no reason to endanger yourself because of me..."

"But you were in my life. I know it was just a little money every now and then, but it told me you never forgot. I appreciate that. More than you know."

Mary inhaled deeply and let the breath out slowly. "Well, I certainly appreciate the help and sincerely hope it hasn't been in vain."

Bobby stood and reached around her, placing his cup in the sink. He gave her a quick hug and turned to the back door. "Be careful when you're around him. And make sure he's tied down real good. I think he will try to hurt you if he ever gets loose."

"Thanks, Bobby."

"Welcome, Mom." Then Bobby slipped out the door and closed it behind him.

Fifty-One

"How's Robert?" Jess asked Madra as she passed the kitchen on her way to the security office.

"Okay." Madra smiled. "He complains too much. Does no good. I tell him he should have been more careful with the children around."

Jess snickered. "Not much sympathy, I take it."

"Not much," she agreed, and smiled. "Him not need sympathy."

"I called Charlie," Jess continued, "to let her know when the 206 would get there. She said Monte will meet them, and if all goes well she'll plan to fly back in the morning."

"West okay?" Madra asked. "Okay with her coming back? And not bring him?"

"The doctors say he'll do fine. I don't know how he feels about her coming home and him having to stay there. I can guess, but I don't know. He's also reasonable and should understand the need for her and Cat to be here where they'll be safe, but liking it, probably not so much. She said that she and Cat stayed with him last night while Monte went back to their house to get their duffels for a change of clothes. He should be back to the hospital before long."

Then Madra cocked her head. "Are you okay with this? With Lenny gone?"

"I guess. I didn't know it before, but when he was in Reno I realized I don't like it when he's away. But I was very surprised when he asked this morning what I thought about him going." Jess smiled and glanced at the papers she was holding. "It's actually the first time he's asked for my opinion when he's had to make a decision."

Madra smiled. "A good sign."

Jess looked up and held her gaze. "Sign? What do you mean?"

She was still smiling. "That he thinks you are part of him. You know, what he does."

"I know he likes me, but—"

"So there you are," June interrupted, greeting them as she stopped at the end of the back hallway. "Morning, Madra."

"*Yáʼátʼééh*, June," Madra greeted in return.

Jess smiled at Madra. "Thanks for talking with me, but I better go."

Madra nodded and then looked at Jess. "We will talk more. After lunch in the garden?" Jess nodded and she turned back to the kitchen.

Jess walked past June and into her office. June followed.

"I was going to go up top," June explained, "but the fellas can't help me right now. Mind if I visit for a few minutes?"

"Not at all," Jess greeted in return and gestured to a chair as they stepped into her office. "I have to deal with some new emails I just downloaded."

"What emails?"

"Hang on while I call Helen."

"Hey, Jess," Helen's voice answered through the speaker as Jess set the phone on her desk.

"Hey, Helen. I have you on speaker and need to tell you about the email dump I just downloaded. June's with me, if that's okay."

"Sure. Hey, June. Since you're going to be living with Ratchet, you'll hear our secrets one way or another, so you might as well be in on them from the beginning. What do you have, Jess?"

"Another batch from Mary on Howard's server. To a new guy this time. An Oscar Delany. He's one we haven't seen before, so I looked him up. He's an attorney. From her email, it sounds like he was her mother's attorney before she passed."

"You can intercept emails?" June asked softly, trying to grasp what Jess was telling Helen.

Jess nodded and smiled.

"From Mary? To her mother's attorney?" Helen repeated, mostly to herself. "And you say she sent it from their server?"

"Yeah. From Mary. And since it came from Howard's server, that means she was close enough to connect to it when she sent the emails."

"I thought Norman said the Detroit Police had hers and Howard's house under surveillance."

"He did. So I'm thinking she must have connected from the street or an alley, if they have those where they lived. It also means that she didn't want to connect to the internet wherever it is she's staying. She must know she could be traced if she did."

"What about the email she sent last week to the investors?"

"Good question." Jess quickly turned to her laptop and searched for the previous email. She studied her screen for a moment, then entered a few more keystrokes. "I was so surprised that she sent one, I didn't check beyond Howard's server. On that one, she did connect through another ISP, and accessed Howard's server from there." She read more and opened her browser. "It's a new service in northern Detroit. I'll have to check the codes and see if I can locate the connection. Or at least get close."

"Wow," June muttered softly. "You can do that? From here?"

"I can," Jess said, and smiled at June. "This is why West and Charlie hired me. I've been tracking various suspicious emails since before the July fly-in when Charlie and Dani were kidnapped. Especially those concerning things Cat's father has been doing."

"So what was the email she sent to this lawyer?" Helen asked before June could ask her next question.

"Copies of the email responses she got from the investors. She asked this attorney to help her plead her case to show that she is not an accomplice or has had anything to do with Howard's criminal or cruel activities. She explained the emails from his investors were all she had at this time."

"That doesn't sound like much of a defense," Helen said, "but I guess if that's all she has, it's all she has."

"Is this Howard the one Charlie said was responsible for Cat's kidnapping?" June asked when a silence developed between Helen and Jess.

"He is," Jess explained. "He's Cat's father and he married her off out of high school to advance his company. It took some time, but she's finally accepted Monte as a good man."

"But Charlie said he had her kidnapped for some other reason. I'm confused."

"Cat had a sister, Emli. She disappeared at the beginning of her third year of college. I think he looked for her when she disappeared, but never found her. Then, last year, he saw Charlie's picture in the flyer from the Alamosa Fly-in and decided Charlie was Emli. And he came after her, kidnapping her and Dani in July."

"She mentioned that they were kidnapped." June slowly nodded. "And he decided she was his missing daughter because she looks so much like Cat?"

She nodded. "We found a series of emails to Howard from some people in South Africa after that, and the timing matched with Howard having Cat kidnapped when he couldn't find Emli or capture Charlie again. He was going to ship her to the South Africans to settle some old debt he owes them."

"My God, nooo." June just stared at Jess.

"We were trying to figure out where Howard took Cat, when Eddie saw her tag on the tracking screen, in Detroit—"

"Her tag? Her tracking buttons?"

"Yes. Mike found one Eddie dropped in Broomfield and put in Cat's purse because he thought it was pretty. Very fortuitous. Mel saw where the button was and recognized the house on the beach as a place where her grandmother and mother had gone when Howard had business meetings."

"And that's when West set up the rescue and went after her," June realized, thinking out loud.

"That's right." Jess smiled. "The tracking button led us to her, just like it told us Mel needed our help last night, riding alone across the mesa, racing sundown."

"I see. Now I see why Charlie and West are so adamant about everyone having them." June smiled and nodded.

"Jess, I've got to go. Ratchet is calling me," Helen interrupted. "I'll talk to you later."

"Okay, Helen. Be safe."

June waited as Jess disconnected and put her phone in her pocket. "How on earth did you learn this email stuff?"

"West hired me out of high school to work in his business. Back then, he wrote security software and I had a knack at writing code. When he sold his business, five of us went with the company and the new owners. West made sure it was worth our while." Jess glanced around the room before she continued. "Then this last spring, he called me and wanted me to meet with him and Charlie. They flew over to Austin and he gave me a software surveillance program he had written many years ago and asked me to modify it. I did and Charlie gave me a server to test it on—Howard's server. I didn't really know what was happening, but after Broomfield, West asked me to come here and work for him. And as a news commentator used to say, 'the rest is history.'"

"And the emails have started again? Since Howard disappeared from the hospital?"

"Yeah. After we rescued Cat, I continued to monitor the email traffic, but with Howard in the hospital, recovering from multiple gunshot wounds, traffic essentially stopped. Until last week.

"There's someone else checking on Howard's server, and we think that it's the South African guys—the bosses of the ones you and Ratchet saw in Reno. But Mary's email last week was a surprise. In Reno, when Cat heard she had escaped her house arrest, she was excited to get back home, back here, and check the security server in her house in Farmington, where they are now. It's linked to Howard's house and we downloaded the video of the night she escaped."

"Wow. She's into this too."

"She's a very capable and talented surveillance expert, writes software code and can handle the hardware as well— especially video. That's one of the reasons why West asked her to come to the ranch and work with us. Besides being safe here." She smiled at June. "West knows what he needs and only hires the best to help him create and implement what is necessary to get the job done. You're included, June. He really wants you, like all of us, to succeed. No hidden agendas. So ask questions and learn all you can. He needs you—the ranch needs you."

"Thanks. I'll do my best."

At 1622 local time, Lenny cleared the engine and shut the T206 down in front of the middle of three hangars just west of the control tower at Oakland County International Airport in Pontiac, Michigan. Helen swung the right-side cabin door open as he secured the cockpit, making certain all of the switches were in their correct positions and the master was switched off. Dani squeezed between the two front seats and followed Helen out.

The medium-build, stocky man sitting on the tug beside the hangar pushed himself up and walked toward the plane as Lenny climbed out of the pilot's side door and came around the nose.

"May I help you?" the man greeted with an outstretched hand, noticing the large Ghost Ranch logo on the vertical tail. "I'm Douglas. You must be the ones Charlie called us about."

"Afternoon. I'm Lenny James, this young lady is Dani Ventura, and this is Helen West, West's mom," Lenny added in his returned greeting. "I figured Charlie would call and tell you we were coming."

Douglas studied the three of them, smiling at Dani. "Didn't you fly another TF in here a couple of months ago?"

Dani smiled and nodded. "Yes, I brought West's *The Beautiful Lady*, and another of our pilots, Ratchet Powers, flew *Hell Raiser*." She gestured to the hangar where she presumed the planes were locked away, out of the public's eye. "Helen wasn't with us that trip."

"Very nice," Douglas said. "It's very nice to have you back. Is there anything I can do for you?"

"Right now," Lenny began, "I just need to secure the T206. A suitable tie-down will be sufficient for tonight. Charlie and Dani will be flying the fifty-ones home tomorrow, and I'd like the T206 inside once they've gone. Helen and I will be here for about a week, if all goes well."

"We can arrange that," Douglas agreed with a nod. "Would you like the 206 fueled before you head into town?"

"That would be nice," Lenny commented. "We can do that while we wait for our ride to get here."

Monte arrived about halfway through the refueling, apologizing for being late.

"Traffic was worse than I expected," he greeted as he shook hands. "Looks like you made it successfully."

"Best way to make it," Helen remarked, and took his hand.

"I suppose it is," Monte agreed, and greeted Dani. "Where are your bags? I can put them in the car while you finish what you're doing."

"I'll give you a hand," Dani said, and pointed to the duffels and Helen's suitcase sitting beside the plane.

Charlie was pacing in West's hospital room while Cat patiently watched her from the overstuffed chair.

"Monte said the traffic was a bear," Cat urged, trying to lighten Charlie's worry. "And you said Dani called when they landed."

"I know, I know," Charlie admitted, and stopped at the foot of West's bed. She glanced at him, sleeping peacefully. "And I know I'm letting this whole situation bother me more than it should. Aside from West being shot and all that that causes."

"Yeah. I know it puts a lot on your shoulders"—Cat sighed—"but I think you have pretty strong and broad shoulders. You'll see. Even though everyone is worried about West, they know you have it under control."

Charlie smiled at Cat, but did not say what she really thought about having things under control. She knew, just like usual, that she had to keep up the image; she had to be strong. It used to be just for her, hiding and using her wits to stay relatively safe, but now she had to prove to West that he made the right choice in trusting her, marrying her; everything she did now was about him and the ranch.

The many footsteps in the corridor caught her attention, and as she turned and Cat stood up, Monte ushered Dani, Lenny, and Helen into the room.

"Mom?" Charlie asked in disbelief. "No one mentioned you were coming along." She caught Helen in a very sincere hug, holding on for an extra-long minute.

"I had to be here, Charlie," Helen explained. "He's still my boy and you need to be back home, so it's my turn to help you both. I know the procedures, so I can work with the nurses to get him what he needs. Especially at night. I'll be here with him until we bring him home. How's he doing?"

"He's still sleeping a lot, but the doctor says he'll do better each day. Thanks for coming. I really don't want to leave him, but knowing you're here makes it easier for me to go."

Cat had hurried to Monte and caught him in a tight hug when he entered the room, easing her unspoken concerns over his tardiness. Charlie hugged Dani quickly and then shook Lenny's hand as Helen moved around the bed and took the chair behind it. Charlie noticed when Helen caught his hand and leaned forward to rub it against her cheek.

"Thanks for coming on such short notice," Charlie said to Lenny, and then looked at Dani. "How's your dad?"

Dani smiled. "He's doing okay. Broken lower left leg and two cracked ribs. Helen says his ribs will mend quickly, but the leg will take a few months—"

"He'll have to keep West company." Helen chuckled, looking up from her study of West's expressionless face. "They can both do their strolling or sitting around together with their walkers and crutches."

"I suppose they will." Dani nodded and chuckled. "He denies it, but Mom says he was showing off for the children."

Cat shook her head. "I've never seen him do anything like that."

"I'm sure he wasn't, but Mom won't give him sympathy." Dani gave them a knowing smile. "Anyway, how's West?"

"Mostly sleeping. The nurses say that's the best thing for him right now. They expect tonight might be a little rough for him."

Monte entered with a straight-backed chair in hand, followed by Lenny and an orderly, each with another chair. Charlie was surprised she did not realize he had left.

"Now," Cat began as she gestured Dani to a chair and settled once again into the overstuffed chair. "Tell us about the children, the details, what they did to earn such praise."

"Explain to me what errand you ran this morning," Bobby demanded, trying to keep his concerns from coloring his tone as he sat, eating lunch, with Mary.

"Just a necessary errand," she deferred.

Undeterred, he held her eyes. "Give."

She sighed and shook her head. "I had to send copies of those emails I received to the attorney friend of my mother's."

"You couldn't do that from here?"

Mary shook her head. "I told you that I sent the request to the partners and investors from here, linking through Howard's business server. Afterwards, I began to worry about someone tracing my emails, finding out where I am. So this morning, I drove by our house and parked on the street one block over. I had everything ready and all I had to do was stop, connect, and send. Then I drove away and back here."

"Do you know how dangerous that was? Going back to your house? The police are watching your house, who comes and who goes by. They are looking for you and Howard, and I bet they know your car."

"No one followed me, if that's what you're worried about."

Bobby let out an exasperated sigh. "It's you getting caught before we finish what we set out to do—that's what worries me. And yes, they could have followed you and you wouldn't know, or they could've just stopped you on the street and taken you away. I wouldn't have had any idea, and I certainly can't help your cause if you keep doing things I don't know about."

"Thank you for your concern, but I have to have an attorney that is not beholden to Howard in some way. So I contacted the only one I know. Oscar isn't. He really dislikes Howard and I consider that a good thing. He was adamantly against Father's arranging my marriage to him—"

"I think I like him already," Bobby interrupted, and smiled for the first time since he had arrived that morning and found she was not there. "Will you give me his contact information? If something happens, I need to know about him and he needs to know who I am." Then Bobby looked at Mary suspiciously. "Does he know who I am?"

"I'm a little worried about Charlie," Cat told Monte softly as they walked back from the hospital cafeteria. "I think when she goes home, it will be the first time she and West have been apart since she first moved to the ranch."

"When was that?" he asked, juggling the carryout dinner order for Charlie as he punched the button for the elevator. When they decided to take a break to eat, Charlie was adamant that she was going to stay with West and asked them to get her something.

Lenny, Helen, and Dani gathered behind them as they waited and Cat turned to Lenny. "When did Charlie come to the ranch?"

"Last fall," he said, thinking.

"October third," Dani finished for him. "A year ago in two more days."

"And have they always been together since then? I thought she said they had been."

"Mostly," Dani admitted. "She's made flights up to the Springs and places like that without West but she's always had Ratchet or Lenny for an escort. West makes sure she's never alone. Why?"

"Just trying to remember," Cat explained. "I think her being back home with him staying here is going to be hard for her."

The elevator door opened and three people exited before they could step in.

"It'll be the evenings and nights," Dani added when the door closed again. "We'll make the days busy enough that she won't have time to think about it. But we can't do much to help her nights."

"It's something we all need to be aware of," Lenny said. "Maybe someone can spend time with her after dinner to make the time go easier."

"We can do that," Cat added firmly as the door slid open again.

When they stepped into West's room, Cat heard Charlie whisper, "Nooo, West." Then Charlie leaned back in her chair and Cat noticed she quickly wiped her eyes with a tissue. She heard West, still speaking softly, imploring her, "Promise me, Charlie. Promise me."

She nodded and smiled at Cat and the rest of them, but her eyes gave her resignation away. Then she looked back at him. "I promise," she whispered, and kissed him, confirming that she would do whatever they had been talking about.

Deputy Minister of Rural Development Karl deVon sat in the ornate padded chair, fingering the loose sheets in his hand. He looked up when Elrich Voster, Deputy Minister of State Security, finished reading the summary he had provided.

"This is troubling," was all Voster said after a long pause. He straightened in his chair and stared at the large portrait that hung on the wall above the credenza placed along the side wall of the office.

"It is," Deputy Minister deVon agreed. "If Agent Schmidt has the information correct, the newspaper reports confirm Howard was involved in kidnapping his own daughter—the older one."

"Yes, which is not the one he promised," Deputy Minister

Voster cited. "But worse than that is that someone knew about it and Collingsworth was stopped before he could deliver her."

"Yes, but we know now that he was shot in the raid and has been in the hospital."

Voster nodded. "Under police guard."

"Does not seem he was considered much of a threat if he walked past the guards."

"I'm thinking there was most likely more to it," Voster continued, rubbing his chin as he thought, "than just walking past the guards. I feel certain he had assistance. What did Agent Brown say when he called you this morning?"

"He said that after checking on Howard's residence and seeing significant police presence in the area," deVon explained, "they stopped at a newspaper archival location. It was after Brown had collected the articles on Howard that Agent Schmidt decided they should watch the daughter's residence."

"That was last week sometime, was it not?"

"Yes, last Monday. In Agent Brown's call this morning, he said the daughter and the lookalike woman returned to her residence with both of their husbands yesterday. He also said Agent Schmidt went to their house last night to inquire if they knew anything about Howard's whereabouts—"

"He what?" Voster sat bolt upright, suddenly rigid, staring at deVon. "He went to confront them?"

"No, not confront. Agent Brown said he was just going to see if they knew anything."

"That...is *not* what they were instructed to do!"

"I know," deVon admitted. "But Agent Brown said that while he was waiting in their rental car, shortly after Schmidt left on foot, two men stopped beside the car and tapped on his window. Brown did not speak with the men, but drove away to wait for Schmidt's call somewhere else."

"And?" Voster asked when deVon did not continue immediately.

"When Brown called it was after midnight in Detroit. Schmidt had not yet called him."

Voster slowly turned his chair a quarter turn and he glanced out the single window overlooking the spring blooms in the small garden area beyond. "When is his next report due?"

"This evening," deVon replied. "He has not given any reasons why Schmidt would not have called."

Voster nodded. "Then we shall wait until this evening to inquire further," Voster said, and turned back to face his desk, changing the direction of the conversation. "What about the emails you mentioned in your summary?"

"On the thirteenth of last month, we noted an email from Howard's wife. She sent it to a name we have not seen before, a Bob Frye." DeVon glanced at his notes. "The next evening, according to the newspaper articles Agent Brown found, Howard's wife disappeared from her home and has not been seen since. Details of her escape are sketchy at best."

Voster looked at a small calendar on the corner of his desk. "That was on a Thursday."

"Yes, the Thursday before Howard disappeared from the police ward in the Henry Ford Hospital where he was being detained. Again, the details of his escape are not explained." DeVon watched Voster for a long moment. "I was thinking we might reassign Stanik to Detroit to help the search for Howard."

"No. I do not want to do that," Voster said in an uncharacteristically soft voice. "Your summary indicates there were other emails."

DeVon nodded. "On Tuesday of last week, Howard's wife sent an email to a dozen of Howard's investors or financial partners. She asked if Howard had ever given her credit for assisting in any of his contracts or project planning. I thought it was a strange request."

Voster shook his head. "With Howard's arrest, I suspect she was arrested as being an accomplice. She is trying to prove her innocence."

"Aah, yes. She sent another early this morning, to another new name—an attorney. The email suggests that he was her mother's attorney at one time."

"Have Brown watch this attorney's office," Voster offered with a nod. "Yes. Maybe, if she goes to see him, Brown can follow her back to where she's hiding and find out who's helping her. Maybe he can discover something about this fellow Frye."

"I will convey your instructions." Then deVon looked up from his notes. "And Stanik?"

"I have some things he can investigate. We shall continue to search for Howard, for he is ours by forfeit, but he still owes us his daughter."

Monday, October 2

Howard woke, like he did other mornings when his IV bottle ran out, before the rays of daylight sneaked around the edges of the room darkening shade. The shade, drawn down and secured tight against the wall, covered the single rectangular window in the wall beside his bed. It was early, and the only illumination was the soft glow from the night light on the wall past the foot of his bed.

He studied the wrappings around his wrists and tugged, but everything remained the same; the raised handrails on both sides of the bed held his wrists tight. He pulled again and this time he noticed the right-side handrail seemed to rock—not inward and out like he expected, but head to foot. He pulled and pushed in that direction and smiled, realizing the rail had some movement; it was definitely looser than before.

Howard continued pulling and pushing on the handrail, first head to foot and then inward and out. Was he making things up or did the rail move more with each try? Something fell to the floor with a soft thump on the rug. Howard stopped with a start; the handrail was still restrained head to foot and inward and out, but it had shifted down.

Careful to not make any significant noise in the predawn quiet of the room—he did not know where in the house he was nor where in the house Mary slept: upstairs, downstairs, in the next room—he gently tried to lift the handrail. He was hindered by the awkwardness of having to use just his arm tied to the rail, wobbling it slowly to ease it up. It moved at first a little, then a bit more. The soft sound of metal gently sliding on metal seemed to fill the room.

Working slowly, expecting the rail to stop at the top of some slotted adjustment mechanism, he was surprised when the whole two-foot-long rail, an assembly of shiny bent tubes welded together and polished, suddenly slipped out of its guides and flopped unceremoniously onto his lap. He inhaled sharply, but the pain was less than he expected; he stared at the handrail and suddenly realized he could unwrap the hook-and-loop binding with his still tied left hand. He began to chuckle softly.

In minutes, Howard had eagerly disconnected himself from the IV in his left forearm and from the urinary catheter and its collection bag strapped to the bottom of the left handrail. He slowly sat upright and bent his legs so he could reach his ankle bindings, his movements restricted by the residual pain and stiffness from the surgeries that removed the six bullets from his chest and abdomen.

He sighed when he dropped his legs over the side of the bed and straightened himself upright. It had been a long time since he was upright, and his lightheadedness made his stomach uneasy. He held onto the footboard and grabbed a handful of sheets to steady himself, waiting for the nausea to pass.

When the slow spinning and tilting of the room subsided, he gently lowered himself onto his feet, hoping he was strong enough to support himself and pleased when his knees did not abruptly buckle. The lightheadedness persisted, making it hard to think clearly as he stood, holding the footboard to steady himself. Then he stepped to the wall near the foot of the bed and leaned his back against it, getting his breathing under control and listening to the sounds of the house as he surveyed the room from his new vantage point. His stomach complained with each movement he made, no matter how small.

Someone made a noise in a room above him, footsteps crossed the ceiling followed by a long silence. A toilet flushed and he decided Mary was getting up to start her day. After a long few minutes, he heard a door open and the footsteps left the room. From the weight of the steps, he figured it was Mary and not that tall fellow that always wore scrubs and a medical face mask, and she would be coming to check on him.

Careful to move slowly, Howard edged himself along the wall and stopped to wait near the corner, behind the door situated in the adjacent wall.

Fifty-Two

It was 0638 when Douglas pulled the tug away from the TF, *My Affair,* a few minutes later than Charlie had requested when she called the main office the evening before. The P-51, *Hell Raiser,* sat on the ramp beside it, in front of the middle hangar. He had just parked the tug and had stepped down when the three petite women in matching gray flight suits and unzipped brown leather jackets walked through the hangar and stopped in front of the tug. The broad-shouldered, taller man with them, wearing a partially zipped black leather jacket over a plain shirt, jeans, and tennis shoes, looked out of place.

"Morning, Douglas," Charlie greeted.

"Morning, Mrs. West." He gestured to the two planes and then to the T206 inside the hangar. "They're ready for you, and the 206 is put to bed until the others need it."

"Thanks. Sorry for making you get up so early."

"No problem," Douglas replied with a wide smile. "We support the aeromedical 'copters next door, so Paul set up a common room for us, with a sleeping room beside it—four bunks stacked in pairs. I was already here. "

"I see."

"Yup. Twenty-four hours on, four nights in a row, then three off. I basically live here."

"Well, thank you again." Charlie glanced at her watch. "We better get ready." She turned to Dani. "Do you have keys to the 206?"

Dani nodded. "I have one and Lenny has the other."

"We need to leave my duffel in the 206 to make room in *My*

Affair for Felix's tote."

Dani took Charlie's duffel and disappeared back into the hangar. A few minutes later, Dani caught up with Charlie as she walked out to the planes with Cat and Monte a short distance behind. Dani and Charlie climbed onto the wings of their planes, opened the canopies, and checked that the mag switches and the fuel shutoff valves were selected to off. Then they dropped back down and began pulling the propellers through to clear the cylinders of any residual oil.

By the time Charlie and Dani had finished their walk-around inspection, Cat had said her goodbyes to Monte and was climbing into the back seat of *My Affair*. Charlie followed her and settled into the front seat, quickly securing the belts and donning her helmet. She waved to Monte and Douglas, where they were watching them from the tug, and then signaled Dani for engine starts.

"Level at 16,500 feet as flight planned," Charlie announced into her oxygen mask as they swung around the southern end of Lake Michigan to miss the airline traffic over Chicago. "Heading 257 true. Westerly winds will switch to the southwest and weaken as we go. I show a ground speed of 308."

"I estimate three hours plus forty-six from Pontiac. Less if the winds really weaken," Dani added.

"Off at 0716," Charlie recounted, noting the time hack she recorded on her knee-pad just after the flight of two broke ground in formation. "Gain two hours...so we should be home around 0900 ranch time."

Charlie suddenly yawned, her words distorted in the doing.

"You okay over there?" Dani asked with a chuckle. "Sounds like someone didn't get much sleep last night."

"Probably right," Charlie agreed, not wanting to admit she felt completely drained. "West didn't sleep very well and kept waking me up."

"Maybe you ought to let Felix fly a little, like you did

coming out," Dani proposed. "She can handle the cruise flying and I'm right beside you. We can talk if we need to."

Charlie thought about Dani's idea a moment before she responded. Felix had flown *My Affair* very well on the trip to Pontiac, and there was no reason she would not do as well now. *So why do I feel reluctant?* Charlie shook her head and asked, "Felix, are you up to taking the stick for a bit?"

"If you want me to," she answered. "I think I can keep us headed in the same direction and on altitude." Charlie heard Felix's smile in her retort.

"Okay, Dani. Felix has the controls. Keep us pointed in the right direction."

"Roger that," Dani replied. "Take us home, Felix."

Charlie relaxed and slowly pulled her feet off the rudder pedals. She studied the instruments for a few minutes, confirming Felix was keeping their altitude excursions to a hundred feet or less and their heading within a degree or two. Her gaze slowly turned to the long, thin ribbons of clouds drifting above them and occasional small cumulus dotting the scape beneath.

Everything was as it ought to be, except West wasn't with her. She felt like she was abandoning him, but she knew that this was the way it had to be. He would be well enough to travel in a week and Helen was there with him, but the thought did not fully appease her sense of despair; she missed him already, suddenly feeling vulnerable.

She inhaled deeply and pulled a tissue from her sleeve pocket, slid her tinted helmet visor up and wiped her eyes.

Howard held his breath as the light footsteps came toward the door to the room where he was being held captive. Absently, he wondered if the man in scrubs was staying in the house also, or if he just came off and on. Was he there, helping Mary, or was it just her?

The doorknob turned and Mary stepped into the room carrying a cup of coffee for him; the door swung open and banged against his toes. Mary gasped, frozen as she stared at the empty bed.

Howard shoved the door closed and struck her across the face as she turned and saw him. The coffee splashed across the wall and the cup broke, falling to the floor. If she tried to scream, it was silenced before she could as she wilted and crumpled to the floor beside the bed. Suddenly, his anger flared and he shouted at her limp form. He jerked her up and shook her.

"How dare you? How dare you tie me to a bed? *Me*?" He hit her face again. "You think I'm going to let you get away from me? After all I've done to provide for you? You owe me, you ungrateful bitch. No way am I going to let you off the hook and tell the authorities that you really did nothing. You are nothing! You're weak, Mary. You couldn't help me if you tried, and I certainly would never let you. But I'll never tell them that! Never!"

He shook her again and slammed her back against the wall beside the door, her head flopping to one side.

"If you know what's good for you, you'll keep doing what I tell you to do. And you'll get your half of whatever they throw at me. For better or worse, remember? I own you, Mary! You remember that!"

He slammed his fist into her stomach, then threw her over the bed. She crashed into the wall beside the window and slumped to the floor, unmoving.

The sudden pain in his chest and stomach doubled him over. Hands on his knees, the fire in his wounds fought him as he tried to catch his breath. He stared at Mary's silent heap, gritted his teeth, and slowly pushed himself upright. Then, with a deep inhale, he opened the door and waited, listening for the man wearing scrubs, but he only heard his own strained breathing.

Howard stepped out into a short hallway and realized his room was just off a small living room. In a coat closet by the front door, he found a dark gray trench coat and slipped it on over the hospital gown he wore. Then, turning to face the room, he saw a pair of men's shoes beside the sofa. They were too large, but he figured they were better than not having any.

He hurriedly checked the dining room and saw his old briefcase on the table. He grabbed it, flipped it open, and saw two bundles of fifty-dollar bills on top of a few of his old papers. As hard as he tried, he could not remember what else was supposed to be in the briefcase, but the cash would make it easier for him to slip away.

He closed the case and clicked the hasps. Mary's car keys lay on the table beside the case and he scooped them up; at least he had some money and transportation.

Howard looked around the room and glanced into the kitchen, feeling like the man wearing scrubs should be coming soon. Then, with the briefcase in hand, he slipped out through the back door, pulled the trench coat tight against the dawn's chill, and got into Mary's car.

As he backed out of the drive, he realized he knew this house and smiled. At least Mary had found a place to take him that was not obvious to anyone looking for her, and now, smiling, he knew where he could find her. Howard drove north, remembering an out-of-the-way strip mall where he could buy a decent change of clothes.

Ratchet and June settled into their chairs at the breakfast table and waited for the other seven to join them and take their places.

"Feels empty," Mike said softly as he sat down, looking at

the other side of the table where Bump and Jessie were the only ones present.

"Yes it does," Jess agreed. "And we're lopsided with six on your side and only two on this side."

Mel giggled. "Not for long."

"That's right," Jess confirmed.

"Dani says they'll be here around 0900 our time," Jess added as Becky and Camila started setting dishes on the table. "Maybe sooner if the winds cooperate."

"Seems like they've been gone more than just two days," Mel thought out loud.

"A lot has been happening," Eddie agreed, and nudged Mel's shoulder. "And you've been very busy. I would've thought that would make the time fly by."

"Yeah," Mel admitted, and glanced at Mike. "But not at night."

"Is West going to be all right?" Mike asked, abruptly changing the subject.

"Dani says he will be. She called in just after they passed Bloomington, Illinois. Charlie stayed with him through the night last night, and they stopped by and saw him and picked her up on their way to the airport. She says he seemed to be in good spirits, and the nurses and Helen were getting him up to walk the corridors again."

"Walk?"

"Hobble is probably a better way to put it." Jess chuckled. "He's having to use a walker and doesn't like it. So be warned for when he gets back home."

"When will that be?" Mike persisted.

"When Charlie called last night, she said that if he gets released tomorrow," Jess continued, "he'll go and stay with your dad at your old house. And if he does okay, he might be allowed to fly home early next week."

"Thank you, Jess," Mike said politely, and began scooping

breakfast items onto his plate.

"You're welcome. I see you're a mite hungry this morning."

"Fences are hungry work," Mike said, and continued eating in earnest. "I'm glad Peter could help yesterday."

"Charlie canceled their flight plan," Jess said as she joined the small group in front of Hangar Five, "when they passed over Great Bend, Kansas. Then she led their flight down to a lower altitude and went south. They settled at less than a thousand AGL and turned their transponders off to avoid Denver radar and are circling south of Clayton. They will be coming in from the southwest."

It was 0900 on the money when Mike saw the two specks over the hills in New Mexico, slowly growing in size. Charlie had slowed the flight and entered a low downwind, crossing the airfield a half mile out from the hangars. Then, in formation, Dani followed as Charlie turned onto their base leg and they reconfigured their planes. They landed together about a half mile east of the hangars and slowed to a taxi, stopping in front of the open hangar without turning.

Charlie raised her arm and the two engines increased RPM; then, with the drop of her arm, they both suddenly fell silent, the propellers whirling to a stop together.

Everyone was hollering happily as Charlie and Dani rolled their canopies open and Charlie stood up and stepped out onto *My Affair's* wing. She quickly turned and helped Felix stand and climb over the canopy rail.

Dani was standing in front of *My Affair's* wing when Felix climbed down and Charlie handed her the duffel and the tote with the servers and cameras inside.

"Welcome home," Jess greeted Felix and then Dani. Then she looked at Charlie as she jumped down from the landing gear strut.

Before either could say anything, Jess caught Charlie in a quick hug. "We're so glad you're back home safe. I take it there is no change in West's prognosis."

Ratchet, holding June with one arm around her shoulders, seconded her greeting with a slap on Charlie's shoulder

"Thanks. He's doing as well as can be expected. Lenny and Mom will keep him in line." Then Charlie asked, "Do you suppose we can talk Becky into fixing a late breakfast for three very hungry pilots?"

"She should have everything about ready for you." Jess gestured to the jeeps and Charlie led the way.

Bobby took off early for his lunch break from the Henry Ford Hospital cafeteria and kitchen where he was the assistant chef—a glorified café cook. He had worked in the food services industry for nearly twenty years and in the preparation side for the past seven, something his father thought was beneath him when he began. Over the years, his father had slowly become accustomed to his son's passion and tenacity when it came to food.

Bobby muttered a curse when he drove into the driveway and saw that Mary's car was not there. He forced himself to accept the fact that she did not need his permission for anything and if she felt she needed to run an errand, she would not listen to his reasons on why she should not. He parked his minivan and stepped up on the back stoop. When he went to open the back door, he realized that she had not locked it. "Damn!" he whispered as he pushed it and stepped into the quiet house. The silence bothered him as much as her car being gone and the door being unlocked.

He slowly walked into the dining room and sensed a difference, but he could not put his finger on what it was. He opened the rolltop desk and saw her laptop, closed and shut off, where she had been keeping it. He checked the top right drawer and saw the two credit cards were still there, the ones she told him were special and needed to be kept secret and safe.

He glanced around the dining room and was about to go upstairs to check her bedroom when he froze, seeing her purse on the bureau by the kitchen wall. *Shit!* Now he was worried— more worried than angry.

He turned to the hallway and slowly pushed the door to Howard's room open, startled to see the empty bed. The catheter lay on the floor like a dead serpent hanging down from the collection bottle, and the light blanket that usually covered him was on the floor near the foot of the bed.

Bobby glanced around and, not seeing Mary, he turned to leave, but the streaks of splashed coffee on the wall caught his attention. Then he saw the broken cup beside the baseboard.

"Mom? Are you here?" he asked, and turned back to the room. He took another few steps and saw her beside the far wall; the bed had hidden her from where he had been standing. "Mom!"

Bobby was down beside her in an instant. He felt for her pulse, and sighed in relief when he found it. He gently pulled her upright, calling her name, trying to wake her up. He kept calling her and gently patting her cheek until she finally began to respond; she moved her head and moaned softly.

"Mom. I'm here," Bobby encouraged. "What happened? Where do you hurt?"

She blinked, and again as she opened her eyes and tried to smile; her hands trembled as she clasped them over her stomach. "Like you told me he would, he got loose last night. He was waiting for me when I brought him his morning coffee."

Bobby looked back at the wall beside the door. "I saw that." He slipped his hands under her arms and lifted. "Can you stand up? I need to get you into the front room and see if you're all right."

Wobbly, she clung to him as he held her up and together they walked slowly out of the bedroom

"He hit me in the face," she said softly, trying to explain, "but I don't remember much after that. From the way my stomach feels, he must've punched me hard."

Bobby turned her head under the light from the front window. "I think your cheek and maybe your eye are going to discolor. I should've stopped by on my way to work and maybe—"

"You didn't know he would get loose," Mary soothed. "Have you checked to see what he took with him? The briefcase? My purse? My—"

Bobby glanced back into the dining room. "Where was the briefcase?"

"On the table." She inhaled deeply and let it out slowly.

"Well that seems to be gone. He missed your purse, the laptop, and the credit cards you hid. But he took your car."

"Well, I took most of the money out of the briefcase," she said, and tried to chuckle, but the muscles in her abdomen complained. She coughed instead. "And I hid his gun and the credit cards, so he has limited funds to move about on. Have you checked the video files?"

"No. I didn't think about them," Bobby admitted as he stood, went into the kitchen, and opened the linen closet.

"Is the DVD still there?"

"Yes." He ejected the DVD and held it up so she could see it.

"Label it with today's date and put a new one in its place."

He was busy for a few minutes and then walked back to her. "Here. Can you watch this on your laptop?"

She nodded and he retrieved the computer, switching it on. After a few long minutes, it booted and the home screen illuminated.

"Get the external DVD drive."

He did and she plugged it in, then inserted the DVD. She selected the surveillance program reviewer and they both watched as the image coalesced on the screen. Mary fast-forwarded until she saw Howard pull the handrail up from the side of the bed.

It was a torture for her to see what he had done to her, but she smiled at the audio. "I think I have what I needed, Bobby."

"I think you do," he agreed, and gently squeezed her shoulders. "Should we give this to your attorney?"

"Yes, but we need to make a copy and keep the original safe. I'll give Oscar the copy." She sighed and slowly worked her jaw, surprised it did not seem to be broken.

"Has he done that before?" Bobby asked as he took the DVD back to the surveillance recorder. "Hit you like that, I mean." In a short moment he inserted the dated, original DVD and a blank DVD into the appropriate slots and pushed the Copy button.

"Yes. Quite a few times. Especially when the girls were young. The last time was when he attacked our youngest, Emli."

"She's the one that disappeared, right?"

"Yes. When I couldn't stop him, I decided I would sedate him every evening that I had a chance. But it was too late; he had already inflicted too much harm and I lost my girls. Their trust was gone, and I'm as much to blame as he was. Catherine was married off after high school and Emli disappeared before her twenty-first birthday."

"You may not have been able to stop him, but you didn't cause the damage."

"But I didn't stop it either."

Bobby removed the two DVDs and reinserted the new, blank one in the record slot.

"We'll not wallow in what might have been," he added sternly as he came back into the room. He sat down beside her and marked the DVD copy appropriately. "But I think I need to get you to a doctor and have you checked out."

"No. I'll rest a little bit, then you can take me to my attorney's office after you get off work."

"What if he comes back before I get off work?"

"He has my car keys, but he doesn't have the house keys. I'll rest and we'll worry about doctors later, if I'm not feeling better."

He started to protest, but Mary raised her hand.

"Don't argue with your mother."

"No. I will argue. Get your clothes gathered up and everything you need to take with you. I have an apartment you can stay in until we figure something else out, but I'm not leaving you here for him to find when he comes back. And he *will* come back, especially if he thinks you have something he needs, like his gun, the rest of his money, his computer. Shall I go on?"

"I really don't—"

"Yes you do." Then he softened his voice. "I need for you to be where I know you are safe. Now get your things."

Mary nodded and slowly got up and climbed the stairs to her room.

Officer Fred Mitchell refilled his coffee cup, smiling timidly at Officer Ableman when she looked up at him as he walked back to his desk. Officer Sally Ableman had been his shift partner while they watched Collingsworth's room in the Henry Ford Hospital. She had not spoken to him since the night he fell asleep and Collingsworth disappeared.

Officer Mitchell settled into his chair, resigned to the fact that everyone in the office, to one degree or another, blamed him for his blunder in the hospital police ward. He set his coffee on the coaster beside his computer keyboard and reopened his internet search for details on the Collingsworth name. He had finished the review and commenting on a patrolman's vicious dog report, one of the many *no-threat-to-the-department* things Sergeant Kilman had assigned him since the hospital incident. But the less-demanding work gave him time to think and he had started looking into any details concerning Howard Collingsworth and his wife that might not be in their police files. Maybe it was his own feeling that he needed to redeem himself, or maybe he was just trying to do something a good cop would do. But whichever it was, he felt like he needed to understand all he could concerning those two.

After searching for information on Howard and finding little to nothing that the department did not already have on file, Officer Mitchell turned his attention to Howard's wife Mary. There were the usual items—the normal marriage and birthdate blurbs: Mary Carole Rothman, age 20, daughter of Mr. and Mrs. Hamilton Rothman of Detroit married Howard Earl Collingsworth, age 23, son of the prominent Mr. and Mrs. Warren Collingsworth of Boston on August 24. He noted that this year was their fortieth anniversary.

For offspring, he could only confirm their two daughters, Catherine and Emli, which he estimated to be about thirty-four and thirty-two years old, respectively.

Then, seeing nothing new, he began to wonder if either Howard or Mary had living relatives that might have been involved in their escapes, or helping them hide. He quickly began a search for siblings.

After another hour of searching, Officer Mitchell set back in his chair and smiled at his computer screen; it was not siblings that excited him, but Mary Collingsworth's family.

He broke for lunch and ate alone in the busy department's cafeteria, enduring everyone's stares and their feelings of condescension. He closed his mind to them and focused, letting his mind rummage through the more positive things he had discovered that morning.

As he finished his lunch, stood, and picked up his tray, he noticed Officer Sally Ableman sitting at a table along the wall furthest from the serving counter and wondered if she also felt the strangeness of being back and not on guard duty. During their duty at the hospital, they had shared time when their shifts

55

changed and either he was coming on duty or she was. They had discovered they both liked many of the same things and had planned on getting together some when their duty was over. But it was over and nothing was happening the way they had expected; she had not brought herself to speak to him, and his sense of guilt stopped him from talking to her.

He turned his gaze away when she looked up and saw him, her expression still blank, and he felt she was accusing him of letting them all down. His thoughts of her reduced opinion of him stung worse than all of Kilman's reprimands had.

He returned his tray and dishes to the conveyor to the kitchen, wishing he could tell Sally that everyone was wrong, that he had not fallen asleep and that he had not been the reason Collingsworth was missing. But that was not the case, and instead all he could think of to do was to apologize—feebly, at best. The reasons were not sufficient to justify his actions.

In the hallway outside the cafeteria, his thoughts returned to his morning's findings and he headed for Sergeant Kilman's office.

Fifty-Three

West ducked as the saucer sailed past his head and shattered against the wall behind him. A plate glanced off his upraised hand and smashed on the floor beside him. When he looked up, Susan, red-faced and with an expression of pure malice, had her arm back and with a quick swing, launched a coffee cup in his direction.

"I've had it, Griff! You can't tell me it's going to be all right! It isn't! And we both know it!" Another plate skimmed over his head and exploded against the wall. "You don't even come home at night anymore! You'd rather sleep in your office than at home with me! Well, I'm tired of being alone! And I'm tired of you! I'm done! And don't bother to call me! I won't answer! Not ever again!"

With her words ringing in his ears, Susan walked through the dining room, past him, and collected her suitcases from where she had set them beside the door. Then, without a backwards glance, she slipped through the door, leaving him to stare after her as the panel swung closed and latched, half their dinnerware a pile of unrecognizable broken pieces scattered around him.

He knew she was right, and for the first time he had not tried to refute her claims. He knew they were *done*. It was his fault, but nonetheless, they were *done*.

Slowly, he walked into the kitchen and picked up the trash can. He knelt down and gathered up the shards. As he transferred the pieces into the can, he became aware of a blond-haired woman kneeling beside him; she was wearing jeans and a lightweight work shirt he recognized instantly.

She turned her head, smiled, and caught his right hand, and he smiled at her. "Charlie..."

The image blurred as he spoke out loud and opened his eyes. Helen was smiling back at him.

"Sorry, Glen," Helen said softly as she squeezed his hand. "Just me, but she'd be happy to know you were thinking of her."

West smiled and looked at his hand, realizing it was his mom's hand that he had felt in his dream. "Yeah, I do almost always." He took a deep breath and coughed. "She's saved me from reliving so many nightmares."

"Nightmares? What kind of nightmares?"

West shook his head slightly. "I just worry about not doing things right this time. I can't let her down like—" He stopped and looked at Helen.

Helen nodded and smiled in return. "I know, and I don't think you've let her down in any way. From the day she came to the ranch, you've done all you could to keep her safe and to show her you love her. I don't think she can have a worry in the world about how you feel about her."

He waded through his thoughts for a moment and then looked back at Helen, his gaze serious. "I was overly stern with her yesterday, and again when she stopped by this morning, and now I can't apologize. She needs..." He inhaled and his shoulders sagged. "There are things I think she has to do and I made her promise me she would do them—even though she was adamant that she did not want to do them, at least not now. I insisted and she finally agreed. I shouldn't have been so demanding, and now, I can't hold her and comfort her so she knows I know how she feels."

"I don't think I've ever heard you talk this way before," Helen remarked. "It's nice to see."

"That I'm being overbearing and forcing her to—"

"No! For caring enough to think of apologizing to her." Helen smacked his shoulder gently. "You mean a lot to her too—enough for her to trust you more than anyone and to allow herself to marry you. And I think she knows she means a lot to you as well, especially after saving her and Cat's lives Friday night. Is the promise something I should know about?"

West chuckled and shook his head, realizing his mother might be hoping for a certain kind of news. "That would not be a secret and I certainly would not have to ask her to promise me anything if we were going to have a child. No, Mother, it isn't anything like that, but it may be just as serious."

"Well then, I believe your cellphone still works, and the last time I looked, your fingers were still working too. Call her—the rest will take care of itself." She handed him his phone. "And while you do that, I'll take a short walk down the hallway. Lenny should be coming back with coffee anytime now."

"Sergeant Kilman, may I have a word?" Officer Fred Mitchell asked as he rapped on the sergeant's office door.

Kilman looked up from the papers on his desk and gave Mitchell a blank stare.

"If you must," he answered, and closed the folder containing the papers. "Did you finish reviewing the dog report?"

"I did, and I have given it back to Jones," Mitchell replied. "But I wanted to speak with you because I did some digging concerning the Mary Collingsworth issue—"

"The detectives are doing that!" Kilman said sharply, his voice suddenly heated.

"I...know, sir. But I found—"

"What? What could you possibly have found that they have not already found?"

Mitchell inhaled and squared his shoulders. "Possibly where she went after she escaped."

"What?" Sergeant Kilman stared at him for a long moment. "You think you know where she went?"

"Yes, sir. Possibly," Mitchell continued, and stepped forward, stopping at the edge of Kilman's desk. He laid a sheet of paper in front of the sergeant. "It seems that Mary Carole Collingsworth, before she married Howard Collingsworth, was a Rothman, the daughter of Hamilton and Carole Janet Rothman. She was named after her mother, her middle name Carole.

"Now her mother, Carole Janet, was a Madison, the daughter of Carl and Janet Madison. Carl was of the Lake Huron Banking Madisons and Carole Janet was named after her mother, Janet Emli. She was a Hancock, the Boston Oceanic Shipping Hancocks, specifically Wilson Hancock and Elizabeth Catherine Fitzpatrick Hancoc—"

"This is all nice and interesting, but what does this have to do with Mary Collingsworth's location?"

"When Janet Emli Hancock Madison passed, Carole Janet Madison Rothman inherited her mother's house in north Detroit. Carole Janet Madison was widowed by then and she kept the house titled in her mother's name, Janet Emli Hancock. And when Carole Janet died, Mary inherited the house. She also kept it titled in Janet Emli's name, her maternal grandmother, but it is her house and no one seems to realize it."

"Okay?" Kilman asked slowly, beginning to accept that Mitchell might be on to something. "So, do you think Mary went to her grandmother's house? I mean her house in her grandmother's name?"

"I do," Mitchell answered. "An interesting aside is that both of Mary's daughters were named after their grands. First was Catherine, named after Elizabeth Catherine Hancock, and Emli named after Janet—"

"—Emli Madison," Kilman said, completing Mitchell's sentence. "Where's the house?"

"On Arden Park Boulevard, between John R. Street and Brush Street. Just two miles by road"—he glanced at the walls, toward the Henry Ford Hospital across the freeway from the precinct building—"from here and the hospital. That might have something to do with why we can't find Howard." He slid another sheet of paper to Sergeant Kilman. "Here's the address I found."

Kilman swiveled his chair, picked up his desk phone, and punched a button from the array on the left side. "Dispatch. I need three squad cars..."

Howard, holding himself as erect as possible and hoping no one would notice his fatigue when he left, stared at himself in the mirror of Jack's Gently Used Garments, a used clothing store in northeast Detroit. The jeans were worn some, but not threadbare. The flannel shirt was a subdued plaid and fit well; he had lost more weight than he realized. He would have to look elsewhere for socks, but the shoes gave him a second pair that fit better than the ones he had found before he fled. But the thing that startled him the most was the thin face under the gray hair and behind a hastily trimmed white beard and mustache that stared back at him. The eyes were still commanding and did not convey the physical weakness he actually felt.

He had parked Mary's car beside the building at the end of a five-store strip mall, backed in so the license plate was not easily seen. Then, with four fifties from the small bundle of cash in his briefcase and the case returned to the passenger side footwell, he had gotten out and entered the store. He had been careful to keep the trench coat from flapping open as he walked slowly into the shop and began browsing. The clerk noticed him and his unorthodox appearance, and began following him as he wandered through the store.

At one point the clerk, possibly the owner, stopped him to enquire as to what he was looking for.

Howard quickly held a fifty up between them. "Hold this until I find something that looks suitable."

The clerk took the fifty, held it up to the light, and nodded. He turned and pointed out the areas of the store where various clothing items were. Howard nodded and followed his gestures to continue browsing.

When he had found suitable jeans, shirt, belt, shoes, and a long-waisted jacket, he tried everything on. Saying the changing room was small was an understatement—he could barely bend over to slip his legs into the pants—but he persisted and, somewhat satisfied, folded the hospital gown and shoes neatly inside the trench coat and then rolled them into a bundle. On his way to the counter, he spotted a display of short-billed felt hats and found one that fit.

The man at the counter checked the items and rang up the total. Howard handed him another fifty and the clerk gave him his change. Smiling, Howard left the store and returned to Mary's car. He had successfully completed the first two things he needed to do: clothes for a disguise and some smaller change in his pocket.

Now he felt like he could move around more naturally and get the other things done that he needed to do before he went back to the house to get his gun, his wallet, and the rest of his money from Mary.

Cat had finished connecting the server that she had brought back from Farmington to the ranch internet network when June poked her head in and asked if she had seen Charlie. Mel answered, saying that she was up top with Ratchet and Bump.

"Thanks, Mel," June replied, and stepped back into the hallway.

Mike had glanced up when June came in but quickly turned back to watch his mother finish wiring the server connections.

Cat had spent the entire morning exclusively with Mike and Mel, from right after they landed, through breakfast, and up until Becky had announced that lunch was ready. It felt to her like so much had happened in the children's time while she was away and she wanted to hear everything they could tell her about the days she had missed. They were growing up so fast, and were spilling over with the excitement and thrills of working on the ranch. Immediately after lunch, she brought Mike and Mel to the security office with its walls of monitors and they began hooking up the server.

"That ought to do it," Cat said, smiling at the children, and set the server unit back on the shelf with the wires hidden behind it. "Let's power it up and see if it will work."

"Yeah," Mike encouraged, and Mel smiled.

Together, they huddled beside their mother as she switched apps on her laptop. The customary security screen came up and Cat selected her parents' server from the drop-down list. In seconds, the dimly lit interior filled the four-screen display. "There it is."

"Are you sure it's their house?" Mel asked, looking closely to see the details in the images.

"Sure am," Cat replied. "Look at the kitchen, the counter and stools. The dining...room..." Cat's voice trembled as the horrible memories of that room flashed through her mind. "...the living room and the family room."

"There's grandfather's red recliner," Mike confirmed.

Cat quickly checked each camera connection and decided their trip had been successful—at least that part of the trip. Then the thoughts of West slipped into her mind.

"How did West get hurt?" Mike asked, as if he could see what she was thinking.

"I guess I'd have to say by saving Charlie's and my life, again," Cat began, and continued to explain how everything that evening had happened. "The doctor says he should recover completely in time, but his leg may make him irritable for a while."

When she had finished, Mike looked up at her and smiled. "I like West more each day. I hope he gets well really soon."

"That's nice to say, and we all wish for his speedy recovery," Cat added. "But when he comes home, he'll still be in his cast and not feeling very well. So you'll need to be on your best behavior."

"We will. We'll fix fences for him and Robert the best we can and be extra helpful when we help up top. We owe him a lot, Mom."

"Yes, we do. We all do," Cat agreed, remembering how much she owed Charlie and Glen.

"God! It feels like I've been gone a month, not just four days," Charlie said emphatically, and set the parts list down on the table. "I can't seem to concentrate. Sorry." She smiled up at Ratchet as he straightened up and chuckled softly.

"I know. I do know how it is, and no one blames you for feeling distracted. I worry about him too, but you will always worry about him more deeply than the rest of us. Don't let the fact that you do, bother you." Ratchet patted her back and turned to the papers. "It looks like Mr. Miles has listed all of the big parts except for engine wraps, a couple of fairings, and a few miscellaneous sheet metal pieces. There are a lot of the smaller items missing."

"Yeah," Charlie agreed, forcing herself to focus on the Tempest project paperwork. "He also doesn't indicate the condition of the major assemblies. I mean, look at his notation on the condition of the wings. There's no notations about any of the attach fittings, or of the many cast parts throughout the structure. He's vague in the same way when he describes the tail group and the fuselage. The details of each major component are glossed over—or at least it seems that way."

Ratchet chuckled again. "I guess that's why Lenny and I are going to inspect what he actually has."

"I guess so," Charlie said, nodding to his chuckles. "I think you really need to look at the condition of the engine. Sabre parts are not going to be easy to find—"

"You must be talking about the Tempest," June interrupted as she came through the hallway between Hangar One and Two and approached Charlie's desk. When she had first arrived, she wondered why Charlie had put her desk out on the hangar floor and not in an office, but she remembered Ratchet had explained that that way Charlie was "in the middle" of what was going on—the work, the inspections, and the flight preparations.

Ratchet turned at June's voice and slipped his arm around her shoulders when she stopped beside them. "We are. Just trying to get a feel for what we should expect when we compare Mr. Miles's parts collection list to your project list. What are you up to?"

"Looking for Charlie," June admitted. "I stopped by the security office and saw Cat and the children working on or hooking up something electronic—"

"A surveillance server," Charlie interrupted. "We flew back to Farmington to get it, hoping that it would work from here."

"Is that why you went?"

Charlie nodded.

"I see. I didn't stay to see if it did, but they seemed to be getting close to trying it out when I stopped by to ask if they had seen you."

"So what can I do for you?"

"Oh, Cappie was talking with Jess about her house," June started to explain. "She had something added and he needed her to go with him to see how it came out. But before they went, he started asking me about things I want in my place. And I thought I should talk to you before I answered him."

"Okay," Charlie said. "And what do you want to talk about?" Charlie noted that June glanced at Ratchet. "Why don't we go up to your office and Ratchet can continue going through the parts list you put together?"

"Sure. That'll be good."

June's expression brightened and Charlie led her to the pass-through into Hangar One and up the stairs.

"Now that we're out of earshot," Charlie began, referring to Ratchet's presence and hearing, "what are you concerned about?"

"First, that you and West are actually going to build me a house." June shook her head to keep from staring at Charlie.

"You'll earn it. We have a number of rebuild projects in stores, and only a couple have enough parts to start a restoration. West reviews each, and when he thinks we have enough parts for a given airplane, he'll start restoring it."

"I was looking at the lists and wish he could give me some guidelines on when there are enough to start."

"Each one is different, but what I would suggest is that you concentrate on the current projects first, and then go through each of the others and just find all of the missing parts you can."

"That's the conclusion I was coming to." June shook her head again as Charlie sat down on the corner of her desk. "But back to the house. Cappie has plans for one- and two-bedroom houses, some with dens or family rooms in addition to the living rooms..."

"Are you planning on having kids?"

June looked at Charlie and slowly smiled. "I want children, and seeing Ratchet with Mel and Mike, I think he'll be okay with a couple. We talk about everything else, it seems, but we haven't actually talked about children yet."

"Probably ought to before you set a date."

"Aah, yes. He did ask me to tell him when I'm ready."

Charlie waited, watching June. "Well, if you think you're going to have kids, I suggest at least two bedrooms and the family room option. You may not want a den and try to keep your work out of the house. I mean, keep your home for the two of you or you two and your kids."

June smiled. "I think that would be good. I'm puzzled though. He said he'd like to start with the digging as soon as he can, and that is why he's asking so soon."

"He wants to beat the first freeze and the usual snows." Charlie saw the confusion on June's face. "The tunnel. He wants to dig the tunnel and have the boys form up the slab."

"He wants to dig another tunnel?"

"All of the houses and barns are connected by tunnels—to be used when the weather is bad, like the last time it rained so hard. You can get to the barn and into the storage areas without going out and driving in the rain. You can also go from one house to another if you want to."

"I see. I hadn't realized there was a network of tunnels. I only knew of the one main tunnel." Then June's expression turned serious as she glanced back at the office door.

"What is it?"

June glanced back at the door. "It's probably nothing," June finally admitted, and looked back at Charlie. "Somehow, talking about the tunnels made me remember, I don't know why. Yesterday after Lenny and Helen left, I was coming down from here and overheard Ratchet and Bump talking. Bump asked if West's trouble was because of the men we saw in Reno and Ratchet said it was, in part.

"Bump asked what else bothered him, and Ratchet told him it was more than that and that he felt it also had to do with a list of Howard's—something to do with the men that were looking for me. I didn't hear any specific details, but Ratchet has been unusually quiet about his trip back to help me. Is there something going on that I don't know about?"

Charlie looked at June and figured her expression was going to give her away. "Yeah, probably." Charlie sighed. "I thought—hoped—Ratchet would have told you, but after his trip back in August, we asked Lloyd to continue watching out for you and another. Lloyd and his man Rodney stayed to watch over you and he sent two others down to North Carolina to watch the other woman.

"Lloyd had Rodney on nights, watching your apartment while you were here at the ranch and at Reno, but Rodney went missing the night your apartment was broken into. They found his body down by Wilmington the day after you got home, and Matt told Ratchet. Rodney was murdered and dumped into the river. The two that the police suspect broke into your place tried again the night you left and came back to the ranch with Ratchet. They were both killed by the new tenants."

"Killed? New tenants?"

"Yeah. Your apartment was rented the day after you and Ratchet moved all of your belongings out. Lloyd said that Matt overheard the two men before they broke in again. They were looking for you because Howard Collingsworth wanted you or Celia for one of his *deals*."

"Collingsworth...yeah, Lloyd mentioned him when he talked to us. Jess said he was Cat's father, the one that tried to kidnap you?"

"He is. And now we know the men you and Ratchet saw in Reno were following Cat and me—probably trying to figure out how to capture one of us in a third attempt."

"A third attempt? I don't understand." June stepped behind her desk and slowly sat down in her chair.

"The first attempt was when they captured me and Dani in Broomfield, Fourth of July weekend. The second was when they kidnapped Cat in late July. What we don't know is how many attempts Howard has set in motion. Counting you and Celia as one, there were nine potentials."

June studied Charlie for a long moment. "And from what Helen told us yesterday, the men from Reno followed you to Detroit and it was one of them that shot West."

"That's about the size of it. That is also why I planned for us to leave the day after we got there. Both Cat and I were afraid they might know we were coming. Lloyd had checked out Cat and Monte's house and neighborhood, and because everything looked quiet and they were close by, we decided to go."

"Wow."

"Jess keeps tabs on Howard's email server and lets us know when anything—"

"Oh shit. Email! Jess wanted me to tell you that Mary Collingsworth sent an email to someone named Oscar to tell him she was coming to his office this afternoon."

"Oh my. That is very risky with all of Detroit out looking for her and Howard."

"Sure is. She also mentioned that she would bring him a video with audio of Howard beating her and admitting she wasn't smart enough to help him. He said she did not help him but also said that he would never admit it to anyone, especially not the police." June looked up at Charlie. "Jess said he said he 'owned her, for better or worse.'"

Charlie slowly closed her eyes and leaned back, tilting her head as if she were looking up at the ceiling. She sighed and wondered if Mary could actually pull it off and escape from Howard's grasp. She opened her eyes and looked at June. "Has Jess told Cat?"

June slowly shook her head. "I don't know, but probably not yet. Cat has been with the children since you landed."

"Okay," Charlie said abruptly, and stood up. "We need to talk to Jess."

Bobby looked past Mary as he backed his dark blue minivan out of the driveway of the south-facing house, into the west-bound lane of Arden Park Boulevard. He swung through the mid-block cut in the grass- and tree-lined median and drove east past Brush Street. Mary glanced down Brush and saw flashing lights two blocks down and coming north, but Bobby drove on, unhurried, as if he had not seen them. At the next street, he turned north and saw the police cars turn west behind them.

"Looks like our timing was better than we expected," he said smugly, and continued to the first street east after the elementary school. He turned and left the neighborhood.

Officer Sally Ableman had had a busy day and decided to retire early. Her wandering thoughts kept her awake and she debated whether she should just get up or keep trying to clear her head and sleep.

She remembered how Officer Mitchell had looked at her that morning, his curiosity begging for some sign from her. But she was torn, wary. Even after she had gotten to know him some during their guard duty at the hospital, she was not certain how she was supposed to react to him falling asleep while he was on duty, resulting in Howard Collingsworth's escape. And then he had figured out where Howard's wife might be hiding, and maybe Howard with her. But the surprise came when she had been assigned to be among the squads checking the address out and he had not.

All in all, she knew he was kind and sincere, not at all arrogant or intentionally intimidating like his somewhat body-builder physique implied. But for some reason, Sgt. Kilman, their supervisor, seemed to hold them both responsible for the loss. Her maybe less than Fred, but still responsible.

It was nearly midnight and she had finally dozed off, not yet fully asleep, when she was awakened by a soft, distinct scratching noise.

What's that? she asked herself as she sat up and studied the darkness, looking first at her bedroom window. She shook her head. *Not there. You're on the second floor.* She grabbed her phone and slipped out of bed.

Shit! One guess what I have here.

In the living room the scratching was louder, though still soft and irregular. She fixed on the front door as she collected her backup Glock from the drawer in the end table beside the hall where she was standing. Then, with a few short steps, she stopped at the door and peered through the peephole. A shadowy figure was huddled low in front of the door, working at the lock, the railing hiding him from passers-by on the walk below.

Be quiet and be patient, she told herself, mentally reciting her training mantra as she stepped back away from the door and touched the icon for her dispatcher. *Don't do anything yet. Let him make his move first.*

"Officer Ableman here," she announced in a loud whisper when the connection made. "I have an intruder trying to jimmy the lock to my apartment. Send assistance. I am armed and waiting."

Then she sat down in the lounger beside the front window, curled her legs up in front of her, and held the pistol leveled at the door. Now, she knew she would wait for the patrol to arrive and either scare the intruder off or catch him, or she would respond when he opened her door.

Fifty-Four

Tuesday, October 3

Charlie tossed and turned for several hours before she finally fell into a fitful sleep.

It was late and her apartment was dark and she heard a faint click. She rolled over to face the apartment door and saw the barest sliver of light creep down its edge as the panel slowly swung inward. She slipped her hand under her pillow, reaching for her pistol. Her eyes never left the door until... The pistol was gone!

She shook her head and turned, flipping the pillow aside, frantically looking for the pistol! Her heart was racing and her brow wet with cold perspiration, but there was no pistol!

Panicked, fearful for her life, she looked back at the door—and suddenly realized the door was closed and her bedroom was dark except for the moonlight streaming through the sliding doors to their private veranda.

She trembled and hugged herself, remembering...she remembered the night in her apartment when she woke up ready to shoot someone that wasn't there. And now she was ready to do it again, only now she wasn't alone in her apartment.

"Nonono." She hugged herself and rocked in denial. "I can't be having that dream again! I can't!" The dream scared her and she knew she was losing it again, unable to completely calm her fears. "Thank God my pistol wasn't there!" Knowing she could be a serious danger to Cat, the children, or anyone around her, scared her more than anything ever had—even Howard.

With tears flowing and unable to stop her shivering, she lay back down and pulled the blanket around her, fervently hoping she could keep herself together until West got home.

Karl deVon walked briskly down the long hallway, turned, and quickly stepped into Deputy Minister of State Security Elrich Voster's office. The portrait of the South African president glared down from its place on one wall and the portrait of the minister of state security glared down from the opposite wall as deVon waved a sheet of paper and hurried across the length of the office, stopping in front of Voster's desk. Deputy Voster looked up with a questioning expression.

"I have just received a message from the City of Detroit in the State of Michigan," deVon stated, and placed the sheet of paper firmly in front of Voster. "They say they have a body identified as Claude Schmidt. His passport and their documentation investigation confirmed that he worked for this department. He was killed in a home intrusion activity, drawing a weapon on four people in their private residence."

"Killed?" Voster's eyebrows rose in disbelief. "By whom?"

"Yes," deVon reconfirmed. "The report summary claims that he entered the residence by deception, looking for information, and drew his weapon when he was asked to leave. One of the guests present shot him when he fired twice at a man and woman, hitting the man with both shots. They were also guests."

Voster's shoulders drooped.

"They want to know when we will come and take possession of the body and responsibility for his actions." deVon glanced down at the sheet of paper. "There are expenses incurred in processing the body and there are criminal charges—criminal assault, battery, and attempted murder by deadly force—that must be dealt with. And there are State

Department issues to be addressed before they can release the body to a foreign government."

Voster picked up the sheet and studied the email for a long moment. Then he looked up. "Leave this to me. I will answer this, and in the meantime, you contact Brown and find out what he knows and where he is at the present moment. I may have new instructions for him in an hour or two."

Winded and sweating, West hopped up to the hospital bed and turned his walker around. He could not believe how difficult it was for him to simply go to the end of the corridor and back, a short distance for him mere days past.

Lenny caught one of his arms, the nurse caught his other arm, and together they gently set him on the edge of the bed. Helen smiled her encouragement from where she stood beside Monte, sitting in the overstuffed chair near the foot of his bed.

Lenny and the nurse swung West up onto the bed and covered his legs, his right leg and cast jutting up like a small mountain under the covers. Helen straightened the sheets around West and wiped his beaded brow while the nurse raised the lower half of the bed, matching the angle of his injured leg.

"Other than being tired, how do you feel?" Helen asked when the nurse had gone and Lenny had taken the straight-backed chair.

"Like an invalid!" West confirmed, softly emphatic. "Four days ago I was fine and doing normal things, and now I can barely hold myself up. At least I can go to the bathroom by myself."

"Why are you acting like this?" she asked. "You know perfectly well why you are this way. And Charlie and Cat are extremely grateful you were there for them."

"I know, I know, Mom. It's just difficult to suddenly be the victim and unable to do what I could do yesterday. But I'll beat this."

"There is nothing to beat," Helen contradicted. "Just do the exercises and you'll be fine. We don't want any complications." She smiled at a happier thought. "How did your call to Charlie go?"

Monte's phone chimed and he got up, glancing at the screen before West could answer. "Sorry, I'll take this out in the hallway."

West inhaled and watched Monte step out of the room as he let his head settle into the pillow. Then he continued. "Very good, I think. She sounded very happy that I called." He sighed, then continued softly. "I am so grateful to have her in my life."

"Did she say anything when you apologized?"

"She just said I didn't need to. She said she still didn't like having to do what I asked, but understands why I asked her to promise me."

"Are you going to tell me what she promised?"

"No, Mother. I am not," West said, and looked her in the eye. "This is between Charlie and me."

Helen smiled. "I just thought I'd ask, son."

"Hey, Lloyd," Monte answered as he stepped out of West's room. "I was wondering about you. What have you found?"

"Morning, Monte. Haven't found out much, but I do have a thought and some questions."

"Okay. Ask away."

"Some updates first. We confirmed what you suspected: the men that followed you from Reno to your home came into the country through the South African Embassy. How they figured out that you were coming here when you did is still a mystery."

"That fits with what we know about Howard's activities and why he kidnapped Cat."

"Yes. And I think his companion, a Cecil Brown, was the

man in the car Saturday night—the one we startled before we got to your house."

When Monte did not say anything, Lloyd continued.

"At first I was thinking those two were brought back to Detroit to look for Howard, based on that email to Howard that you showed me, but it seems something changed. I know you said the one that came to your house was asking about Howard, but I have been trying to figure out why he suddenly decided to shoot at your wife and West's."

"We've been trying to figure that out as well."

"I don't have an answer yet, but because they still seem to be in danger, I need to ask you if you still have that rental in Colorado Springs—the one you said you were going to use as an office."

Monte hesitated, trying to guess what Lloyd was thinking. Finally, he admitted, "Yes...I do still have it, but I won't—"

"I know, but if you still have it I'd like to send Matt out, and if you are agreeable I'd like for him to stay there and keep watch of you and you and your wife when she's with you in town."

"That would certainly be a relief to have him around..."

"Good. I'll take that as a 'yes,' and I can keep tabs on Cecil with others I know here. So I'll send Matt to help you in Colorado, and I'll try to find leads on Howard."

"Okay. I'll continue getting everything ready to move, and Matt will have some time to study the landscape before I get back. Probably will be another week, maybe longer. When do you plan on sending him out?"

"As soon as you agree and you give him a key. I'll text you his number and you two can communicate directly, set up a meeting with him, give him a key and the address and so on. I don't need to be in your conversations unless you need for me to be. Thanks. I'll be in touch."

Monte smiled, suddenly relieved to know Matt would be close by. The connection broke and he returned his phone to his pocket, absently nodding. He would agree to just about anything Lloyd suggested if it would help keep Cat safe.

"Sorry, Mitchell," Officer Sally Ableman said in greeting as she passed his desk at the start of their shift. "After Kilman mentioned that you figured out where to go looking, I was surprised he didn't include you when we went to check the address out."

"Hey," he remarked in reply. "I wasn't. It's still my fault that Howard is on the lam and not in custody. Kilman won't let me forget that for a long time."

A strained moment passed between them, and then he continued.

"Thanks for saying hi. I was thinking maybe my blunder had turned you away also."

Sally smiled. "It was terribly unfortunate, but I do understand how it can happen. Even on days, it was hard to stay alert."

"Thanks."

"So what does Kilman have you working on during your penance?"

"Fact checking and reviewing the daily reports that are submitted." Then he looked up at her and smiled. "But"—he gestured to the chair at the end of his desk—"while you were away yesterday looking for the elusive Mary Collingsworth, I reviewed the charges we have against Howard."

Sally took the chair and twisted to face him.

"The one I was looking for was concerning Howard kidnapping his own daughter, Catherine. It was during her rescue, led by a private investigator, that he was severely wounded."

"Yeah. I read the Port Huron Police report."

"Well, what snagged my attention was that no one's seen his

daughter since her rescue, until"—he slipped a sheet of paper to her—"last Saturday night. She and her husband and another couple and two men showed up at their home in Farmington. I understand they came back to prepare their house for sale."

Sally nodded absently as she listened.

"That evening, the Claude Schmidt we have in the morgue came to their house and talked his way inside, where he shot a man named Glen West. He and his wife were the other couple. The same private investigator that rescued Catherine killed Claude."

"Wow. That's a lot of coincidences."

"Yeah. Too many." Fred nodded. "I also found out that Mr. West is at the Bradmont Hospital in East Farmington, but when I called for general information, I was told Catherine and the other woman have quietly gone back home, but what was strange was that they told me the hospital has not admitted anyone by the name of West."

"Really? Glen West was shot, but not admitted to the hospital? Does he have a different name? Anyway, how's this connected with Mary or Howard's disappearance?"

"I don't know yet, but I think we're only seeing the top part of the iceberg. Could you check and see what you can find out about the Wests?"

Sally nodded again.

"Thanks. I decided to look at the other charges and realized a significant number of them, many unrelated to the kidnapping, had been filed by an attorney, Norman Kent, of Colorado Springs, Colorado, on behalf of Catherine. Of particular interest is one that accuses Howard of arranging the kidnapping of Mrs. West and another woman in Broomfield Colorado last Fourth of July weekend. The report indicated Mrs. West is a lookalike for Howard and Mary's missing daughter, Emli."

"Lookalikes? How can Mrs. West look like Collingsworth's daughter?"

"I don't know."

"That sounds so weird."

"Yeah." Fred looked down at the sheets in front of him and then smiled. "Sorry. I'm going on and on and haven't given you a moment's breath to tell me what you found out yesterday. I heard Mary wasn't there."

Sally nodded and smiled back at him. "Kilman is going to have a briefing this morning, but no, she was—"

"Ableman! Mitchell!" Sergeant Kilman's voice echoed down the main hall and spilled into the offices. "Briefing room! You're late!"

"I guess he's called his meeting," Sally chuckled, and quickly stood, sliding the sheet of paper back onto Fred's desk.

"Seems like he has," he agreed with a sigh, and gestured for Sally to lead the way.

"But Mooommm—" Mike complained.

"Michael Ralph Williamson! Stop!" Cat snapped, and stared at him. "Celina gave you two the day off from your schooling yesterday so we could be together. Is this how you show your appreciation?"

She held his eyes until his head bowed. Then she looked at Mel's startled expression. Mel had quickly glanced in surprise at Mike beside her and back again, her shoulders squared and her back straight and rigid, trying to silently distance herself from her brother's inappropriate outburst.

"No," Mike admitted softly. "There's just so much to get done before the snows start..." He let his words die as he saw his mother's icy stare.

Cat held her stare for another minute before she slowly let her shoulders drop and she glanced at Charlie, ashamed of the scene her son had created when she told him fences and work up top had to wait. Charlie had covered her mouth, but Cat could see her eyes were dancing.

Cat sighed and turned back to Mike. "Have you seen anyone else here act so unruly when they disagree with something?"

"No," he replied softly.

"Then I suggest you apologize to Charlie and everyone else for your lapse in manners and then we can discuss the situation more calmly."

"Yes, Mom." Mike turned to Charlie and offered his apology, and then did the same to everyone else at the breakfast table.

"We accept your apology, Mike," Charlie said gently. "And we all understand there is a lot to be done. There always is, and I appreciate that you and Mel have taken such an active role in helping around the ranch and up top. But your mother is absolutely right: school first. There will be plenty to do after you have finished your time with Celina."

"Thanks." Mike paused and glanced at his mom. "I was worried we won't get the fences inspected, and Robert was telling us we need to be moving the cattle into the fields in the valley west of the main house. It feels like we're running out of time, with it getting dark so very early now."

"I know how you feel," Charlie agreed, and smiled at Mike. "Tell you what. You and Mel go and do what you have to do this morning and when Celina has finished, you two and your mom come and find me. I'll see if Peter can have the horse trailer and a jeep ready for this afternoon."

Mike's eyes lit up as he smiled. He looked across the table at his mom and at his sister beside him, and then back to Charlie. "Thank you. We'll get everything done best we can and be ready. Is that okay, Mom?"

Cat nodded and smiled at Charlie. Then to Mike she replied, "Yes, dear. That will work out fine. Now eat your breakfast before Becky thinks you'd rather complain than eat." She smiled to take the sting out of her words.

"Now that that is settled," Woody began, and looked at Charlie, "what's on the agenda this morning?"

Charlie glanced around the table, noting the three empty chairs: West's, Helen's, and Lenny's. She cleared her throat and forced herself to smile. "We'll talk while we eat. Please pass the scrambled eggs and the ham."

"We have all of the major components for the C model moved up into Hangar Two," Ratchet began. "Mike and Mel have been helping us sort and clean parts when they've had time, and June has a pretty complete list of what we have in stores." He winked at her and took a bite of his breakfast.

"We still need," June added, picking up the conversation when Ratchet stopped, "a few hydraulic system components, an aileron trim tab, and a number of coolant system tubes and parts, including a header tank. Bump says we have some damaged ones we can cannibalize and make a good one." She smiled at Bump and saw Dani's grin. "We'll see how he does repairing the old parts. And, I called Buck and two other possible sources to see what they might be able to find."

Bump smiled and nodded. "I can make a serviceable part."

"I'm sure you can," Charlie agreed, and sipped her coffee. "Woody?"

"I'll need time with Felix this morning," he replied, and glanced at Cat. "I picked up a Cessna Bird Dog over the weekend, and since she's back, I need her to take me to get it and I'll escort her home—a sorta solo cross-country."

"An O-1? Obviously it's flyable."

"Yup. This one is actually an L-19E, but converted to removable dual controls."

Charlie nodded acknowledgement.

"Not nearly as nice as your 180 was. It needs a bit of work, but it's airworthy." Woody smiled at Charlie's question. "I figure we need something better to use to check on the cattle, make general checks on the fences, and anything else around the ranch that needs checkin'. It'll make a good trainer, and with oversized tires it can land almost anywhere on the ranch. Besides, we need another taildragger with a stick in the stables."

"I see." Charlie nodded and chuckled at the thought of *needing* another taildragger; the rented 172 and her Legacy were the only tricycle-gear planes on the ranch.

"You can have her," Jess added, then looking at Charlie, "after I get a chance to talk with her and you, Charlie. Sorry Woody, but I got an email from Norman and I need to talk with them after breakfast. I'll try to keep it short."

Charlie looked at Woody and then at Cat, and when she smiled, Charlie agreed.

"Let's get you inside," Monte said as he opened the front door to his and Cat's house. Lenny helped West negotiate the steps. "I hope the memories won't be too bad or keep you awake."

"Shouldn't," West retorted as he positioned the crutches and hopped up the first and then the second step. "I don't remember anything after the fact—just the falling."

He crossed the porch and took the last step up into the house. Monte led the way and stopped in the living room.

Helen followed them in and went into the kitchen, setting her sack on the counter.

"Where would you like to be?" Monte asked, and gestured to the dining room and the kitchen.

"I think the dining room." West started hopping in that direction.

"I hope you're as hungry as you said you were," Helen remarked from the kitchen. "The portions look very big."

"I am, Mom," West answered, absently rubbing the deep,

lightly scabbed and itchy abrasion on his right temple as Lenny helped him settle into a chair. He looked at Monte. "Thanks for stopping."

Helen pulled the plastic containers from the deli bag and placed them in front of the chairs around the table. "Drinks?"

"Just water," West answered, and Lenny and Monte agreed as Monte began filling glasses with ice.

Lunchtime passed quietly, and finally West began to glance around the combined open rooms. His focus kept returning to the splintered hole in the cabinet just to the left of the kitchen sink, just above eye level.

"What happened to the cabinet?" He gestured and Monte turned to look.

"Don't know." Monte got up and opened the door; broken glass and plate shards fell to the counter below. "Looks like a bullet hole. Must've been a third shot fired." Monte shook his head and grabbed the trash can that sat near the mudroom door. He chuckled, catching the dish towel, and began wiping the debris off the counter into the can. "Now there's less stuff to be packed."

Lenny looked puzzled and reached up, turning West's head. "Helen? Could that explain the cut here on the right side of your son's hard head?"

Helen got up and came around to look.

"Oh my! Looks like it could at that," she agreed, and glanced back at the cabinet door. Her hands suddenly trembled. "No one said that man fired three shots."

West tried to act nonchalant and forced a chuckle. "Don't look at me, I only remember the first one."

"We'll have to start calling you 'Lucky' instead of West," Lenny jested.

West looked at him for a long moment, realizing how close that one had come, then shrugged. "I'm just glad I saw what was happening soon enough and Charlie and Cat didn't get hurt." He suddenly yawned hugely.

"I think you need to lie down for a little while," Helen remarked, changing the subject.

"We'll put you in the downstairs guest room," Monte said, and got up. "Let me see if the bed is still made up."

"He went down easier than I expected," Lenny commented as Helen came back into the living room and settled into an overstuffed chair.

"Obviously he's more tired than he wants to admit," she said. "And I think that third bullet got his attention. It certainly got mine."

"Yeah," Monte chimed in. "That one was too close for comfort."

Helen nodded and, still trembling, pulled her phone out of her pocket. "I think I'll give Charlie a call."

"Let her know he's out of the hospital?" Monte asked absently.

"She already knows that. I know she's been watching the buttons. But I thought I'd see how she and Felix are holding up."

"So, what does Norman have to say?" Charlie asked as she settled into an extra chair at the end of Cat's desk.

Jess switched her laptop on and gestured to the screen. "It seems that a police officer in Detroit contacted him yesterday afternoon with questions."

Charlie nodded. Police officers and lawyers would seldom contact anyone if it was not for questions.

"The officer had been reviewing the charges brought against Howard, and when the report of West being shot reached his desk, he realized that you, Felix—well, you, Howard's daughter—were in town. He tried to find you at home and then at the hospital, but you'd already left. It was the charges filed by Norman on your behalf that suggested how he might reach you."

"So? What does the officer want to know?" Cat asked, and glanced at Charlie.

Jess looked at the screen and clicked the mouse a few times. "His first question is whether you know of any properties your mother might own under a different name—ones other than your father's."

"A different name?"

"Like her maiden name, or under a relative's name. Norman thinks they are trying to find anything that might lead them to places where she might hide. He also suspects she was involved in Howard's escape from the hospital."

Charlie pulled her phone out of her hip pocket and punched an icon. "Hey, Eddie. Got a minute?" She nodded when Eddie said something. "Do you remember where you and Mom filed that list of properties we put together in July, when we were trying to figure out where Howard had taken Felix? Uh-huh. Sure. We're in Jess's and Felix's office. Okay."

She tapped her phone and put it back into her pocket.

"Eddie's coming. She was visiting with her dad, but says she can pull up the files I remember."

"I thought," Cat began when Charlie looked at her, "you said it was the tracking button that led you to me."

"It was. But before Eddie freaked out over seeing her icon in Michigan, we had started a search for any properties connected to Howard or his business' name. We thought he would go somewhere that was familiar and where he might feel confident that no one would know to look. We were actually right, and it seems the officer in Detroit has the same idea."

"Well," Cat added, "I guess the Gratiot house is a good example. It belonged to Howard, but he kept it listed publically as his uncle's."

"Did your mother have any like that? Especially any that she kept private or even secret?"

"Hey guys, *Yáʼátʼééh*," Eddie greeted as she stepped through the office door. "Jess, may I use your computer for a minute?"

Jess turned the laptop to Eddie. "Help yourself. We're just discussing and looking for places where Felix's mom might be hiding."

"We can run a search on her maiden name," Eddie said as she clicked through the folder tree.

"Rothman, Madison, Hancock, or Fitzpatrick," Cat announced softly as her own laptop booted. "Those would be the most likely on Mother's side."

"Here's the file we made up in July." Eddie turned the laptop back to Jess.

Charlie thought a minute, watching Cat dive into the hunt and Jess review what had been found before. She suddenly wondered if Cat would remember the property northwest of St. Ignace that her great-grandfather Carl Madison had passed to her and Emli when they came of age: six hundred and forty acres of mixed farmland and wooded acres in Michigan's Upper Peninsula. Should be mostly covered in trees by now. She cocked her head, wondering why she remembered that. The house and barns were long gone, so there was nowhere to hide—and besides, it wasn't Mary's. It belonged to Cat and Cat's sister.

When she brought her thoughts back to the scene in the office, Charlie realized Eddie was watching her instead of the others.

"*Ni yínííl naʼadá?*" Eddie asked softly.

Charlie nodded. "Yes, *shí yínííl naʼadá*—I be troubled. I be *very* troubled," Charlie answered literally in a voice just above a whisper, holding Eddie's eyes as she spoke. She knew the others did not know that Dani and Eddie had been coaching her in a few Navajo phrases. "By many things, especially Howard and his wife being on the loose and West not being here. I don't feel right—pressured by old memories and fears."

"I know those are big worries. But you and Felix are home

and safe from them, and I think West is in the best of hands and will be home soon too."

"I know," Charlie sighed, and shook her head. "I should be glad he's recovering and doing well, and that all of their buttons moved from the hospital to Felix's house about ten our time. He's been released."

"That's good," Eddie encouraged softly as the printer clicked and spit out a sheet of paper. "But worries and the past have a way of holding on." She gestured with her fingers curling into a fist. "*Dah yootįįł.*"

Charlie nodded.

"I found seven," Cat announced cheerfully, oblivious to the conversation Eddie and Charlie were having.

"Seven?" Jess asked, surprised. "Addresses?"

"Yup," Cat confirmed. "On my mother's side and listed under her mother's and grandmother's names. I'll put the satellite pictures up on the array."

"Do you have any properties that they might have access to?" Charlie asked, trying to sound like she did not know she did.

"No." Cat looked at her with her eyebrows pinched together. "Yes, I actually do have a place. It's really my sister's and mine up in the UP."

Cat clicked her mouse a few times and the aerial views of the seven addresses and the Upper Peninsula property coalesced as individual images, nested on the merged screens.

"Whoa!" Cat zoomed in on the house and barn near the north side of the UP property, and Charlie stared at the screen in equal surprise but caught herself before she blurted anything out. "When did these get built?" Cat asked softly as the image settled. "There was nothing there when we last visited. I was eighteen or nineteen."

Charlie realized there was only one person besides Cat and her sister that could get permits to build anything on that property, and she wondered if she should drop a hint to

Norman so he could pass it along. But just as quickly as she had thought of that, she knew Cat's mother wasn't the one they needed to worry about. It was Howard, and they still did not know where he might be hiding.

Fifty-Five

Agent Cecil Brown paced in his small motel room with two queen beds, a dresser under the TV, and a straight-backed and an overstuffed chair. He was still thinking about Saturday night, when Claude had left him and gone to the Williamsons' house. He knew Claude was wrong to go, but sometimes there was no way to stop him when he made up his mind to do something. So Cecil had just settled down for the wait near the street corner by their house, until the two men knocked on the car windows and startled him out of his Wellies.

Everything had unraveled after that. He had bolted and fled the neighborhood, but when Claude had failed to call to be picked up, he had realized something more regrettable had happened.

He had called and left a voice message for Karl deVon that night, but it was nearly noon the following day before deVon had returned his call. But it was today's call from him that had Cecil distressed: Claude had shot someone in the house and was killed during the shooting.

What were you thinking? We were supposed to be listening and watching. We had no reason to approach any of them, and certainly no reason to shoot one of them.

Cecil grabbed a burger at a local drive-through on his way to Farmington and the neighborhood where he had last seen Claude. He slowed and turned the corner, surveying the Williamsons' house; the car that had been there that past

Saturday night was gone, the drive empty, but the front window drapes were pulled aside, indicating to him that someone was probably there.

He had no sooner made his observation than the garage door lifted open and the man with the athletic, football-player physique carried a trash bag to the collection cart beside the garage. He recognized the man from Reno—the darker-haired woman's husband.

Cecil continued past and drove out of the neighborhood, thinking he should come back a few times to see if the women were still around.

Howard's irritation slowly grew as he ate lunch in a nondescript diner two blocks from the shabby motel where he had been able to secure a room without a credit card. He cursed his hurry at fleeing the house without searching for his wallet or phone and without checking to see how much of his cash was actually in the briefcase. With the three months that had lapsed since he had been shot and arrested, he was certain the police had seized his accounts or at least frozen them. But he had taken some satisfaction in the fact that much of his wealth was off-shore, hidden in accounts abroad, and the cards for those accounts should have been in his briefcase.

But they were not.

He knew only one other person knew of them: Mary.

She knew *of* them, but he was surprised she had known enough to find his briefcase and take it, along with the cash, the cards, and his gun. But then after he had overheard the man at the house and Mary talking, he was surprised she had managed to affect her escape from the police. He had never noticed that she was particularly resourceful or talented in anything, and the fact that she obviously was, at least in this case, irritated him further.

Howard got up and paid his bill, then, shaking his head at his thoughts, he stepped out onto the sidewalk and studied the street. She may have surprised him, but he was determined to get back the things he needed: his phone, the cards, the money, and his gun.

It was nearly one thirty when he swung Mary's car onto Arden Park Boulevard off Oakland Avenue, just a block and a half from the house. As he slowly approached and crossed Brush Street, he realized there was an unfamiliar car in the driveway beyond the sidewalk. It was foreboding; black and unmarked, ominous to say the least.

Then he glanced at the house, and the yellow ribbon stretched across the front porch and the portico on the west caught his attention.

"Shit!"

It was obvious the police had discovered where Mary had been hiding, and now the things he needed were most likely in their hands. He cursed again, pounded on the steering wheel, and drove on past, turning north on John R., quickly leaving the neighborhood. He could think of only one other place he could look.

Mary was pacing slowly around the coffee table in Bobby's apartment when she heard the distinctive sound of his minivan. The fact that he had finished his workday and was back made her feel much better. The long day in a strange apartment, at least one that was strange to her, had made her tense; her situation and worry of discovery did not help. There were a couple of things she had decided she needed to do, especially now that Oscar was reviewing her position and she now just had to stay out of sight.

"Hey," Bobby greeted as he opened the front door and stepped in. "Did your day go all right? No one bothering you?"

"Went fine," Mary acknowledged. "No one dropped in and no one called. I guess it was a good day." She was slowly wringing her hands.

"Sorry we didn't get a chance to talk this morning, but were the accommodations okay?"

"They were fine. I told you they would be." Mary gestured to the second bedroom, the one she had used. "I should have gotten up when you did—"

"Why? It was too early and I know you couldn't have slept very good. Sleep in and enjoy the time you have while you're carefully hidden away."

"That's part of the problem."

Bobby raised his eyebrows in question.

"Me being here. It makes things worse for you. If they find me—"

"I'm okay. I said I would help and that's what I'm doing."

Mary smiled and looked at him for a long moment, trying to decide how to continue. Then she nodded. "I do need your help. Two things."

"Sure," Bobby agreed, and settled onto the cushioned chair as Mary settled on the love seat sofa. "What can I do for you?"

"A haircut and clothes. I need to change my looks."

"Aah, I see. I think I know just the person that can help with the hair and where we can go for the clothes. What else?"

"A car. I need to buy a car."

"What?" Bobby half rose from his chair but Mary raised her hand to stop his objections.

"I know what I'm doing and I have the cash. I want something simple and reliable. Older and used, but reliable. I need for you to help me pick one out."

"But...but what about the title and registration? Everyone is looking for you."

"They're looking for Mary Collingsworth, wife of Howard Collingsworth." Mary chuckled. "I haven't worn his wedding

94

ring in almost nine years." Then she handed him her driver's license. "They aren't looking for Carole Madison. I've had a second license for almost the same number of years now. Just in case.

"One night after the girls were gone, after Catherine was married and settled with Monte and Emli had disappeared, Howard was unusually upset over something that happened at his work and he took it out on me again. That was once too often. The next day, I made a decision and started making plans."

"Plans? Madison?"

"Yes. Yes, after my grandmother. I knew I would never survive serving him with divorce papers unless I had a place to go and a way to protect myself from him. So I started setting things in motion."

"You have a place?"

"I do, but not here." She smiled at the sudden hurt in Bobby's expression. "I can stay in contact through Oscar, but I cannot involve you more that I already have. In some ways, Howard's injuries and arrest makes my next moves easier. But his escape from me has made things more difficult for him." She smiled. "Now I just need to look like my license picture and get a car for Carole. Then I'm ready."

Sally Ableman turned her sports coupe off Lake Shore Drive in Grosse Pointe Shores, into the drive of her parents' palatial home on the west shore of Lake St. Clair. Compared to the larger estate on their north, her dad's lake shore home was modest with only a swimming pool and lake access; they did not have a tennis or a basketball court since her dad was not athletic and she was not a boy.

The house sat back from the road north of the marina, just above a short, sandy strip of beach with a boathouse and pier extending out into the water. She always thought it ought to be called a *yacht*-house instead, because her father's 34-footer was not a mere boat by anyone's standards.

She stopped halfway around the circle drive, in the niche formed by the house's recessed front wall, centering the main entry doors flanked by two small gardens. The upper story of the modern home extended over the drive to form a portico. Closing her car door, she slowly looked around and once again embraced the memories of growing up in a place where the floor-to-ceiling glass walls provided beautiful views of the tree-shaded lawns, the swimming pool, and the lake itself to the east.

Then she remembered her father's displeasure when she had completed college with a degree in business and had told him her life's desires had changed: she intended to become a police officer instead of working in his firm. His displeasure was even greater when she applied and was accepted.

Shaking the unpleasant memories from her mind, she pushed the front door open. Time had passed and slowly he had grudgingly accepted her choices. The door swung away from her; her mother was pulling the handle from the other side.

"I thought I heard a car drive up," her mother greeted warmly, embracing Sally with a tight hug. "I was surprised when you left a message saying you were going to stop by."

"I know you just got back a couple of days ago, and I hope it's all right to come by."

"Of course." She eyed Sally suspiciously. "Is something wrong?"

"No, nothing wrong." She had chosen to ignore the previous night's intruder, considering it a random intrusion attempt. "Work's been frustrating and I just wanted to get away and clear my head. With all that's happened in the last two weeks, I've been very busy."

"From what we've seen on the news, I figured you were

busy. Well, in a way I'm glad you're not sitting in that hospital all day long anymore."

"Me too. It was a long eight weeks. But Fred and I wish it was over for different reasons."

"Fred? Is that the young man you were trading spots with?"

"Yup." Sally nodded and turned her mother toward the kitchen and family room at the back of the house. "He was nights and I was days at the hospital, and we had two weeks left before we were to be relieved by another team."

"And you wish it was under different circumstances?"

"Yeah. I'll talk about it later. I'm sure it will come up." Sally looked around the family room. "Where's Dad?"

Her mother swallowed. "Your *father* is upstairs changing. He got home a couple of hours ago to do some cleanup in his office. He went up to change just before you got here."

"Okay," Sally commented absently as she stopped in front of the wide, full-height windows looking out over the back yard and lake. After a number of minutes, she turned at the sound of her father descending the stairs.

"Well, well. Good to see you, Sally," he greeted as he stepped into the family room. "How're things in the policing world?"

His words had an edge to them, but she chose to ignore it.

"Busy, as always," she replied. "How're things in the investment banking world?"

"Busy, as always." He smiled, mimicking her response as he gave her a gentle, though brief, hug. "Can you stay for dinner? I'm not sure what your mother is fixing, but it smells heavenly."

"It does and I was hoping," Sally admitted. "I have no other plans, except to get some sleep for a change. I just wanted to spend some time with you two since you're back in town. How was your trip? Vacation or business?"

"Both," her mother explained. "Your father had a little business in France, and the rest of the time we vacationed— France, Switzerland, and northern Italy."

"Very nice."

"Well, if you were working for me like I wanted," he continued, smiling as if to take the sting out of his words, "you could have been with us, enjoying the beautiful mountains and Italian beaches."

"Thank you, Dad," Sally bantered. "I enjoy my work and feel it's necessary."

"More necessary than—"

"Let's have a drink," Sally's mother interrupted, forestalling the potential of an impending argument. "How about you, dear?" she continued smoothly.

Sally inhaled and smiled. "Bourbon Old Fashioned...please." She was actually glad that her mother had interrupted. Her father needled her over her career choices every time she came home. His manner was so predictable, she was surprised that it still piqued her.

He got up and slowly walked to the cabinet and counter below the staircase. He fixed their drinks, then one for himself—bourbon, on the rocks.

"So what has you so busy these days?" he asked congenially as he served her and her mother. He went back to the cabinet and retrieved his glass. "Are you working on the case of the prisoner that disappeared from the hospital?"

"Yes." She took a sip. "But I can only tell you things that have appeared on the news and in the papers. Someone rigged an explosion in a utility room just off the police ward and everyone went to help the orderly that was injured by it. Even our officer on duty went to help."

"And the prisoner just hobbled out during the confusion."

"Not quite. The detainee did not set the explosion and we have proof there were two others involved. The department released pictures of the two men from the security videos; two men in scrubs, caps, and gauze masks hid in the stairwell, slipped in, and in minutes, pushed him out in a wheelchair. They exited down a service elevator before anyone knew it."

"All set up and executed neatly," her father scoffed.

"We know he did not make any contacts or set the escape up himself, so it had to be someone that wanted him more than we did."

"Who would that be?" her mother asked.

"Not sure. Possibly someone that he owes, maybe money, or as a result of one of his deals that had gone sour." She sipped her Old Fashioned again.

"Could it be someone that worked for him?" her father asked.

"It's possible, but doubtful." In her mind, she quickly reviewed the possibilities they had discussed during the investigation. "Then yesterday, my sometimes partner, Officer Fred Mitchell, figured out one possible place where he might have been taken, and our sergeant set up a raid. That information was on this morning's news and in the paper. We didn't find anyone, but we know Fred had figured right. No matter why, we missed them."

"Where was that?" her mother asked.

"I can't disclose the address." She looked at her mother and smiled. "And I can't tell you how he figured it out."

"And you said your friend, Officer Mitchell, figured it out," her mother said. "Good for him."

"Yes. It is."

Her father stood up and walked back to the counter. He fixed himself another drink. "And why is this prisoner, aah, *detainee,* so important?"

Sally straightened her shoulders and considered his question a moment, and then, admitting that she would not be disclosing anything that had not already been reported in the local news, she continued. "He was arrested on multiple counts of trafficking, murder, kidnapping, and numerous charges of spousal abuse. One of his daughters brought charges against him for raping her and her sister. There are other charges, but those top the list. I understand the daughter's attorney has

99

compelling evidence..." Sally hesitated when the oven timer chimed from the kitchen.

Her mother stood up and followed the sounds. "Come, give me a hand setting the table. All of this police talk makes me uneasy and glad I've never had to deal with anything like what you're talking about."

When the table was set and the Hawaiian-seasoned spare ribs with mashed potatoes and fresh garlic asparagus were plated, Sally went to tell her father that dinner was ready. She found him in his office, staring at a sheet of paper he was holding.

"Dinner's ready, Dad."

He did not move or look at her, and she wondered if he had somehow not heard her.

"Did you hear me, Dad? Dinner's ready."

Slowly, he turned his head and nodded. "Sorry. Yes, I heard you."

"What is it? What's wrong? "

"I was wondering about your work and you confirmed my suspicions. After dinner, I want you to come back here with me and read this." He shook the paper and laid it on his desk. "Let's go enjoy dinner with your mother and then we'll talk, just the two of us. There is something you need to know."

She turned to lead the way back to the dining room, suddenly awash with uncertainty and anxiety, worried that her father was not acting like the confident, demanding man she knew him to be.

After a pleasant dinner and non-job-related conversation, Sally helped her mother clear the table. She was appreciative, but sent Sally to chat with her father.

She obeyed and followed her father into his office. "So, what's all the mystery?"

"Please close the door and come sit with me," he remarked,

his tone somber as he picked up the sheet of paper he had been previously studying. He sat down in one of the two chairs arranged for quiet conversation off the end of his formidable desk.

She closed the door, then followed his lead and settled into the second chair. "What's this all about?"

"While you were talking about the case you're on, I realized that you were talking about Howard Collingsworth. Tell me, when was he arrested and why?"

"What do you know about Collingsworth?" Sally eyed her father suspiciously.

"More than I'm supposed to, I think." He hesitated and watched her.

"You're right. I was talking about him. He was shot in a raid that killed one, Sonny of Sonny's Collections in Melville, and two others that were helping him were severely wounded. The case has not gone to trial, but it is alleged that he kidnapped his married daughter, Catherine, intending to use her to settle a deal that had gone badly. A private investigator led the raid to rescue her on the thirty-first of July."

Her father nodded. "And did you know that in the two months that followed, his henchmen have been looking to kidnap others? Probably because of arrangements that were set in motion before Howard was shot and captured."

"Why do you say that?" Her mind was suddenly aswirl, trying to understand how he could know anything about Howard's activities. "How...how well do you know Howard?" She was not certain she wanted to know the answer to her question.

He inhaled, looked down at his hands in his lap. "As I said, too well, I'm afraid. I don't know how to say this but to say it. I was very foolish when you were a little tyke."

She saw his tired, almost defeated expression when he looked up at her—it stopped her heart mid-beat.

"Howard came to me with an investment opportunity in

a project he was doing many years ago. He had all the pieces in place but was short on finances and I thought it looked like a good deal—good returns on a resort development with the support of the local dignitaries. The returns were guaranteed at a minimum of twenty percent, but they turned out to be closer to thirty percent.

"I reviewed the draft contracts one evening, and the next day he brought the finals to my office for signatures. He pointed out two or three things he had changed from the draft and I agreed. So I signed up. But later I found out that he did not point out everything he'd changed."

"What did he change?" She held her breath, feeling something was seriously wrong.

Her father handed her the sheet of paper. "This is an email sent almost two weeks ago, but I wasn't here to open and read it. All of the emails with Howard are through his private server, and for some reason I cannot receive them on my phone when I'm away from here or my office in town."

Sally took the sheet and leaned back into the chair. She glanced at the header and saw there were multiple recipients, and then began reading.

Gentlemen:

As investors or interest holders in Howard Collingsworth's International Opportunities, this email is being specifically sent to each of you: H. Carlton, W. Lunas, R. Newit, C. Olgana, S. Myers, D. Ableman, G. Dufmat, W. Gibbings and F. Scott.

We have singled the nine of you out because each of you have signed contracts with clauses that obligate you to provide certain assets, your daughters, to Howard whenever he needs them to reduce progress hindrances in Opportunities' business dealings. In straight talk, to reduce his company's expenses by providing their services to the stakeholders.

This email is to also inform you that Howard has been injured and arrested in a kidnapping and trafficking attempt that has failed. When he could not locate his missing daughter Emli, he kidnapped his daughter Catherine to be used in her place. He was severely wounded in the raid that rescued her, and has been hospitalized until he is well enough to stand trial on numerous felony charges ranging from murder to human trafficking.

At this time, all of Howard's business activities have ceased, assets frozen or confiscated, but his collection contracts are still active, obviously paid for in advance. We have no idea who his connections are and no way to stop those hired from attempting to complete their missions. It is imperative that each of you try to keep your daughters as safe as possible.

In order to validate what we have said, we offer the following incidents: In August, a kidnapping attempt was made on Walter Gibbings's one remaining unmarried daughter, June. The attempt failed because someone was with her to protect her; three attackers died, and one defender was wounded. The second incident was on September 15, when June's apartment was broken into in a second kidnapping attempt. As luck would have it, she had moved and the two attackers were killed by the apartment's new occupants.

For the record, Howard's daughter Catherine and her children, and Walter's daughter, June, are safe and can no longer be harmed.

This email is a warning to the eight of you that remain obligated, that Howard's reign of evil still persists and your daughters are in very serious danger. Please be vigilant and keep those precious to you safe.

We hope you will heed this warning.

Sincerely, June Gibbings and Catherine (Collingsworth) Williamson

She inhaled deeply. "What is this?" Her voice suddenly pitched. "This is a joke, right?" She looked at her father and saw his depression-filled expression deepen. "This can't be true. You'd never…"

Her father slowly nodded. "It's true. That clause is what Howard added to our nine contracts and maybe others, and then he cajoled us into signing them by not telling us. I felt like I'd sold my firstborn to the devil himself when I found out."

She stood up sharply and stomped away from him. She wanted to scream, curling her fingers in to a fist, wanting to hit him, pound him for his duplicity. Her indignation flared, her irritation threatened to burst out in a fury, but she fought to control herself. Waving her fists at nothing, she forced her training to take over and kept her emotions under a tight rein; tears ran down her cheeks, the only remaining outward sign of her inner sense of betrayal. Then, barely above a whisper, she asked without turning, "What about the rest of this? The kidnapping and…"

"It's all true. I did some research today and verified the incidents in the email, and then you further confirmed them tonight. Catherine was kidnapped to fill her sister's place."

She turned to look at him, still seated in the chair facing hers.

"Years ago, I found out that he was supposed to deliver his younger daughter as part of a project he had in South Africa. She must have found out and she either escaped or was caught trying to. As far as I know, she hasn't been seen or heard of since the start of her third year in college, over ten, eleven years ago."

"Where was this sent from? Obviously it was written before they knew Howard escaped." She tried to force her emotions down so she could think.

"Obviously." He nodded. "It was sent from Howard's private server, from his email account. As far as I can tell, the message is authentic, but I cannot believe his daughter Catherine or June Gibbings are where they have access to Howard's email."

"But..."

"On more than one occasion," her father continued, "I have heard that Catherine is rather clever with computers. She was the president of her school's computer club when she was in high school."

Sally stared at him for a long moment and grimaced; the thought of the previous night's intruder suddenly had darker, more sinister possibilities. "God! This makes me furious. Partially because you did what you did and mostly because you kept it hidden from me all these years."

He nodded. "I know. But I thought that if you came to work for me after college, you would be close enough that I could provide some kind of protection."

"What could you do besides shadow me around everywhere I went? Is this why you've given me so much grief over the years?"

"I'm sorry, but yes. I knew in the police force you would be exposed more than ever to the dangers around us. I couldn't begin to help—"

"How? How were you going to help? You don't even know how to shoot a gun, and from this email and from what I know about Howard, it sounds like these guys are playing rough."

He smirked and she waited, one eyebrow raised.

"What?"

"I do know how, and do carry one for personal protection. Shortly after I realized what was in that contract, I enrolled in a self-defense and concealed-carry class. I planned to be ready if anything did happen."

"Shit! And you never told me that either."

"It was wiser not to—not until you were old enough to understand—but since you graduated and changed your mind on your career, we haven't had situations when we could talk—at least not civilly."

She inhaled and nodded. "You're right. We haven't." She looked at him and held his eyes, unsure of how she felt. The initial flash of indignation had subsided some and the pounding in her heart had slowed, and now she felt uncertain again. "I need to go and think on this a while. May I have a copy of this?"

"Sure," he agreed, and stood up. He took the sheet and walked to his copy machine. "I want you to know I really do want the best for you, and if police work is what you want, then please try to work with a partner, as much as you can. For me and your mother, if for no other reason." He handed her the copy.

"I'm still hurt, upset, and mad at you for letting this happen. But thanks for finally telling me." She turned to the door. "God! I can't believe I'm in a situation like this." She glanced back as she opened the door, gave him a thin, tight smile over her shoulder, and shook her head. "Damn."

Fifty-Six
Wednesday, October 4

Agent Arthur Stanik had been in Denver for two weeks, watching the news, visiting the local airports, even asking local airport business operators if they had any idea when the beautiful planes from West's Ghost Ranch might reappear. In each instance, the answers were all the same; everyone's crystal ball was foggy and no one knew when or where Glen West might put his planes out on display.

After a week of wandering the streets and airports of Denver, and now, after Cecil Brown had called him to explain what Claude Schmidt had done and that he was dead for his efforts, Arthur decided he needed to be more proactive in his searching. He stopped in the Denver Central Library on 14th Avenue Parkway and, wandering through the uniquely designed facility, nosed out the computer research area. The room was full of octagonal tables, each with eight monitors and keyboards. He settled down at a table near the information counter under the large 'Ask' sign and in front of a computer terminal situated at one of the table's facets.

Pulling his attention away from the beautiful architecture of the library, he thought about his purpose and returned to the airplanes he had seen at the Reno Air Races, especially the ones where he had seen the two lookalike women: a P-51, two TF-51s and a Spitfire, displayed under the Ghost Ranch business name.

With his notepad as a placeholder, he got up and asked the research clerk how one would look up airplanes owned by different people. The clerk suggested the FAA's website and a few others, sending Arthur happily back to his terminal.

It took him nearly twenty minutes to navigate the FAA website and to figure out how the search engine worked, and after another few minutes he found a listing of registered North American P-51s, their registration numbers, and owners. He scrolled down the list, searching for the Ghost Ranch in the list.

Nothing.

He shrugged and tried to think of the woman's name, remembering her last name at the same time he noticed West Restorations LLC for one of the airplanes in the list. He smiled and ran a second search, filtered for the restoration business name, and a number of different World War II airplanes popped onto the monitor screen. He smiled at the eleven planes, but when he asked for more information on the business, he was greeted with a nearly blank screen: a web address and a message stating the address information was restricted and not publically accessible were all that displayed.

Arthur printed a hard copy of the short list of airplanes and decided he would think about how to use his findings over lunch; somehow, he felt this information might help him find the elusive Ghost Ranch. Abandoning the terminal, he collected his list from the clerk, left the library, and stopped at the Restaurante de la Santa Fe, near his cheap motel.

Charlie stood behind her chair like West would have done with his if he were there. She tried to be calm and reserved as she waited for everyone to arrive, nodding and greeting them as they took their seats along the length of the new table. Her night had again been tortured, restless, and fitful, with more dreams of past fears and unsettling memories. She clung to the chair, wondering if one of Howard's men might actually figure out where the ranch was.

The expanded dining room and the reoriented table made their lunchtime meetings pleasant, and the sense of community helped her calm her jitters. When Ratchet followed June in and they settled between Woody and Eddie, Charlie sat down.

"Helen called today," Charlie began. "West was released from the hospital yesterday and they are recuperating at Monte and Felix's place in Farmington—"

Everyone interrupted, expressing their happiness and encouragements at the news.

"And," she continued, looking at Woody, "I see Woody and Felix are back. I presume that means this morning's training flight went off without any unexpected issues."

"Yes," Woody agreed. "The flying was very good and Felix got another cross-country logged. This one was technically a solo cross-country, even though I was following in a rather loose formation."

"How's the plane? All you expected?"

"Yup." He smiled and glanced at Felix. "We did some low and slow formation work around South Fork, refueled in Alamosa, and then home."

"Where was the plane?"

"Mineral County. Northwest of South Fork and just outside of Creede."

"A wide, empty spot along the river," Felix added as she took another serving of roast.

Charlie nodded and turned her attention to Mel. "I see our fence-mending team is here. Anything to add, Mel?"

Mel did not say anything at first, but looked at Charlie for a long moment.

"Mel?"

"Sorry, Charlie," Mel said, clearing her throat. "Our morning wasn't as good as Woody's and Mom's."

"How so?" Charlie asked softly, suddenly worried as Mel placed a folded map on the table beside her plate.

"We found a spot along the north fence, between our mesa and Dalerose Mesa, where the fence was cut and posts were removed—"

"What? Intentionally cut?" Charlie voiced the questions everyone was murmuring.

Mel nodded. "I thought Peter told you."

Charlie shook her head slowly.

"There were a lot of tire tracks, like trucks going back and forth through the gap, from the road coming down from the north. They're fresh, like since the last rain. Peter followed the road a ways while we"—she glanced at Mike—"started clearing the area to get ready for new posts. When he came back, he said he went a couple of miles and the tracks just kept going. The road goes east of Fallas Mesa and joins Highway 160."

Charlie looked at Jess. "I know we've been preoccupied, but has anything shown up on the surveillance monitors?"

Jess shook her head. "No alerts, but you're right. I haven't done a full visual in a couple of weeks." Then she nodded. "After lunch I'll check again, search the archives, and try to see why we haven't had any alerts."

Charlie inhaled and forced a smile as she looked back at Mel. "Thank you, dear. You were able to secure the fence?"

"Not yet." She shook her head. "We didn't have enough posts or wire with us. That's why we came back in—to get what we need so we can go back and get it fixed." Suddenly Mel's eyes got very wide and round. "They were stealin' our cows! Weren't they?"

"Might be." Charlie chuckled at her possessive regard for the cows. "And that used to be a *hangin' offense* here in the Old West. We'll find out what they were doing and then act accordingly. And...I will discuss it with the Las Animas County Sheriff." She glanced at Ratchet, Woody, and Bump. "I'll talk to Robert."

Jess stared at Charlie. "Doesn't West have the cattle chipped?"

"I don't know."

"Well, I think it would be very easy to implant a tracker that sends a number so the computer can continuously record them. It would even make it easier to find them for roundup."

"Good idea. Maybe you and Felix can work on that." Charlie smiled. "And maybe the computer can keep count and send an alert if any are outside the ranch boundaries."

"Sort of like closing the barn door after the horses get out," Jess admitted with a chuckle. "But it'll sure warn us in the future."

Ratchet climbed up on a small boulder and surveyed their work, looking west along the newly replaced section of fence. He smiled at Mel and June and gave them a thumbs-up. "Looks great." Mel grinned from ear to ear and he nodded to Mike and Peter as they walked back from the far end of the repaired section.

Ratchet and Peter had driven two jeeps pulling their horse trailers to the edge of the mesa, stopping opposite Dalerose Mesa. Below them was the valley between the two mesas and the break in the north fence. June had accompanied him in one jeep and Mel and Mike rode with Peter in the other, leading the way for the easy, forty-minute, ten-mile trip from the hangars to the rim. At the lip, they had unloaded the five horses to take them, their tools, the wire, and the three fence posts and had begun another thirty-minute trip descending the steep canyon to the gap. There, they spent the afternoon setting new posts and stringing the barbed wire.

Ratchet retrieved his phone from his vest pocket and connected a patch cord between it and the camera box on the short pole hidden near a creosote tree. He tapped Jess's icon on the maintenance screen that appeared on his phone.

"Hey, Jess. Are you where you can check the proximity sensors and cameras one eighty-six, -seven, and -eight? Okay. I can wait or you can call me back. Okay, I'll hang on." A couple of minutes passed. "Okay. You have us on the prox-sensors. Good, good. And you can see us on one eighty-six and-seven. Yeah, hold on."

He lowered his phone and shouted. "Hey, Peter. You and Mike check eight. It's looking the wrong way."

Instantly, Peter led Mike to their horses and they hurried off to the west. After a few minutes they stopped a quarter of a mile down the long fence and waved back. Peter disappeared behind a stand of trees and a moment later Mike waved.

"How's that? Yeah? Okay." Ratchet raised his arm and swung his hand in wide circle over his head."

Another moment and then Mike waved again.

"Okay? Okay. That's good. So, you can just see us at the repair and you can see the trace where the trucks went? Good," he continued to Jess as June and Mel joined him on the boulder. "Thanks, Jess. Looks like we're about done then."

He grinned at June and Mel, then waved to Mike, signaling they had fixed the problem. He hugged June and then disconnected the patch cable and coiled it around his fingers before he stuffed it in his hip pocket. Then he tucked his phone back in his shirt pocket.

"Looks like we can tidy up and head back up the hill." He glanced back down the long fence and realized neither Peter nor Mike had mounted; they hadn't started back. "Actually, it looks like we should go and see what's keeping the boys."

When they reached the boys, Peter was just coming down off the slope below the camera pole.

"That should hold it until I can come back with a new pole," he was explaining to Mike as Ratchet, June, and Mel stopped beside their horses. "Oh, *Yáʼátʼééh*. I was just telling Mike that something bent the camera pole. I straightened it the best I could and made a splint out of a tree branch, but it won't hold long. Branch and barbed wire, not that strong."

"See anything that might have caused it?" Ratchet asked,

suddenly wondering if the *something* might have been a some*one*.

"I think *nílch'i* and *ts'in*—sorry, the wind and tree." He smiled. "More likely from the storms. Mike and I will come again in a couple of days and set a new metal pole."

Ratchet nodded. "Okay. Let's get our stuff picked up and head back up to the jeeps. I'll give Robert a status when we get back tonight or tomorrow. Are you ready?"

Peter smiled with a nod. "For now." He mounted his horse and, smiling at Mike, reined his ride around. They joined in behind Ratchet and the girls.

Back up on the rim, they loaded Peter's, Mike's, and Mel's horses into the larger of the trailers, but when Mel questioned why Ratchet wasn't loading his or June's, he smiled.

"Mel, I think June and I are going to ride back. It's a beautiful afternoon and I figure we should get back just about dinnertime. You drive the jeep with the empty trailer and follow Peter."

Mel stared back at him without moving.

"Now don't give me that look. I know that Bump and Woody have taught you how to drive the jeeps and tugs. Here on the ranch, it's completely okay for you to be driving. So whaddya say?"

She swallowed and then smiled. "O...kay. I...I can do that."

"I know you can." Ratchet smiled and then turned to June. "Are you ready?"

When she nodded, he led the way back toward the hangars, leaving the youngsters to get themselves started.

"Are you sure that's the right thing to do?" June asked as Peter and Mike, in the first jeep and the long trailer slowly, drove past them. "I mean letting them go off on their own."

"Can't hurt," he chuckled. "Besides, Peter has done this many times in the last four years and he can help Mel if there's a problem. And I like it that she takes the initiative and isn't afraid to try." He smiled and sighed. "She reminds me a lot of Charlie, only a lot younger. Cat's—sorry, I mean Felix's getting better, like she's beginning to feel like she's fitting in."

"I see that makes you happy," June said softly. "I mean, that you like it when everyone feels like they fit in."

"It does," he replied with a nod.

"Do you think I'm fitting in?"

Her question surprised him and he cocked his head and looked at her for a long minute. "You tell me," he finally said.

"Okay," she continued after considering his answer. "I think I feel like I am. I still miss some of the things I had in Jersey: the night life, the occasional steak dinner, the after-work drinks with friends, the trips to the clothing and the grocery store—"

"Grocery store? Really?" He chuckled. "I guess two out of three isn't too bad."

"Two out of three?"

"Yeah. Dinner and drinks are things we did together back there and can do here anytime you'd like—especially after we get you a house built. And trips to the grocery store can be arranged if you want to ride along with whoever draws the short straw."

"I didn't know you drew straws to decide who goes for groceries."

He chuckled again. "We actually don't, but you get the idea. Each month we volunteer for the grocery runs, but West told me to wait and volunteer last when our workload is high. When it isn't, I jump in just like everyone else and so does West. Well, he did and will again when he's back on his feet."

June smiled. "I know you feel odd with him away, laid up. We all feel the same way, and I've only known him for a little while. He'll be home before you know it."

"Yeah, I know. Charlie's good at keeping things moving and under control, but yeah, it feels odd."

June nodded, thought for a moment, and then changed

the subject. "Have you thought any more about us getting married?"

He sobered his expression and looked at her, a tight smile on his lips. "Nah. Not much. Only a when I wake up in my bed by myself, or when I walk back to the bunkhouse by myself at the end of the day. And a few other times when my work allows."

"You haven't said anything about it, and I was wondering if you were having second thoughts."

"I'm not. I asked you to tell me when you're ready, not the other way around." He sighed with a wide smile. "I was waiting on you, trying to give you time to decide."

"Do you like that I'm here?"

"Of course. Isn't it obvious? I like that you're here and we can talk about your work and I can answer your questions and that you can enjoy our friends, old to me and new to you. I like that you are here and can experience the new things that happen and the continuation of old things still going on. Personally, I think you fit in at the ranch very well, but only because of what I see and what you tell me." He studied her face carefully, hoping he wasn't missing something. "If you don't feel like you do, or that you've changed your mind, please tell me what bothers you and I'll try to get it fixed."

"That's just it," she remarked in a pleasant tone. "I keep waiting for something to come up and bother me, but it hasn't happened."

"Well, I hope you realize there will likely be some things over time that you might not like, and that they are usually temporary. I want you to be happy here and I want you to feel at home."

"Everyone has made me feel welcome. I just worry that I'll wake up one morning and realize that all of this was just a dream."

Ratchet laughed and June stared at him.

"Me too. I guess I still think it's a dream," he explained.

"Each day is unbelievable, sometimes more serious than others, but never really routine or mundane. There are always challenges and things that need to be done."

"I can see that." June smiled and glanced away, looking across the mesa at the two jeeps and trailers, barely noticeable except for the light trail of dust rising behind them. She turned back to him with a devilish smile on her face. "How about you spend the next few nights with me in the main house and we discuss ideas for a date?"

He reached across the gap between the two horses and took her hand. "I like that idea very much."

Thursday, October 5

It was early, still dark outside, when Charlie rolled over and reached across her bed, feeling the empty spot where West usually slept. She was instantly depressed, remembering why he was not there, the night he had protected her and Cat from the shots fired by the man at Cat and Monte's house, the panic she had felt when he did not respond to her urgings for him to get up, and the long, anxious, pacing hours in the hospital while he was in surgery.

It was a few minutes past three a.m. and her mind kept repeating the memories. After what seemed like hours, she finally fell into a troubled sleep, again waking as the dim morning light seeped into their room. Exasperated, she got up, donned her robe, and went downstairs for a glass of water, hoping the activity would make her drowsy.

But with her drink in hand, she aimlessly wandered around the main floor until she found herself in the security and tracking room. She sat down in Helen's chair, switched on the large monitor array, and keyed up the tracking program, hoping that just seeing the tracking button's display would help her relax. The screen array illuminated and the image coalesced, focused on the last place searched, the Farmington area.

Charlie's heart stopped. The tracking button icons were not at Cat and Monte's home; they were back at the hospital!

Her shaking hands fumbled in panic, trying to access the phone console, and through sudden tears, she sought the keys and Helen's speed dial button, her breathing suddenly deep and worried as she cradled the hand unit against her ear, waiting for the connection to make.

"Mom? What's wrong? What's happened?" she urgently asked when Helen answered her mobile phone. "Everything was fine last night when West and I talked."

"Charlie? What are you doing up at this hour?"

"What's wrong? Tell me." Charlie tried to hide the rising panic in her voice, but she felt like she was turning hysterical.

"Calm down, Charlie. He's going to be all right," Helen's voice encouraged soothingly.

"What is it? Why're you back at the hospital?"

"Charlie. Calm down. He's going to be all right. He had a coughing fit this morning and it sounded like his lungs might be congested. We brought him to the emergency room to have it checked out and they're giving him some intravenous diuretic medication to reduce his tendency to retain fluids in his lungs. They'll keep him today to be sure he responds to the medication."

"You're sure he's going to be okay?"

"Yes, dear. I was going to call you before breakfast, when I figured you would be awake," Helen continued. "Please listen to me. Often there is a fluid retention problem when someone has had chest surgery. He's doing remarkably well for having surgery on his lungs as well as everything else."

Charlie inhaled deeply and noticed Cat, her robe hastily wrapped around her, as she slipped into the room and closed the door behind her. Cat pulled a chair up beside Charlie as she continued speaking to Helen. "Is this going to delay him coming home?"

"Probably by a few days," Helen admitted. "We'll know more after he responds to the medication. The plan is to take him back to Felix and Monte's this evening. I'll let you know how things stand then. And maybe he'll feel up to talking with you."

"Okay, Mom." She swallowed and tried to smile. "I know it's only been three days, but even though we talk each day, the waiting and being without him is killing me."

"I know, dear. I'll keep you informed. And the best thing you can do now is to get some rest and stay busy when you're awake. "

"I'll try. The busy part is not hard, but the resting is difficult. Tell him I love him. Talk to you tonight."

"I will, and be assured that he knows that you do. He wants to get home as fast as you want him to come. I'll call tonight. Get some rest if you can."

"Thanks. Later."

Charlie sat unmoving, staring at the console for a long minute after Helen had hung up. Then, slowly, she turned to Cat.

"Sorry I woke you, but I woke up feeling something wasn't right. At least I waited to get up and check the tracking icons. When I saw they were back at the hospital, I almost fell apart..."

"It's all right. I know how you feel," Cat soothed, and put her arm across Charlie's shoulders. "I heard you get up, but it wasn't until I heard you on the phone that I realized what was happening. Helen knows what's going on and she'll keep you in the know. Trust her."

"I do, more than you know." Charlie sighed. "For most of my life I've lived alone, not needing anyone, but now, I just realized how much I rely on West being here, us being together. He always has my back, watching out for me, helping me adjust..."

"I'll listen if you need someone to talk to," Cat added as Charlie stood up. "But it's up to you."

"Thanks." Charlie opened the door. Smiling, she barely shook her head as she looked back, forcing her voice into its normal tone. "Looks like it's getting light outside, so I think I'll go up, shower, and get ready for the day. Come on and I'll meet you for coffee before the others come to breakfast."

"I know what you mean when you say you were alone most of your life," Cat remarked as she sipped her coffee. Only the two of them occupied the dining room, with their coffee and a piece of coffee cake on a dessert plate in front of them. She had taken Helen's chair and Charlie sat in West's. Charlie was listening. "Since high school, Monte has been my companion, my husband, yet until this summer, almost a stranger. I think I told you once before, I wouldn't let him in. It took years before I shared his bed, and a number more before I became pregnant with Mel."

"Yeah. You did tell me that," Charlie conceded, and a brief smile crossed her face as she spoke. "I think your being alone was tougher than mine, having him around every day and not liking it. I'll break ten thousand flying hours before Christmas at the rate I've been flying recently. Except for training and the flying I've done since I came to the ranch, they were the only time I could really be safe, out of reach of anyone that wanted my time. Those hours aloft were my sanctuary, my secure time away from other people." Charlie looked straight into Cat's eyes. "A woman in this world of aviation—especially a single one—can trust very few men she meets—I can count all of the trustworthy ones I've met on one hand—and that keeps her wary. I was so preoccupied with taking care of myself, I nearly missed seeing West for who he really is."

Cat chuckled at Charlie's smile, wondering about what she was not saying. She knew Jess had been recruited before the Broomfield kidnapping, specifically to follow Howard's email traffic, but no one had said how they knew where to look for his emails.

She was about to ask Charlie where she was going with their

discussion when the children entered and quickly interrupted, hugging her in a bright good morning.

"Good morning to you also," Cat answered as she released their embrace.

Jess and June entered, followed by Ratchet, and Charlie stood up and moved her cup and dishes to her place. Cat quickly followed her example, keenly aware that their quiet time together was over.

When everyone had entered and taken their places, Charlie sat down. Suddenly, the food platters were being passed around and conversation became happily animated. Charlie tried to raise her mood to match the pleasantries, but worry kept a tight rein.

"Ratchet," she interrupted softly. "Have you talked to Hubert Miles about when you're going to meet with him?"

Ratchet turned and smiled at her. "I talked to him on Tuesday, and with West being away, we decided more toward the end of the month would be appropriate."

Charlie nodded. "Good, good." She glanced at Jessie. "Sorry that it will mean Lenny will be gone again."

Jess nodded and forced a smile. "I understand. Maybe there will be a little time before he has to leave again."

"And speaking of West," Woody said when Jess had finished. "Any updates? When he might get to come home?"

Charlie tried to smile when she looked at Woody, and then at each of the others, but it was forced at best and she knew everyone saw her uneasiness. She cleared her throat. "He didn't have a good start to his day. Helen says he has some fluid accumulation in his lungs and they took him back to the hospital early this morning to have it checked out." She inhaled and then continued. "They put him on some diuretic medication and she said she'll let me know more after they've had some time to see how he responds."

"Sorry to ask." Woody reached across the table and

squeezed Charlie's hand. "We're all worried, but West's a tough bird. Hasn't been sick a day since I've been working for him. He'll be okay."

She smiled grimly. "And he's never been shot before." She softened her expression and glanced around the table. "I know you're all as worried as I am. Thank you, each of you, for helping me keep a positive attitude." She inhaled deeply, shook her shoulders, and looked back at Ratchet. "So what are the plans for today?"

Ratchet, Woody, and Bump went through the list of things to be done that day, and when they were finished, Mel statused the fence-mending they did the previous day, then mentioned a conversation she had with Robert: he wanted the cattle moved to the west pastures that coming weekend, and everyone was going to be needed.

"Everyone?" Charlie asked, vaguely remembering Robert talking about the roundup the previous fall. She was so new to the ranch then that she had not paid it any mind and just focused on the jobs West had given her.

"Yes. He said the boys and Mike and me will ride the horses and get the cows up out of the ravines and canyons, and everyone else will use the jeeps and the pickups to move them across the mesa." She looked at Woody. "Robert asked me to ask you if the L-19 was flyable. If so, he asked if you could spot the cows in the canyons for us—to save a little time, of course."

Woody chuckled and nodded. "I'll take your mama and we can do the spottin', girl. You bet we can. She shouldn't be riding horseback for long hours or bouncing around in a truck, but she can fly."

Mel smiled hugely and thanked him. "I'll pass the word to Robert. He's getting a little testy, being cooped up and all and not doin' the doin', if you know what I mean."

Woody chuckled again. "When you go to tell him, mind if I tag along?"

"No, sir." Her smile widened even more. "He'd like that, a

lot."

When breakfast was finished and people began leaving to start the day, Cat called Mel aside. Charlie caught Ratchet and they stepped away from the table. "I want to remove the drop tanks off *My Affair*. I think I need to go unwind a little, get my balance back."

He nodded. "I remember West telling me you needed to do that every once in a while. Bump and I can get that done as soon as we get up top."

"Thanks. I'll be up shortly. I need to check on the building progress with Cappie and then I'll be up."

"Mom! Stop fussing," West demanded. "I just need to sit up. Help me with the pillows." He swung his good leg off the bed and then gently lifted his other leg by the cast at the knee. "They took the IV out and said I could move around, so I'm moving around."

"I know, but don't try to do too much too soon."

Lenny stepped in from the corridor. "The nurse said you can have coffee, so I brought some." He smiled and set a cup on the table beside the hospital bed and then handed one to Helen. "I hope I fixed it like you like it."

She took a tentative sip, then smiled. "You did very well, Lenny. Very well indeed."

"Thanks." Out of the corner of his eye, he caught West reaching for his crutch. "Hey! Hey, ask for some help." He grabbed the crutch from beside the cushioned chair and handed it to West. "Where're ya going in such a hurry?"

"For a walk." West stared at him as if he were going to try to stop him. "I was going to sit up and stare at the walls, but changed my mind. Morning's a wasting. I need to get strong enough to get out of here."

"Why the hurry? You can't go until the doc sees you and says it's okay."

West sighed and dropped his stare. "I just need to do all I can so we can go home."

With that, West lurched on the single crutch and walked, as best he could, out of the room and up the corridor. Helen quickly hurried after him, trying to not spill her coffee.

It was midafternoon when Helen sat down beside West, upright in the cushioned chair. Lenny was getting antsy himself, and West told him he should drive up and check on the airplane, even though they both knew it was secure and that Douglas would not let anything or anyone bother it.

"So," Helen began, interrupting West's deep thoughts, "what is so important that makes you so irritable and in such a hurry?"

"I just need to be there for Charlie." He glanced up from his hands and smiled.

"She's strong and will take care of things while you're gone."

"I know that, but there's something that has driven her for so long, there are times it seems to take over before she can do anything about it."

"Whatever are you talking about? I haven't see—"

"I know you don't know everything about Charlie and her past, but she lived in fear for nearly eleven years, and I've seen how she is when she feels trapped, or even just overwhelmed." He saw that Helen did not understand. "The last day of the La Plata County Fly-in, Lenny called us to tell us about the guys that had been searching for us—the ones that he had arrested. When Charlie heard that they had planted a tracking beacon on the plane, she left the room. I found her a few minutes later, trying to pack her bags so she could disappear. She felt like she was a threat to the safety and seclusion of the ranch and that she had to leave.

"Fortunately, I was able to talk her out of it and got her to realize she was not the cause of people trying to find the ranch. But I heard that same frightened tremble in our last two phone calls, and after what you said about her call to you this morning, she's on the ragged edge. No one there knows how to talk her down safely.

"Since we met, she's let me soothe the beast within and she's let herself trust me to guide her back home. With me here and her there, I don't know if I can."

"Call her and see how she is. I think she needs to hear your voice more than I realized."

"I will, but I'm worried. I can't lose her, Mom. I need her."

Charlie thought about the sleepless nights and the recurring nightmares, her inability to stay connected and comfortable at night. The sudden change left her adrift and she thought again and again of how she was burdening West and everyone at the ranch, how much simpler and uncomplicated their lives would be if she were not there. She had tried to leave before, and each time, West had convinced her she belonged there, with him, and she had stayed.

She enjoyed every minute of being with him and being there on the ranch, and she knew she was being unrealistic. But something inside kept pushing her, driving her, and with him gone she was suddenly unable to keep her hold on herself. It was different now; he had changed everything. Before, she knew what to do: she only had to protect herself, stay out of sight, keep moving.

But West had changed all of that. He was with her when she had seen Cat again, supported her after her kidnapping and in finding Cat after her kidnapping. She owed him for so much, for staying with her through everything, the good and the not so good, but now he was too far away. She talked to him, but only had her memories of his arms around her, his warmth and steady support. She had never been close to anyone before, not since she was a young child, and was surprised at how much she needed to be with West.

She needed his physical touch, and knew what she could do to get it. But that would mean fueling *My Affair* and heading east. Or she could simply disappear. She knew how to do that, but then everyone would know she could not manage on her own and she knew that would reflect badly on West's character and judgment. That was as depressing as being at the ranch without him. And if she did leave, she knew she would lose him forever.

Lost in her thoughts, Charlie marched across the open hangar and up the ramp to her waiting airplane, completely oblivious to Mel, also dressed in her flight suit and with her helmet tucked under her left arm—a slightly thinner, nearly identical copy of Charlie—following briskly behind her. At the top, Ratchet and Bump were waiting beside *My Affair*.

"You're taking a copilot?" Bump asked, amused by Mel's rigid and purposeful posture as she stopped behind Charlie.

"What?" Charlie turned and saw Mel. "Ooh, Mel. I can't take you today. I'm sorry, but—"

"I need to go with you, Charlie."

Mel's determination caught her by surprise. "What? I don't understand. I need to work out my tensions. I—"

"That's why I need to go. So you'll come back."

Charlie stumbled back a step and looked at Mel, then quickly glanced at Ratchet and Bump, then back at Mel. "I'll be back, Mel."

Mel shook her head. "Mom and I can see it in your eyes. We know you're worried about West, but you can't just go back to see him and we can't let you go. Take me with you and you can still work out your tensions."

Charlie stared at the girl, wondering how much she knew, how much she and Cat might have deduced. What did they really know?

"Mom said I have to go and keep you from doing something

you shouldn't do. So I'm going." Mel pulled her helmet smartly down on her head and climbed the left landing gear strut, leaving Charlie watching after her, a bit bewildered.

"Better get up there and go get yourself unwound," Ratchet said, and caught Charlie's arm, pulling her gently toward the plane. "And don't let your admirer see you doing anything you shouldn't be doing."

She snapped her head at his words, and saw the teasing smile firmly set across his face.

"Dammit, Ratchet! She shouldn't be going." She glared at his smirk. "Bah, you're no help at all." Charlie pulled her helmet on and climbed up on the wing. She glared back at him before she swung her legs over the canopy rail and dropped into the pilot's seat.

Once *My Affair* was running and idling smoothly, Charlie pushed the throttle forward and taxied to the east; the winds were straight out of the mountains.

"What was that all about?" Bump asked as they watched the plane taxi out.

"Looks like Felix and Mel are worried about Charlie," Ratchet admitted. "I saw the look in her eyes when she asked us to get her plane ready. I've seen it once before, and it seems what she says is true—that she needs to fly, fly hard, to get her balance."

"Balance? She's always on top of things, always dedicated and determined. What's with the balance thing?"

"All I know is that West told me once that sometimes situations or circumstances get her on edge and she has to fly to get herself under control. I've only seen her that way once, and she all but tore the wings off the poor plane." He smiled as she turned *My Affair* into the wind and did a prop and mag check. "Having Mel along will help her a lot, I think."

Bump opened his mouth to say something more, but stopped to watch as the TF raced toward them, light, tail up and airborne a quarter of a mile away. It stayed level, barely higher than when it was on its landing gear, and streaked past, the huge propeller clawing the air for more speed.

They watched as it raced over the lip of the mesa, nosed up slightly, and spun to the right in a fast roll—one turn and then three quarters. The roll abruptly twisted into a sharp left turn, then reversed into a continuous left-hand aileron roll as the flight path angled up and away from the mesas in New Mexico.

Fifty-Seven

Charlie swung her legs over the canopy rail and dropped heavily into her seat. She quickly buckled the parachute straps, clasped her lap belt, and tightened the shoulder harness as she scanned the cockpit gauges.

"Fuel check." Mel's soft voice in her headphones startled her. "Left tank first then the right."

Without answering, she glanced down and confirmed they were indicating full.

"Flap handle up and carburetor air control forward to RAM AIR position," Mel said softly and unperturbed in Charlie's headphones, voicing the steps in the before-starting checklist. Charlie touched the flap handle and the air control, silently confirming their position.

"Trim tabs set five degrees right," Mel's voice continued softly, "ailerons zero degrees, and elevator two degrees nose heavy."

Absently, Charlie nodded as she double-checked the trim knobs and the indicator settings.

Mel's voice called off each step, moving to the starting procedures checklists, and Charlie responded by silently checking each item and assuring the controls and switches were properly set. Somehow, the sound of Mel's voice eased her initial frustration and she began listening for her next item.

"Oxygen reading, four hundred PSI."

Again Charlie nodded in response and reached to prime the engine a second before Mel announced she should. She smiled and held the switch for three seconds, raised the starter switch guard, and held the starter switch in the START position.

The plane rocked in response and the propeller began turning. The exhaust pops came together and she pushed the Mixture control full down to the RUN position, Auto Rich. The Merlin stumbled once and then settled into the steady purr she desperately needed to hear.

Charlie scanned the instruments and confirmed the oil pressure, the idle RPM, the vacuum reading, and that all of the engine instrument indications were where they should be. She waited, and when the coolant temperature began to rise, she cranked the canopy half closed and pushed the throttle forward. *My Affair* started moving.

A half-mile east of their starting point, Charlie swung *My Affair's* nose into the wind, closed the canopy, and conducted the requisite propeller check and magneto checks. She nodded to herself and called the ranch.

"Ghost Ranch, Ghost Two is departing west and southwest. Two souls onboard." Then she glanced around the pattern and pulled her lap belt and shoulder harness tight.

"Cinch your belts and shoulder harness really tight." They were the first words she had spoken to Mel since they had gotten into *My Affair*. "This isn't going to be a walk in the park, and I don't want you banging your head and cracking my canopy." She pushed the throttle forward aggressively to 40 inches to get them moving, then at 80 mph, she pushed the throttle up to 55 inches initially, slowly adding another five as the tail came up and the bouncing stopped.

She held their altitude, their wheels merely a few feet off the ground, and retracted the landing gear. She heard Mel inhale through the headphones and was absently pleased that her aggressiveness had surprised Mel, at least a little.

The airspeed indicator needle passed 170 miles per hour as the rim of the mesa flashed beneath them and she eased the nose up, establishing a shallow climb. Then, sharply, she snapped the plane into a fast aileron roll to the right, one turn, then three quarters of a second turn, controls centered and a hard pull to execute a left turn from their original flight path. Then, as soon as their new heading was established, she snapped the plane into a continuous left aileron roll and climbed for more altitude. At ten thousand feet, she pulled into another rolling turn, this time to the right.

"Oxygen mask on." Charlie stopped the roll, wings level and still climbing. She expected a complaint from the back seat but was completely unprepared when Mel screeched in her headphones, "Oh, WOW! Can we do *that* again? That was sooo cool..." and her words dissolved in to unrestrained laughter.

Smiling hugely at Mel's unexpected, exuberant reaction, she pulled *My Affair's* nose up into a loop with a snap roll at the top and a series of rolling turns on the way back to level.

"Take a hold of the controls," Charlie instructed with calm acceptance, and immediately felt Mel's hand on the stick. "Feet on the pedals. Follow me through as I do an aileron roll. We'll keep the nose pointed at the same spot on the horizon through the roll, but I know you won't be able to see that clearly. As we roll, we have to keep *My Affair* from turning or changing altitude, so we'll use a combination of stick and rudder to oppose those tendencies. Ready?"

"Okay, Charlie. I'm ready."

Charlie smiled, hearing the anticipation and sudden seriousness in Mel's voice. She had shifted from her role of being Charlie's conscience into her eager and attentive student mode.

For the next hour, she and Mel danced in the skies over northeastern New Mexico, Charlie calmly explaining and demonstrating each maneuver, then following Mel as she attempted to repeat each on her own. Charlie was completely back in her element, lulled by the comforting power and soothing sound of her mighty Merlin, her worries of the morning swept away in the laughter of a little girl and her unswerving confidence that everything would be all right.

Mary, with her freshly bobbed black hair and wearing jeans and a plain printed blouse, followed Bobby into the main offices of Freddy's Auto Sales on Gratiot Avenue, northeast of the Colman Young International Airport. He led her to the end of the row of cubicles and knocked on the open door of the end office.

"Freddy," he said as he led her into the office and extended his hand to the man rising from behind the steel office desk in the center of the room. A single file cabinet stood in the corner opposite the door. "This is Carole, the woman I told you about that is needing an inexpensive ride in descent condition."

Freddy smiled, shook Bobby's hand, and then extended his to Mary. "Nice to meet you."

"Same, I'm sure," she greeted in return.

"Come with me."

Freddy led the way from the office, down the corridor they had come in through, and back out into the lot. He turned to his right and walked to two cars parked beside the building.

"I have this six-year-old Accord and the five-year-old Fiesta." He handed Bobby the keys to both cars. "Look them over, drive them, and let me know what you think. I'll be back in the office, so just come back in when you're ready." With that, Freddy left them and Bobby popped the hood on the Accord.

"He must know you fairly well," she commented softly, watching him as Freddy walked around the corner of the building and out of sight.

"A few years now. We went to culinary school together, but he dropped out when his father fell ill and subsequently died. He got the car business from him and has been trying to keep it going since then."

Bobby took his time and thoroughly looked at each car, and when he had finished, he handed her the key to the Accord. "Let's see how it drives."

She got in, started the car, and pulled out onto Gratiot Avenue, then turned left and drove northeast for a half mile or more, turned into a neighborhood, around a few blocks, and then into a school yard to check the turning and backing. When nothing abnormal appeared, she drove back to the dealership and they test drove the Fiesta.

In the end, knowing the Fiesta was likely the cheaper car to operate, she preferred the comfort of the Accord, and comparing the "friends" prices Freddy had given Bobby, she thought the Accord would satisfy her needs better.

When Freddy had filled out the appropriate papers and she was ready to sign them, she glanced quickly at Bobby and then back to Freddy.

"Can I use an investment credit card or do I need to get cash?"

Freddy stared at her and then smiled. "A credit card will work just fine."

She signed the papers as Carole Madison when Bobby smiled.

Bobby leaned against the bedroom doorjamb. "What address did you use?" he asked, watching as Mary packed her clothes into the suitcase she had purchased that afternoon.

"Cathy's," she answered without turning. "Years ago, when I got my second driver's license, I had used her and Monte's Farmington address so Howard would not find out what I was doing. Then, when Monte was helping Howard in his renewed search for Emli, he discovered that she had bought an airplane and had done the same thing, using his and Cathy's address for the registration. Probably for the purchase also, but he never said whether he found a bill of sale or not." She stopped and straightened, staring at the wall beyond the bed. "I often wondered about the coincidence of it all, the like-mindedness, but I dismissed it, since Emli was gone before I made my move. She couldn't've known that I was doing the same thing. Nor did I know that she had done the same thing when I did it." She absently shook her shoulders.

"How will I contact you?"

She turned to look at him. "I guess just email me. Don't mention or call me by my new name, in case someone sees the email thread."

"Can I text you?"

"If you do, please remember to delete our conversation from your phone when you've finished. Don't leave any crumbs for anyone to follow. I'll do the same."

"Where are you going to go? You can't go from one motel room to another."

She turned back to her packing. "When I started making plans years ago, I made a place to stay if I should ever need to have one. I guessed right on that one."

"You're not going to tell me, are you?"

"No. For both of our sakes, you shouldn't know where I am. Sooner or later the police will realize we're related and come to talk to you. And you can't tell them something that you don't know."

"Okay," he reluctantly accepted. "I don't like it, but if that's what you want. I'm just getting used to having you around."

"Thanks, Bobby. But save that sentiment for your girl when you get one."

"Okay. Promise me you won't sneak out in the middle of the night. I'll get up early and fix you a light breakfast to hold you into the morning."

"All right. I want to get on the road before sunrise."

"I'll wake you at five." He turned and went to the kitchen to set the coffeemaker.

It was nearly nine thirty and the last vestiges of the day's sun were gone from the sky when Howard walked down the street, one block off from his and Mary's house. He listened and checked every car parked along it to be certain no one was in them. He didn't want to stumble into a police stakeout, knowing there should be one but hoping there was not.

His day had not started well, and had not improved as it matured. He needed money and was not certain of where he was going to find it, or get access to it. But either Mary or the police had what he needed and he did not know where Mary was and he most certainly could not ask the police to give them back. He had cautiously made contact with a few that he knew would not turn him in, lest they themselves get drawn into the whole trafficking trial, but none had agreed to help him. He knew they were just trying to distance themselves from him, but it made him angry.

So, as risky as it was, he did not have any choice other than to fix things himself, like he always had. He had to try to get back into his own house and hope his safe was still undiscovered and secure. There he had his last resort access to funds, cards for a second identity, and more. Even Mary did not know about them—he hoped.

At the dark corner where the crossing street nearest to his house intersected with the street he was on, Howard turned and stepped off the street, onto the grassy side yard of the house behind and to one side of his. He waited in the shadows of a large bush that he recognized, but did not know its name. He never took the time to learn such triviality, and only knew that it flowered in the spring and looked green the rest of the year.

He watched the illuminated street corner near his house and the shadows as he approached the alley, thankful that his house was not in a newer part of the neighborhood without alleys. Slipping around the corner of the backyard fence and into the mouth of the alley, he stopped and leaned back against the fencing, keeping to the shadows as he studied the dark, ominous length. A dimly silhouetted car blocked the far end of the alley, parked with a purposeful air. If anything looked like a stakeout, this was it—blocking the exit so the occupant could easily see anything or anyone that appeared in the darkness.

Howard crouched down and waited beside the fence. During the next hour, he noted the car was indeed occupied; the occupant lit cigarettes and he counted the glows of the puffs to ease his own boredom.

Finally, unable to remain still, Howard slowly edged along the fence and around trash carts until he was directly behind his house and the gate beside his garden shed. Another cigarette was lit in the car, and Howard fought his stiffness and slowly lowered himself onto his hands and knees, hoping the person in the car was reading or doing something to stay busy or awake. He crawled forward, stopping often so a glance would not see his dark shadow moving.

Finally, at the gate in the fence, he rose up and felt for the latch string. With the faintest clink of metal on metal as the panel jiggled, he pulled the small ring and unlatched the gate. It swung silently into the yard, pulling him with it. He exhaled, realizing he had been holding his breath, as he knelt and studied the yard and the back of the house.

Satisfied he was the only one in the back yard, he followed the side fence and stopped at the door in the back wall of the garage. The spare key was still under the rock in the flowerbed to the right of the door. With the door unlocked, he returned the key to its hiding place, stepped into the garage, and closed the door behind him.

After dinner, Charlie settled on the front veranda with

Dani, Felix, June, and Jess, catching up on the home progress issues. Since she and Mel had cleared her head in the morning, Charlie felt like she needed some personal time with the other key women on the ranch.

"Where's Eddie?" Charlie asked as Dani sat down on the love seat beside her. Felix, June, and Jess were in the wicker chairs forming a half-circle in front of her.

"Not sure," Dani answered. "She said she wanted to talk to George and went off right after dinner."

Charlie chuckled but did not voice her thoughts about Eddie and George, both eighteen and having known each other for all of their lives. She changed her line of thinking and turned to Felix.

"Thanks for sending Mel this morning."

Felix smiled. "She wanted to go, and I told her you could use the help. I'm glad it worked out for you."

"It did," Charlie admitted cryptically. "I cannot believe how much she liked that kind of flying."

"She's my wild one. She's always liked things like roller-coasters—the taller and twistier, the better."

"I can see that. Where are they now?"

"Out with Peter, Camilla, and Billy. Robert was talking about some new horses coming in, and they wanted to see them."

"How are you doing with the changes in Mel and Mike?" Charlie asked.

"Changes? You mean Mel's new independence or both of their possessive attitudes?"

Charlie nodded.

"I'm okay with her independence as long as she's polite and respectful. I reminded her that if she wasn't, I suspected West would have words with her"—everyone chuckled—"and she might not like what he'd say. But their possessiveness worries me some. Are you okay with them talking like they belong here as much as everyone else that has been here a lot longer?"

"Personally, I like that they feel at home and that they feel like they do. And I was hoping that was because they were getting that feeling from you, that you might be feeling like you belong here too." She glanced around. "I hope you all feel like you belong here as much as we want you to."

She looked at Jessie. "How about you?"

"Me? Oh, well. Please don't take this the wrong way, Charlie, but I felt like I was coming home when you and West asked me to come. I enjoyed working with West before, and now, with all of this"—she waved her hands wide, as if gesturing to everything—"I've never been more happy, more challenged, or more at home. And last week Cappie said my place is ready and Lenny said we can go get my stuff from Amarillo as soon as he gets back."

Charlie smiled. "Bump or Ratchet could help get your things."

Jess shook her head and coyly smiled. "I'd rather wait for Lenny."

Charlie nodded and then cocked her head at Felix. "I talked to Cappie when I got back and he thinks your den or office space addition will be finished by the first of the week. Has Monte given you any idea when he will be ready to ship your furnishings?"

"He has the movers ready and waiting until West can travel. We've had two lookers on the house, but he figures he'll have to leave that with the realtors if it hasn't sold before it's time to come back." She smiled and glanced at each of them. "And to tell you the truth, I think when our stuff and Monte are here, then I'll feel like I'm home. I really do like everything we have here."

"You don't miss your friends back home or miss the city?" June asked softly.

"In a way, I do. Friends, not so much. I had a few, but my life wasn't structured around my friends. It was around the parents of Mel and Mike's friends—mostly just our neighbor, their two children, and those in their school. But what surprises me the most is the way they have taken to Celina and their schooling here and how little they talk about their old friends. They haven't even asked to write or text them." She absently shook her head in dismay.

"Now, as for the city, I guess my situation has made it easy to let that go. I don't feel comfortable in the city anymore. Not like I used to. Maybe someday, but now its unknowns scare me, and unless I'm with people I know, I don't want to be there. I've seen the worst, with witnessing Charlie's and Dani's kidnapping, their rescue, my own kidnapping and impossible rescue. Charlie, Dani, and Jess know the details of my ordeal and I will leave that at that, but I'm thankful to be accepted by my best friends—friends that had compassion and were willing to face dire odds to rescue me. I'll always be happy to be in their company, at home with them."

"Sorry, Felix. I think that was insensitive of me," June admitted. "I also felt a fear of the city, for the first time the night in August when Ratchet was wounded protecting me from potential kidnappers. And when we got back here this last time, and knowing that the ones that kicked my door down while I was at Reno broke into my old apartment again, looking for me, the night after we left, I suddenly realized that I was not safe there, in the city, any longer. I'm very glad Ratchet wanted me to come here, especially since it was for the right reasons." She absently smiled and twisted her engagement ring around her finger. "I like it here very much."

"It is different," Dani said with a smile. "Peaceful and rewarding in its way. And very much home if you listen and let the land speak to you, comfort you. It teaches you how to listen to what is around you, and that helps when you are back in the city. Knowing has helped both Eddie and me when we are there."

"Very philosophic, Dani. I will try to learn." June smiled.

"Very peaceful indeed," Charlie agreed, and then she smiled.

"Except when the still is broken by the sounds of Merlins, and the occasional Allison, Pratt and Whitney, Wright, Continental, and Lycoming engines."

They all chuckled.

They chatted about general things—life on the ranch and other less important things—for a while longer. Dani was the first to leave, explaining that she wanted to talk with her dad before she turned in. Jess left next, to check on the surveillance videos and check for any warnings before she called it a night. June left to find Ratchet and Felix got up to leave just as Charlie's phone chimed.

"It's West," Charlie announced and quickly tapped to answer.

"See you later. Gotta put the kids to bed," Felix whispered loudly, and waved as she went to the door and Charlie put the phone to her ear.

"Hey stranger," she greeted as she waved to Felix. "I hear you've been making the docs and nurses work for their living."

"I have," he replied, his cheerful voice comforting to her. "It's been hard, but someone has to remind them and keep them on their toes. How are you doing? Last time we talked you sounded a bit down, tired."

"Lonely, I think. I'm better, knowing Mom and Lenny are there and you're getting the best care we can get you."

"Are you sure? You sounded...so..."

"I know, and I was getting that way. But I went out and tried to twist the wings off *My Other Man.*"

"Not really, Charlie." His voice had a sudden edge to it.

"No. I did work him pretty hard, but Mel wouldn't let me go alone. She was in her flight suit before I knew she was there, and in the plane before I could argue. I was mad at her until we got to the end of a rolling climb to ten thousand and I told her to put her mask on but she was laughing so hard she could hardly speak. She wanted to do *more*! I was beyond surprised. She was genuinely eager to do more. So, I gave in and we danced, more rolls, loops, Immelmanns, spilt-esses, rolling turns, tail slides, stalls, snaps, everything...and she still wanted more. I let her try to do the loops, rolls, and everything, but I think I'll have to get Woody to teach her the basic maneuvers. Too hard for her to see from the back seat." Charlie took a deep breath. "I miss you. More than I can tell you. If it weren't for Mel this morning"—her voice dropped to a whisper—"I don't know how things would have worked out."

"I'm here, Charlie. Talk to me whenever you need to, and I'll be home before you know it. And please, try very hard, and don't let this push you the wrong way. I miss you also; I miss being with you, touching you, having you near. So please be there when I get home."

She inhaled suddenly and held it for a minute, realizing how well he knew her, and how well Cat and Mel knew her, making certain she'd stayed and hadn't gone away. "I'll be here. I'll be here unless I'm there with you."

"Thank you, but we need you there. Lenny will get me home as soon as we can convince the docs that's where I need to be."

"Mom said they might keep you a few extra days."

"They said they might, but I'm exercising as much as I can and trying to not be a bad patient. Mom says I'm still grumpy enough they might kick me out early."

Charlie laughed. "Well, it can't be soon enough for me."

She sighed and changed the subject, feeling she should be telling him about the happenings around the ranch. She told him about the break in the fence that Mel, Mike, and Peter had found, and that Ratchet and June had gone with them to help them repair it. She explained that Robert wanted the cattle moved down to the west pastures soon and they would do a headcount when they did. She mentioned Jess's thoughts about microchipping the cattle, and West seemed receptive to the idea.

Then she mentioned that Woody and Felix had gone and picked up the L-19 he bought and was surprised that West seemed to know all about it.

"Well, he says he and Felix are going to use it to spot the cattle during the roundup and that he is going to transition her into taildraggers early. She only has three more cross-countries to finish before she's ready."

"Wow, already?"

"Yeah. And she's talked to Monte about buying herself a plane."

"Does she know what she wants?"

"Yeah. But I'll let that be a surprise. I think you need to help her decide on a good one."

"Sounds like something to look forward to." He paused and she could hear a voice in the background. "Shucks, the nurse is here to give me more pills, another shot, and a snack before the lights go out. I have to go, but remember, I love you. I'll call tomorrow after we talk to the doc and see if he's getting any closer to letting me out of here."

"You're sure it's me you're missing and not the sounds and smells of the airplanes?"

He chuckled. "Goodnight, Charlie."

"I love you, too. Goodnight."

She had just switched her phone off when she heard Jess holler for her and Felix.

Felix caught up with her as she grabbed the doorjamb and swung into the security office.

"Felix, dim the lights please," Jess said by way of greeting.

Seeing the wide array of monitors and the dark yet familiar dining room and kitchen, Charlie asked what was happening.

"Felix, there's someone in your father's house," Jess explained. "When I checked, I noticed the shadow cross the kitchen from the garage mudroom. I think that was what you said was there between the kitchen and the garage."

Charlie and Felix leaned closer and studied the dark image.

"Where are the kids?" Charlie asked absently.

142

"I had just put them to bed when Jess called. Brighten it some, Jess."

Jess adjusted the image as they saw the shadow cross to the family room.

"He's going down to the basement," Felix whispered, as if speaking out loud would be heard by the image.

"Did you—"

"Yes, I put three cameras in their basement, two looking from opposite sides. There he is." Felix pointed to the screens as she shifted to the basement cameras. "He probably won't turn on a light. The basements have windows up near the floor above. Aah, yes. A flashlight. He's under the living room and… now the kitchen."

They followed the shadowy figure as he crossed to his left from the stairs, walked purposefully to the wall, and turned left again. Two large circuit breaker boxes hung on the back wall; he stopped and shone his light on the left one.

Charlie caught her breath before she spoke. She thought carefully and then asked the obvious. "Why does he need two electrical boxes?"

"One's a dummy," Felix answered. "There's nothing in the house that needs that much power or that many circuits."

As they watched, he opened the cover door on the left breaker box and threw the fourth breaker down on the right side. Nothing seemed to happen, but he turned to the left again and stepped to a closet door under the stairs from the family room. He opened the door and, once inside, followed another flight of stairs down into a dark room. Felix switched to the third camera as a light snapped on in a small bedroom-sized room, and he looked around as if to get his bearings.

Felix inhaled sharply. "He's changed his looks. A beard, a different haircut. Clothes are different and he's carrying a hat. We'll need to get a picture of him to Norman."

A daybed was aligned along the right wall, and a narrow dresser with a mirrored cabinet above it stood against the left wall. He walked straight to the far wall, past an occasional chair and opened a foot square door, then entered a code in the exposed keypad. The square vault door behind the keypad snapped open.

"You knew about this room?" Jess asked softly.

"Yeah. Emli found it somehow and I found a note from her in our grandfather's trunk," Felix explained, flicking her eyes at Charlie.

"Looks like a strange place for an extra bedroom."

"I know. I was able to put a camera in it when he and Mom were on the East Coast this summer."

After a moment, he closed the safe door, pocketed a bulging six-by-nine envelope, and slipped a gun into his other pants pocket. Then, feeling his pockets again, he closed the safe and looked around the room a second time. Satisfied, he donned his cap, walked past the hidden camera, and the lights went out.

Jess followed him as he left the sub-basement room, reset the switch in the electrical box, and closed the panel door. When he turned to the stairs and climbed them to the family room, everything looked like it had before he had been there.

"Felix, call Norman and tell him Howard's at his house. He can call the Canton Police," Charlie added as she watched the screen array. "Tell him we'll give him a picture of Howard's new looks later tonight or first thing in the morning."

"I'm calling, but make stills of the daybed and the room." She turned and watched the screens until the phone connections made. "Norman? Hey, this is Cathy Williamson. Sorry to call so late, but I have some urgent news about Howard Collingsworth that you need to know..."

Fifty-Eight
Friday, October 6

"I can't eat any more," Mary said as Bobby offered her the bowl of fruit. "Eggs, bacon, fried potatoes, and fruit. You outdid yourself."

"I just want to be sure you start out properly fed." He smiled—a worried smile, but still a smile.

"I'll be fine." She reached out and patted the back of his hand. "And I'll text you this afternoon, once I'm settled."

"You still won't tell me where you're going?"

"Uh-uh. I'm not going to do that."

Finally, she sighed and pushed herself back from the table, picking up her plates as she stood.

"I can get those," he said, and reached for the plates. "I'll clean up later, before I go to work."

She relented and he took the dishes to the kitchen sink as she straightened her chair and turned to the spare bedroom. Then, after a stop in the hall bath, she picked up her suitcase, and with her laptop case slung over her shoulder, she walked back into the living room.

"I guess I better get started," she said. "If I take too much time, I might change my mind. And that wouldn't be good."

Bobby stopped in front of her and gave her a long, tight hug. "It's been good to spend time with you, even if the situation is not the best. Maybe someday."

"Yes. Maybe someday." She forced herself to return his smile. "And don't do anything foolish. We'll let the cards fall as they may now. I appreciate all that you have done for me, but from here on out, you have to stop worrying about me. Take care of yourself and stay out of trouble."

"Yes, Mom," he chided. "I'll try, but the same goes for you. Keep in touch with your lawyer and keep a low profile."

She nodded and turned to the front door. Bobby opened it and followed her out into the dawning day, down one step and across to the driveway. When the cases were in the trunk and Mary opened the driver's door, he bent to give her one last quick hug. She kissed his cheek and smiled.

"That's for caring. I love you, son," she admitted softly.

"I love you too. Now off with you, Carole." He gently pushed her into the car, emphasizing her *new* name, and closed the door behind her.

Bobby stood and watched as she backed out of the drive and turned up the street. When he started back to the house, he saw his neighbor was out picking up his paper.

"Who's that?" the neighbor asked as he walked back to his house.

"An old friend," Bobby said, swallowing his surprise. "The mom of an old girlfriend."

"Pretty nice-looking *mom*."

"Yeah, she's taken care of herself," Bobby chuckled.

"Haven't seen her around before," he added as he stepped up on his front stoop and pulled his storm door open.

Bobby nodded in the dim light. "Told her years ago, if she or her husband were ever passing through, to give me a call." Bobby waved and stepped up to his own door. "See ya."

"Yeah. Have a good day."

Mary glanced back in her rearview mirror and saw Bobby step back into his house. She smiled, thinking about how much he had helped her, the mother he barely knew. But as she turned west on the 696 freeway, the thought of her daughters filled her mind and the memories of how Howard had treated them threatened to unsettle her stomach. If only she had been strong enough...

She deviated from her route to connect with Interstate 75 and drove through Catherine's neighborhood in Farmington. Knowing she could not stop to see them, and would most likely be unwelcome if she did, she could not help herself and wanted to at least drive by and see their house one more time before she left the city.

She stopped at the familiar street corner and studied the home she had visited so many times in the years since Catherine and Monte married. The house looked the same as it always had, its stone and brick warm and appealing, but it was the *For Sale* sign in the front yard that startled her.

Officer Fred Mitchell poured himself a cup of coffee and glanced up from the breakroom coffee bar counter as he set the pot back into the coffee maker. He was startled when he saw Sally walk in with her utility and pistol belt slung over her shoulder. She stopped beside him, and with her free hand grabbed her cup from the rack, set it on the counter, and filled it from the same pot he had just used.

"What's wrong?" he asked softly, quickly passing her the jar of sugar packets and a spoon. He tore a packet open for her. "You look like you didn't get much sleep last night."

"I didn't," she answered without looking at him. "Too much on my mind. Finally got a little and was late getting up."

He noticed her auburn hair was not as neat and clipped as she usually wore it; this morning she had pulled it back into a ponytail in her obvious rush.

"Turn around a sec." When she did, he tugged on the strands of her hair and centered the clasped tail. "Sorry, it was a bit off to one side. You might want to straighten your blouse. It's a little wrinkled around the middle."

She turned back, expressionless, and looked at him, running her free thumb around the front of her waistband in an attempt to flatten the wrinkle.

"Collingsworth, or something else?"

"Yeah, Collingsworth." She stepped past him, carrying her coffee in her free hand. "And a lot more than you can imagine."

Fred followed her into the room full of desks where they worked; she turned right to hers by a north window and he turned left to his next to an inside wall. He knew that her curtness meant that she did not want to talk about what was bothering her, so he settled into his chair and scooted up to his desk without saying anything more. But he could not help but watch her; something in her manner had him worried.

Sally knew Fred was watching her as she unfolded the sheet of paper she had gotten from her father, but she stayed focused and did not look back at him. They were not close, but she knew he knew her well enough to know when something bothered her. The last two weeks of their hospital duty had been different from the rest of their time—visiting longer at shift change, talking more. She had even brought him a couple of car magazines at the beginning of his shift in what turned out to be their last week of surveillance.

But he had never asked her out and she figured it was because he had the night shift and she had days, and since Collingsworth had disappeared, because he was spending his time trying to figure out a way to get back into the good graces of their sergeant. His finding the Arden Park house had helped, surprising them all by his deductions, ultimately pointing to where Collingsworth had been hiding.

Sally turned her thoughts to her computer and began searching the newspapers around Cherry Hill, New Jersey. She wanted her own verification of the accounts the email mentioned concerning one June Gibbings.

It was after nine when Sergeant Kilman called her, Fred, and four other officers into his office. She folded the sheet and slipped it into her breast pocket, buttoning the flap over it as she closed all of the open programs on her computer. With the department's flash screen up, she picked up her notepad and stood. Fred was waiting by the hallway door and fell into step with her as she hurried. His expression was sober and she could not tell if he knew anything about the meeting. Before she could ask, he was gesturing her to two chairs by the outside window.

"Victor," Kilman started, looking at the officer in the chair farthest from Fred. "Sorry to bring you straight in after a long night, but I have to ask: did you happen to nod off sometime last night?"

"What?" The officer straightened stiffly. "No, sir! I called in every half hour like I'm supposed to. Why do you ask?"

"You were posted in the alley behind Collingsworth's home, right?"

"Yes, sir. Bob and I"—he glanced at the man beside him—"took our position in the alley at nine o'clock and left this morning at eight thirty when we were relieved by Officers Clark and Walnut."

"Higgly? You and Connors were on the street?"

"Yes, sir. We began at seven last night and we were relieved at six thirty this morning."

"Did either of you report any activity?"

"No, sir, none," Higgly replied. "Neither of us did."

He glanced at Victor and Bob, both shaking their heads.

"Hmmm. I see." Kilman paced once behind his desk and then turned, his gaze starting with Victor and strafing all six of them. "At twelve forty-five this morning, the Canton Police received an email from a Norman Kent in Colorado Springs and they sent it on to us. Mr. Kent is the attorney for Catherine Collingsworth, now Williamson. He represents her and her suit against her father, Howard Collingsworth. He wrote to tell us that Howard Collingsworth was inside his home last night from nine thirty-eight to ten minutes after ten, Mountain Time. Add two hours for our time zone and that makes it eleven thirty-eight till twelve ten our time. We are told he entered and left through the garage."

"How could he get in?" Victor asked. "If he came down the alley, we would've seen him. And with Higgly—"

"That is why you are here," Kilman explained abruptly. "To figure out how. Higgly, how much of the side street could you see?"

"A couple of blocks along the street in front of his house and down the side street to the alley. We could see if anyone climbed over his neighbor's fence to the east, and no one came to the front of the house."

"We were about the same," Victor volunteered. "The side street on the west and the entire alley."

Sally looked at Fred as he turned slightly to face Kilman. He nodded to her and raised his hand. "Sir? If I may ask, how did an attorney in Colorado know he was in the house when our stakeout did not? Does he have some kind of surveillance system set up?"

"I think he must—"

A clerk entered and handed him a sheet of paper. Fred recognized the clerk as a woman from the communications room.

"Thank you, Amie," Kilman acknowledged. He turned to the officers and turned the paper around for all to see.

"Obviously he does have some kind of surveillance. This is a picture of Howard, as he looks now, beard, hat, and nice but very casual clothes. It was taken last night at three after ten mountain time, while he was inside the house. Pass this around."

Resigned, Fred felt Kilman's continued displeasure over the hospital incident when he handed the picture to Victor first, ensuring that he would be the last to see it. Then Kilman turned to him.

"Mitchell. I want you to spend some of your weekend off thinking about where else Collingsworth might be hiding. See if you can surprise us again."

Fred sat down in the chair at the end of Sally's desk as she closed and locked her desk drawers; it was the end of their shift. She looked up and smiled.

"What brings you to my desk at such a late hour?"

He smiled back. "Two things, actually."

"Oh?"

"Is the attempted break-in part of what's been bothering you?" He cocked his head. "I saw the incident report on Wednesday. I thought maybe you'd have said something."

"Yeah." She held his eyes and the smile slowly vanished. "It's just one of the many things."

He nodded, a tight smile forming on his lips when she did not explain further. "Okay, then for my second reason for my stopping. I was wondering if you would accompany me this evening. Pizza and a beer, my treat?"

"And why would I do that, Officer Mitchell?" Her smile returning in spite of her trying to not look too agreeable.

"I thought you might enjoy some time non-work-related." He smiled. "Unless there is something else you would like to discuss."

"No, no. Non-work-related would be fine," she admitted quickly, unsure if she wanted to talk to him about her visit with her dad.

"I can pick you up—"

"Not necessary," she interrupted. "Tell me where and I'll meet you there. I need to go home and change."

"Okay. I do too. Do you know where Earnie's is?"

She nodded. "On Kelly, south of Harper Woods Mall? Yeah.

Is that close to where you live?"

"About a half mile or so. I have a house near Rex and Tacoma."

"Hmm, Regent Park. About the same distance for me. I'm in a small apartment in Eastland Village, east of the mall, off Balfour." She stood up and pushed her chair under her desk. "Give me an hour? Traffic is sometimes heavy on a Friday night."

"Sure," he agreed, and escorted her out of the room, down the long hallway, one flight of stairs, and out into the parking lot. He turned toward his car. "See you there. Watch out for the idiots on the roads and don't let anyone take a pot shot at you."

She shook her head as she walked to her car, amused that his words were more meaningful than he could possibly know.

She slipped into her car and watched as he waved and got into his not-quite-new-model Mustang. She continued watching as he drove out of the lot and merged into the traffic. *Maybe I should talk to him about this.*

Howard had risen early and packed his few clothes into his tote bag. This was the day he had needed to move to a different motel, buy a cheap cell phone, and find a replacement for the license plate on Mary's car. He had showered and dressed for the day and then, glancing at the small pocket notebook lying on the nightstand, he had thought about the calls he needed to make.

About two miles west, he had stopped at a bank drive-through ATM and withdrawn the maximum amount of cash the machine would give him in one day. Another couple of miles north, he had stopped for breakfast at Carl's All-Day Diner, a nice sit-down affair with booths and counter seating. Over a cup of coffee, eggs with griddle-fried ham slices, and hash-brown potatoes, he had started planning his day.

The cell phone had come next; he had stopped at a respected mobile phone service and looked at their lowest-priced, pay-as-you-go phones suitable for receiving emails and texting. At first the clerk would only consider setting up a service with a credit card, but Howard had finally talked him into a cash deal, but had to settle on a six-month plan to get it. Howard used his mother's maiden name for the account.

A laptop had come second ,and the neighborhood big-box electronics store had solved that need with a cash sale.

By noon he had secured a room at the small 8-Mile Motel in a heavily industrialized part of town, just west of the railroad tracks and the expansive auto salvage yard on 8-Mile Road, near Groesbeck. He had paid cash for three nights—a small, modest room that at least smelled nice and promoted clean linens and cable TV. Several small diners and clubs dotted 8-Mile Road, but he knew he would have to drive for most things he would want. *At least,* he sighed to himself, *it's a respectable distance from last night's room. Maybe I'm far enough away that no one will recognize the old man wandering around in a new neighborhood.*

Back in the motel after a quick, albeit late, lunch, he settled into the straight-backed chair by the round table near the window. Then, taking a folded sheet of paper from the envelope he had retrieved from his house, he opened the laptop and waited for it to boot.

He established an internet connection and opened the computer's email program. In the settings, he entered the server information from the sheet of paper and tapped the Enter key. Slowly, a listing of old emails filled the screen.

He scanned them quickly, pleased to see the list stopped in late July, his account showing no further activity as he opened his pocket notebook. Scanning the pages, he quickly found the number he was looking for and entered it into his phone's keypad.

"Tyler? Howard Collingsworth," he said when the phone

connected and the familiar voice answered.

"Howard? How in hell are you—"

"Long story, but let's just say I'm out and needing information. What happened concerning the Gibbings woman?"

"I don't know for sure. The first time my men tried to get her, she wasn't home, and the second time in the next week, they were both killed."

"What? They're dead? How—"

"They were shot for breaking in! There's no 'how,' Howard. And when another of my men tried to pick her up at her office after work one evening, two men joined her and interfered. I know you're going to ask, but no, I do not know who they were. And now, it is apparent that she has taken a hike—she's moved. That's what I know."

"And now she's disappeared also! Damn! You know she moved because? I presume you called the apartment office and I'll bet she left no forwarding address."

"I did. Nope. Nada."

"We have to think about this. I need to find that woman."

A long silence fell between them before he finally continued.

"Okay, the main reason I called is that I also need someone to go out to Colorado and start looking around for me again."

"I can have a man there by Monday. Where do you want me to send him?"

Good, good. Denver area. Here's what I got from Tony Bellini in July."

Dressed in jeans and a long-sleeved sweater top, Sally threw her fleece-lined jacket on and stepped out onto the landing, closing her apartment door behind her. She double-checked that the door was locked and pushed against the panel to be sure it was latched. Then she reached under her coat and adjusted the gun and holster in her waistband. She descended the stairs and crossed the lawn to her car.

Getting home had taken more time than usual and she chalked it up to being Friday night with everyone in the city hurrying to start their weekend. But if everything worked like it should, she would still be on time, or within a couple of minutes.

Monday night's intruder and her dad's disclosure had raised her situational awareness, and she watched her surroundings more than normal. She noted the people walking to and from various apartment buildings and cars. She also watched the two cars that turned out onto Balfour behind her; she turned left and one, a red coupe, and the other, a blue van, both turned right. Taking the mall's south side perimeter road, she turned southwest onto Kelly Road—Earnie's was only five blocks down.

When she crossed the median and pulled into the parking lot, she noticed a blue van make a U-turn behind her and head back toward the mall. It startled her, looking a lot like the van that had followed her out of the apartment lot, the one that had turned north.

She shook her head, wondering, and parked her car in a spot beside Fred's Mustang, deciding she had better keep up her vigilance, just in case.

When he saw Sally enter and look around, Fred stood up beside the table he had picked near the back of the diner. He waved and she waved back, smiling with a nod as she worked her way through the closely spaced tables.

"Can I help you with your coat?" he asked as he caught the collar.

"Sure," she agreed, and shrugged out of it. He spread it over the back of her chair as she sat down. "Not too packed."

"Not yet. I think we beat the crowd, but probably not by much," he answered as he took a chair across from her. "I like your shirt. Nice colors."

"They call them blouses," she said, but smiled to take the sting out of her words. "Thanks."

He ignored her jab, knowing it was a reflex, which he suspected was due to her upbringing, and not a criticism. "Are you a beer type, or would you like something else?"

"Beer's fine, especially with pizza. But I also like anything with bourbon or rum. You know, the sweeter drinks."

"How 'bout I get a pitcher? What's your choice?"

She studied the extensive beer list long enough that he was beginning to think she wanted something else instead. He started to make a suggestion when she looked up and smiled. "The Kölsch."

He blinked in surprise and smiled. "Very nice. I'll be right back."

Fred got up and walked around a few tables and up to the bar. He placed the order and then turned, scanning the room like he always did. Some things in his training stuck, and he always checked and rechecked. Finished with his initial appraisal, he stopped his turn and smiled. Sally looked up from the menu and smiled back just as the bartender set the pitcher and two mugs on a tray. He paid and carefully carried the libations back to their table.

"Have you decided on a pie?" he asked as he set the tray on one side of the big-enough-for-four table and began filling the mugs.

"I have my favorites," she answered, and smiled back at him as he sat down, "but I want to know what your favorites are."

"Aah." He opened his menu and quickly pointed to three choices. "I like everything, but I tend toward the meatier ones. The Tiger's a good one"—he pointed to the city's baseball namesake—"or the Mets or the Diamondback, if you like one with a bite."

Sally giggled at his grimace. "So, I take it you don't like hot or spicy foods?" She cocked her head in question.

He smiled and shook his head. "Actually, I do. I thought you probably didn't."

"No, I do too, some. I mean, I like the spiciness, but not so much the burn of the hotter food." She glanced down at the menu and then back at him. "I come here and get the Diamondback on occasion, usually after a stressful day."

Fred smiled, knowing what she meant. "After my debacle at the hospital, I came here and ate a large one by myself, with suitable amounts of liquid tranquilizer to go with it." He watched for her reaction, but when she said nothing, he continued. "Sorry, that was a bad day anyway you look at it."

"You probably don't have too many of them," she finally encouraged. "You know, I think this is the first time I've seen or talked to you when you're wearing something other than your uniform." She thought about his wide shoulders, solid upper body, and narrower waist. "You look like you spend a little time in the gym."

He smiled. "I try to stay fit."

"Yeah, I saw your name on the rosters for the last two fitness demos. You must be doing something right."

"Thanks," he said as a waitress stopped beside their table.

"Sorry. Have you ordered yet? I'm late and just got here."

"No, we haven't." He glanced back to Sally. "The Tiger okay?"

She nodded.

"We'll have a large Tiger with extra Canadian bacon and sausage." He looked at Sally again. "Anything else you'd like added?" When she shook her head, he turned back to the waitress. "I guess that's it. Thanks."

The waitress nodded and hurried off to place the order.

Sally watched the waitress for a long moment and then turned back to him. "I know you said no work talk, but I've been wondering what happened that day. You seemed a bit off when we changed shifts—not like you usually were when you came on duty."

"I guess I wasn't." He sighed and took another sip from his mug. "We had another fitness demo scheduled for the next Thursday, and so that afternoon I'd spent in the gym. I was tired, but I didn't think I was that tired. Besides, there wasn't anyone available to substitute."

"I figured as much, but"—she studied his face—"I couldn't help but think there was more."

He was surprised to see the plea in her expression as she waited.

"I remember that look. You looked at me that way just before you left that night. It almost broke my shell."

"Your shell?"

"Yeah. You know, my façade. How I let other people see me. But to explain, I need to go back a few years." He took a longer sip from his mug. "You sure you want to hear this?"

She nodded. "I want to know more about what makes you tick."

He smiled, liking the sound of that. "Okay. To start with, my dad was a career police officer in Ypsilanti."

Sally nodded absently.

"Mom died in her fifties and dad passed four years ago. My older sister, Julie, had married a police officer, a beat cop in Ann Arbor, when she was nineteen, and fought cancer for the last three years. They had two kids, Jimmy and Elizabeth. They're eleven and twelve now." He took a deep breath and another long sip, emptying his glass. He reached for the pitcher, but Sally beat him to it and refilled his mug for him.

"Thanks. I don't know how to keep this from sounding like I'm making excuses, but that Tuesday, midmorning, Pete, my sister's husband, woke me up. He called to tell me Julie succumbed to her cancer late in the night and he wanted me to know as soon as he could tell me. She was going to be thirty next month." He inhaled and realized Sally was holding his hand.

"Sorry, Fred. I knew something wasn't right."

He nodded, but held his countenance. She did not let go of his hand. "I knew you did, but I couldn't talk about it. Not right then." Then he chuckled ruefully. "At least there was a bit of a bright side to my dozing off in exhaustion." He smiled at her. "I had a day off and got to go to her funeral and be with her family that Sunday."

She chuckled with him and slowly pulled her hand back. "Does Kilman know?"

He shook his head. "No need."

She nodded slowly and took another sip of her beer. "Thanks for telling me. I know it isn't any of my business, but… thanks."

He smiled and inhaled, taking another quick look around the dining room. "It's fine. I don't mind you asking. Anyway, after college I bounced around a few years and then I joined the Third"—he referred to the precinct—"about a year ago, thinking I could work my way into a beat or patrol work. Now, I think Kilman would prefer I get there as quickly as possible."

She chuckled. "But you're good at data analysis, putting things together and seeing things we don't see. The Arden Park house, for example." She gave him a coy look. "I wouldn't be too quick to jump out on patrol."

"Okay." He nodded. "I'll think about it, but only because you brought it up. But for now, I want to know a little about what makes *you* tick."

"One more question first." Her large, bright brown eyes and teasing smile made it impossible for him to say no. "Was your brother-in-law a beat cop two and a half years ago when that other beat cop, Lieutenant Marrow, and his wife were killed?"

"Yeah. Pete walked nights and he was to take the shift from Marrow that afternoon. Julie and Pete were actually friends with them. Why do you ask?"

"Just wondering. I keep up on things like that, especially when I know that guy, O'Brien, that did it hasn't been caught yet. Anyway, I heard about it from a guy I know that was in the park that day." She sighed and forced a smile.

"Your expression says there's more to that story." He waited.

"Yes, but not for tonight."

"Okay. I didn't mean to pry—"

"I started with the Third Precinct," she began abruptly, "just after that incident happened, and my dad was not happy! Well, he has never been happy that I chose police work over working with him in the office."

"The office?"

"He's an investment banker, partnered with Grandmyre and Sons, up in Mt. Clemens. He always said he dreamed of the day I would come and work with him. So, I went to college for a business degree, but added a second major in law enforcement against his will."

Fred listened, sipping his beer.

"I've been doing investigative and data analysis, digging through evidence to help the actual investigators with their cases. I like doing it."

The waitress showed up with their large Tiger and a pie stand. Fred moved the pitcher to make room as she placed the stand and then the pizza between them. Another waitress handed her two plates and silver wrapped in napkins.

"Anything else I can get you?" she asked, and Sally shook

her head.

"I think we're set, thank you." Fred smiled at the waitresses and then turned to plate a slice for Sally, but again she was ahead of him and passed him a plated slice. He took it and topped off their mugs.

Sally sank her teeth into her slice and he could tell by the roll of her eyes that they had made the right choice.

"Tell me," he began after swallowing his first bite, "what does a pretty investigating officer do in her free time, or days off?"

She smiled and took another bite, making him wait until she had finished and taken another sip of her beer.

"Well, if that's your way of asking if I'm involved with someone—"

"It wasn't, but..." He cocked his head. "Are you?"

She smiled again and shook her head. "No," she acknowledged softly. "Not for a long time."

"Are you?"

"Not since college. Most of the girls I knew couldn't see themselves in a relationship with a policeman." He sighed and smiled. "They might have a point."

Sally chuckled and slid another slice onto her plate.

"I take it you had the same sort of reaction from the men you knew."

"Pretty much. One actually tried to dissuade me from continuing my training, claiming he could take care of me better," she explained.

"From what I see, you do pretty well taking care of yourself."

"What does that mean?"

"I just *happened* to see something on your recurrent training scores. High marks in martial arts and self-defense—"

"You just *happened* to—"

He quickly held up his hands. "Easy, easy. I wasn't snooping.

161

Kilman was reviewing the reports on all of us and he absently laid your sheets down next to mine. That's all. When I picked mine up, I noticed how well you'd done."

She stared at him a long moment and took another bite of her pizza. "Really?"

"Really. But I'm glad to know you can defend yourself. With your smaller body mass, I knew you had to be good."

Slowly she smiled. "I like to think I can handle what life throws at me, but I sometimes wonder."

"We all do." He grinned a slightly crooked grin. "We just do the best we can."

She pushed her plate back and sipped her beer. "I don't think I can eat any more."

"Do you like cold pizza?"

"Not really. Not since college. Why?"

"That's okay. We'll split the leftovers. I still like cold pizza for breakfast."

She made a face and then smiled. "I'll nuke mine. But back to your question, my evenings are usually nice and quiet at home, mostly reading, and since it's gotten cooler, my weekends are spent mostly indoors. At home, an occasional movie or shopping, mall time, sometimes TV if a good game is on, but otherwise, reading or napping. Sunbathing, swimming, and sailing will have to wait until next summer."

He cocked his head, thinking how much he'd like to take her sunbathing. But instead, he said, "I know we're both off until Monday, so...would you happen to be free tomorrow?"

"Maybe. What do you have in mind?" She pulled her mug in front of her. Then she leaned up to the table and studied his face.

"I'd like your help brainstorming some things. Can I pick you up around nine?"

"Brainstorm? What are you up to?"

"Kilman's orders, but no talking work tonight, unless you won't go with me tomorrow. But I did promise not tonight."

She waited, but when he did not say more, she caved. "Okay, okay. Tomorrow. Nine is fine. I'll text you my apartment number." She sighed and shook her head.

"Good." Then he leaned back in his chair. "You were telling me a little about what makes you tick when we got sidetracked. Please continue. Favorite colors, foods. You know."

They talked for another hour, and sometime during that conversation, the waitress came to their table and placed their leftovers into two take-home boxes. They barely knew she was there.

When they finally called it a night, Fred paid their tab, then helped Sally up. She followed him to the end of the bar, where Fred motioned to the bartender.

"Hi." He flipped his ID and badge for the bartender to see. "I'm Officer Mitchell of the Third Precinct, and I'm wondering if you've seen this man." He held his phone up to let the man look. "We'll be sending bulletins out over the weekend, but I thought I'd ask."

The bartender studied the picture and zoomed it up once, slowly nodding. "He was wearing a plaid hat, beret style. Yup, I think it was him. About four thirty or five this afternoon. He bought a growler and a small pie. Natalie, your waitress, took his order."

"You're sure? He was here?" Sally asked as she stepped closer.

Fred slipped his arm around her so she could get all the way up to the bar. "This is Officer Ableman. We're trying to keep a low profile, but if you see this man again, please call the Third Precinct or your local police neighborhood office. We don't know if he's armed, but he's known to be dangerous."

Sally slipped the man one of her business cards. "Don't try to hold him, but please let us know."

"Will do," he said, and smiled at the card. "He was driving a big black car, Chrysler or Lincoln. I remember getting a glimpse of it when he backed out and drove off."

"Thanks," Fred said, and stepped back, pulling Sally with him.

She looked up at him, puzzled, and when he did not react, she glanced at his hand and arm across her shoulder.

"Oh, sorry." He dropped his arm and stepped back again. "Just wanted you to be close to the bar...so you could hear...and all."

He turned and led the way to the front door, then opened it for her. Outside, he walked her to her car and waited as she got in.

"I need to call dispatch. See you tomorrow then?" he asked, and smiled.

"Only if you promise to behave yourself." Then she smiled and closed her car door.

"Charlie, can you come to the security office?" Jess asked, speaking into her phone. "Thanks."

Jess was studying her computer screen when Charlie stepped into the office.

"What do you have?"

Jess looked up and shook her head. "Howard's active again." She tapped her monitor. "Two new emails from his server. He must have set up a new computer."

Charlie leaned closer to see. "He probably had money stashed at his house and got it last night. Who are they to?"

"New names. One is to a Lee Bishop and the other is to a Rick Murray. He's looking for a status on two of his collection contracts." Jess looked up and caught Charlie's eyes.

"The women," they both said together.

"The ones we warned, but we don't know which two are they trying to collect?" Charlie asked, almost absently to herself.

"I'm checking the headers, and...it seems Bishop is...in the Detroit area somewhere, and Murray...give me a minute." Jess entered another string and studied the results. "Richmond, Virginia, maybe. At least that's where the server is."

"Olgana in North Carolina," Charlie whispered. Then in her normal voice, continued, "We need to send them another warning. Who's in Detroit?"

"Ableman. Let me confirm these server locations and I will draft another email. Give me a half an hour?"

"Sure. Call me when you're ready."

"Uh oh," Jess whispered. "Here's another one."

Charlie bent to look again.

"It's to someone named Tyler." She hesitated, reading the email, and then looked at Charlie. "He's giving this Tyler information on where Tony last saw you. Looks like the information was before they kidnapped Felix."

"So he's sending someone else to look for me," she surmised with heavy thoughts and an equally heavy voice.

"That's probably what that means. You better warn Felix."

"Yeah. I think I better."

Matt Morgan parked his rental car in front of the double garage door to the right of the house Monte had leased. Widefield, a small suburb, was situated five miles south of the Colorado Springs Municipal Airport and two miles east of the US Army training and deployment installation, Fort Carson, "the Mountain Post." The house looked much like all of the other houses in the area, though its location in an older section in the southern portions surrounded it with mature trees and shrubbery.

He carried his two suitcases and laptop bag and stopped inside the front door to get his bearings. The house was modestly furnished, with the living room to his right and a hallway to his left. The dining room was straight ahead and the kitchen to its right, behind the living room. A second opening connected them at the garage wall. There was another door there and he assumed it was to the garage and possibly to the back yard. A quick investigation revealed the bedroom wing was a typical three-room layout with a hall bath and the en suite master at the back.

Smiling, he put his things in the master.

Once he had confirmed the services and appliances were working, he tapped Monte's icon on his phone.

"I'm here," he said when Monte answered. "Nice house."

"Thanks. Glad you made it. Any trouble?"

"None. Landed half an hour ago, got a car, and just finished walking through to be sure everything is working."

"I'm glad it's going smoothly. Closest gas, groceries, and other stores are about five miles north on Academy and Hancock Expressway. I'm sure you'll find others."

"Okay. I'll call if I need anything."

"Okay."

Fifty-Nine

Saturday, October 7

"Good of you to meet with me, Cecil," Hermidt Ernst, Special Liaison Agent for the State Department of South Africa, said as he greeted Cecil at the restaurant's front door.

Cecil nodded. "I was surprised to get your call."

He followed the special agent as a petite waitress led them through the dining room to a corner booth.

"Anything new on this Collingsworth fellow?" Hermidt asked as he slid onto the bench against the wall.

"Not really. I contacted deVon when I saw the newspaper article about a police raid on a house on Arden Park."

"The one where they found where he had been but wasn't there when they raided the house?"

Cecil nodded.

"I saw that one. Did any leads come from it?"

"Nothing public. The police aren't talking, if they know anything. I emailed deVon when the article came out. He said I should just continue waiting."

Hermidt smiled.

"I suppose you are here for Claude."

Hermidt nodded as a middle-aged waitress stopped at their booth, passed them menus, and took their drink orders. "What's good here?" he asked as the waitress left them.

"Breakfast menu's on the back, but everything is good if you like Mexican."

"Mexican, not Spanish?"

It was Cecil's turn to nod. "I eat here three or four times a week. With Collingsworth keeping a low profile, there hasn't been anywhere to go to search for more details."

"Maybe that will change when deVon sends you some help." Hermidt glanced up as the waitress brought their coffee and juices.

"Some help? Am I getting a new partner? DeVon has not said."

"He mentioned that Stanik or that someone else might come to help. DeVon said he figured two here would be better than one."

"Stanik?" Cecil shook his head. "No, that would not make sense. He seems like a good sort, not very talkative, but—"

"I do not know Stanik."

"Before Claude died," Cecil continued, "deVon said they were still looking for the lookalike. I was surprised, thinking he was just looking for Collingsworth for defaulting on his contract, but that's what Stanik is doing."

"I know nothing of contracts. I know deVon is looking for this Collingsworth, but that is all. My task is to try to deal with the mess Claude has left for me and get him home."

Their conversation halted when the waitress brought their orders and left them to their meals. Cecil nodded in agreement. Finding Collingsworth would be hard enough, and he knew he had no time to hunt for the missing daughter or the lookalike. They ate in silence.

"Well," Hermidt said on a soft exhale as he finished his breakfast and picked up his tab. "This is never easy, but I guess I should go to the police station and answer their questions. If I am lucky, I can get arrangements made to have Claude's body prepared for shipment before the day is gone. I'll call you, and if I am finished and you're not too busy, maybe I can join you for dinner."

Cecil nodded and they both stood and went to the cashier

to pay for their breakfast.

"Mel, there are three down in the ravine on your right," Woody directed, speaking into his handheld two-way radio as Felix guided the L-19 low and slow over the rugged northern edges of the ranch.

Listening with the radio's earphones, Mel got Woody's message and answered. "Thanks, Ghost Six. I see them."

"Mike, in the stand of trees fifty yards to your left." A moment later he continued, "George, three in the hollow at the south end of the cut ahead of you." Then, in the hot mic, he commented to Felix, "Have you noticed how at ease that daughter of yours is on a horse? She rides as good as she flies."

"Yeah. I've been amazed at how she's growing and the things she can do," she replied, sparing the briefest of glances as Mel started down off the lip and down into the ravine Woody had mentioned.

Everyone that was able to help with the roundup had gathered for an early breakfast in the main house, and by sunrise they were scattered along the northern ranch boundary. They slowly worked along the fences and into the ravines and canyons to gather the cows and herd them up onto the mesa to start the southwestward trek across the plain toward their winter pastures, west of the main house and in the valley between the northern and southern mesas. This was their second day; on the first they had pushed the cows up out of the eastern canyons and ravines.

The hardest part of the roundup was flushing the cows up onto the open plain of the mesa. Of course, those on horseback had to find them first. This time, Felix and Woody's assistance was making that job much easier. Felix flew and Woody scanned the area outside the plane's wide window with his large binoculars, reporting any hidden clusters or stray cows that he saw.

Thus was the routine for that day and the next four, firmly establishing Felix's, Mel's, and Mike's undeniable place in West and Charlie's and the Ghost Ranch family.

"Where are you taking me?" Sally asked when Fred turned his Mustang left off Vernier Road onto northbound Harper Avenue, leaving Harper Woods behind as he took the on ramp on the left to I-94, the East Edsel Ford Freeway, north.

"Coming home last night," he began explaining as he checked traffic and merged onto the freeway, "I crossed Gratiot Avenue and remembered that Gratiot was where Collingsworth had held his daughter. That's where two PIs and a number of civilians found him and rescued her."

"I remember some of the report, a little sketchy in places. I hadn't thought too much about it since I read it."

"Well, I thought that if we could see the place, in person, we might think of something else—maybe something important."

"You mean more important than finding out he was in the same restaurant that we were in last night?" Sally smiled and turned slightly to face him. "That was an incredible find."

"Sure was. Dispatch had a car from the Ninth Precinct office on Gratiot out to my place a few minutes after I got home." He smiled at her and nodded. "I gave them what we knew and they relayed the information to their other cars."

"How late did they keep you up?"

"It was near midnight when they left." He chuckled. "Aren't you glad you could go home and get some sleep instead of dealing with them?"

She nodded absently. "I couldn't go to sleep, not right away. I was caught up in thinking about him being in the nearby area." She glanced out the side window, thinking about the other things that had kept her awake.

Fred changed the subject. "I got up this morning thinking about the report. It said Collingsworth arrived in Gratiot late in the afternoon and joined the others that were already there—Sonny and his man Stan. We're not sure when Tony Bellini arrived, but he was there also."

"So, if he drove there"—she added, thinking out loud—"then the police would have impounded his car along with Tony's and Sonny's. Three cars, if we assume Sonny and Stan were together." She looked at him. "So, he must be driving—"

"His wife's car." He smiled at her and nodded. "The bartender said he thought he was driving a black Chrysler or Lincoln. Would you open my glove box and get the folded envelope out?"

She complied, noticing that besides the envelope, he only kept the essential registration and insurance paperwork and an extra pistol in the compartment.

"This is the only one."

"Open it. There are copies of two reports—the one on Collingsworth's capture and the one on his wife's arrest. I thought I saw a listing of key assets in one of those, with her car noted. It was in the garage."

Sally studied the short, factual document on his wife and quickly found the list. "Yes, a two-year-old Lincoln sedan, black, with the license plate number noted."

"I'm sure he's swapped plates by now, but we probably ought to tell dispatch what we think he's driving. Unfortunately, there might be more than one black Lincoln sedan in the Harper Woods area."

She was on her phone and connected with the Third Precinct's dispatcher before he finished his comments.

"There's the canal," Fred commented as he followed Pine Grove Road north. The trip had taken a little less than an hour and he was feeling anxious as they got closer. He glanced at his notes. "Kraft Road should be coming up. We turn right there."

A couple of minutes passed and Sally pointed. "There it is."

He turned and followed Kraft until it dead-ended into Gratiot Avenue. He turned right again.

"It's on the north side of the canal."

"Yup. See it," Sally said in confirmation. "Turn in here."

Fred slowed and turned into the drive of the house that sat between Gratiot and the shore of Lake Huron. They both noted the police warning signs adhered to the front door and the windows as they walked along the beach access drive around the south side of the house.

"There's the dock where the report says the unusable boat was moored." Sally pointed.

"Odd thing about that."

"What?"

"The boat. The report said it was unusable, but the Canadian crew had just used it to come ashore to retrieve Collingsworth's daughter." He smiled at her and shook his head. "I know it's trivial, but what happened to it? Why was it unusable?"

"The PIs and the others must have been waiting for it to arrive before they sprung their surprise rescue." She cocked her head, and with one eyebrow raised, continued. "I suspect they disabled it once the crew was ashore. They would want to be sure he couldn't take Catherine out of the country."

"You're probably right," he agreed, and walked over to look down on the pier. After a moment, he descended the steps and walked to where he suspected the boat would have been moored. Then he looked at the heavy plastic cofferdam retaining wall behind the dock, holding the beach sand back from the canal. Startled, he stared at the six-foot-wide random pattern of cracked and splintered holes in the wall.

"Come and look at this," he called as he realized the dock had been splintered as well, the pattern reaching across from where the boat would have been.

Sally quickly joined him and studied the pattern. "Bullet holes? You said they disabled the boat after it got here, but"— he smiled and patted her back—"bullet holes? Big ones." She looked back over the canal and the waters of the lake. "Where did they shoot from?" She looked back at Fred and saw him scanning the bright sky. "Oh my! Is that what you think?"

He nodded without voicing his thoughts.

"Now I understand why this trivial detail was not in the report."

"Let's just say I have a hunch," he said, and turned to the steps. "I'll be right back. I need to get something out of my car."

Sally sat on the sandy beach beside Fred, studying his find. The metal detector lay beside him, opposite Sally. She focused on the six items in her hands.

"They're fifty-caliber slugs. Military style, jacketed, designed for use in machine guns," he explained as she studied the nearly perfect bullets they had found in the sand.

"Machine guns. I don't think I've seen any bullets this large before."

"Do a search on your phone. The whole cartridge is huge"— he chuckled—"not a personal weapon, and they are very restricted, even illegal almost everywhere."

"So how is it that someone used one here, legally or illegally?"

"I don't know, but we'll do some digging. Everyone involved in the rescue of Collingsworth's daughter knew about this and chose to leave the details out of the report. For now, for me, I'm not going to upset the cart unless I uncover something that says they shouldn't have thought it was okay. But I'm very curious."

"So you're not going to say anything?"

"Nope. Not now, but we'll see what we uncover." He smiled at her with an odd twinkle in his eye. "Just remember, the guys that did the shooting were the good guys. They stopped the bad guys and rescued Catherine. But we'll take these with us." He winked at her. "I have a use for them."

"You have? And you're not telling me what you're going to do?"

He waited.

"Since I seem to be your partner in all of this, you need to tell me." Her voice pitched as she finished with a punch to his arm, startled by the solid muscle that resisted her attempt to show frustration. She paused and looked at him as he studied the other seven bullets in his hand.

"Partner, huh?" He smiled without looking at her. "I like that."

She was sure he was going to say something more, maybe more personal, but he did not.

"Okay partner," he announced abruptly, "let's put our thinking caps on. Who was in the rescue party?"

She unfolded the report and scanned the list. "The PIs were Lloyd Smithson and Sam Peuler. They were assisted by Glen West, Charlie West, Norman Stold, Dani Ventura, and Monte Williamson." She looked up at his sharp inhale.

"Catherine's husband was part of the rescue team? Isn't that a little odd. And who are the others?" He smiled. "I looked up people named West, Stold, and Ventura in the Detroit area, but did not find anyone that would've been involved. They aren't from Detroit, but they're obviously people Monte knows."

"What's Monte do?"

"Financial investments. His dad owns Openlands Financials, a very large commercial investment group, and Monte has an investment firm that supports some of his dad's customers."

"Dad might know them," she volunteered, "Monte or his dad."

"Let's head back into town." Fred stood up and offered her

his hand. "There're a few other places we should go and see if they trigger any thoughts."

As they passed Port Huron, Sally studied her phone; making quick searches concerning the raid and rescue but seeing nothing new, she turned to the names.

"An internet search has a number of posts on a Glen West. Nothing very informative."

"I sure wish I could find someone that showed that much interest in me instead of her phone." He smiled when she looked up at him.

"Huh?" Then she smiled and stared at him without moving, flinching, or blinking. "That good enough?"

He started laughing and shook his head. "Not quite what I had in mind. What've you found?"

"The first post indicates a Glen West owns a restoration business in Colorado. Numerous Second World War airplanes, but it does not say how many."

"And nothing that might tell us why he was here."

"Oh shit! We gotta find an internet café." She quickly started a new search. "There's a Big Boy a mile off the exit in Marysville. I can use it. Next exit."

"Yes. ma'am," he responded as she pulled her satchel from behind her seat and extracted her laptop. "Did you find out anything about Charlie? Is that a brother, son, or—"

"Wife," she answered, and switched the computer on. "All I can get on my phone is a headline. Glen West was shot at the home of Monte and Catherine Williamson. That was a week ago on September thirtieth. I need an internet connection and can use the Big Boy's visitor internet."

"Charlie's his wife? Is she a Charlotte or something?" he asked as he slowed and drifted onto the exit ramp. Moments later he pulled up next to the Big Boy hamburger diner.

She quickly connected and searched for the article. "Here

it is. A man entered Monte and Catherine Williamson's house asking for information—what information is not mentioned—but at some point he pulled a gun and West stepped in front of Charlie and Catherine, taking three hits clearly intended for the women. PIs Lloyd Smithson and Matt Morgan were visiting the Williamsons and shot the intruder. Glen West was taken to the local Bradmont Hospital in Farmington."

"Lloyd Smithson again. Hmmm," he murmured, rubbing his chin as he thought. "They must have had a lot happen to have a PI as their close friend."

"Yeah, looks like it." She quickly switched windows and linked with her account at the precinct. "Okay, what do we have for photos..." she asked herself in a loud whisper. "Oh my! Charlie isn't just a lookalike to the missing daughter, she and Catherine are twins!"

"What? How can that be?" He leaned over, his head an inch from touching her shoulder as he tried to look. The soft fragrance of her perfume suddenly captured his full attention.

"You okay?" She noticed his sudden silence and tipped her head, nudging him to see what was wrong.

"Sorry. Yeah, I'm fine." Then he saw the photos. "Are they related?"

"I don't think so, but I need to search our records for Charlie."

As she settled into her search, he asked if she would like a drink. She nodded and said she'd like a cola. He slipped out of the car and went inside.

"You won't believe this," she said as he settled back into the driver's seat and set her drink in the console cup holder. "One of the charges being brought against Howard is the kidnapping of Charlie West and a Dani Ventura at Broomfield last July the second. Suspected reason is that Charlie looks a lot like his missing daughter Emli, Catherine's sister, younger by two years." She clicked on another tab. "I called up another article on Charlie and found a newspaper magazine about airshows. She is shown in the cockpit of..."—she zoomed the image and read the print below the picture—"a...P-51D. The article further indicates that she is a certificated airplane mechanic and commercial pilot, and that Glen West, similarly qualified, occasionally takes his planes to public shows for their historical value." She looked up at him. "I wonder how long the Williamsons have known Charlie."

She took a sip of her drink and leaned back against the door. She hesitated and then, deciding, she looked at him. "Fred, there's something else going on that you don't know about."

He looked at her and she knew she had his full attention. Suddenly, seeing the concern in his expression and in his eyes, she knew she had already gotten his *attention*.

"Tell me," he answered softly.

She took a deep breath. "Last Tuesday night, my dad hit me with a real bombshell. It seems that the other charges against Howard for human trafficking are also likely true. He has been using various investors' sons and daughters as assets to expand, improve, or otherwise benefit his business dealings."

He did not say anything, but she saw the surprise on his face as she picked up her laptop case from the floorboard and pulled out a folded sheet of paper.

"I want you to read something and then I'll explain more."

"Okay," he agreed as she handed him the sheet.

She waited, watching him as he read the email message her dad had received. His body language told her a lot about him; he was not startled or disbelieving, but calmly took in what she had to show him. His face reflected his growing concerns, and finally he closed his eyes and lowered the sheet.

"Your father is on this list. Does that mean you're..." He slowly opened his eyes and looked at her.

She was nodding. "Yes," she replied softly.

"Shit!" he whispered.

"Dad was duped into signing a contract with that clause in it and he's worried for me—"

"He should be, and...and now I am too." He reached for her hand.

Absently, she watched him take her hand and pull it to him as she continued. "It seems that Howard has had problems with other projects and has called for some of those *assets*, as he calls us, to be collected. After seeing this, I began thinking the intruder that tried to get into my apartment Monday night might be connected with his contracts and not just a random happening. I checked on the incident concerning June Gibbings. Most likely, they did not go after her sister because she was recently married. She's the wife of the attorney Catherine hired.

"And we know about Catherine's kidnapping and rescue." She sighed, looking at his hand, his fingers gently rubbing her palm. "At some time, Catherine met Charlie, and I'm thinking it was after the newspaper article came out with Charlie's picture." She pulled her hand back and quickly searched the police report on Charlie's kidnapping in Colorado. She paused to read the list of names involved. "Oh my. Catherine's lawyer, Norman Kent, and Monte are listed as the ones that stopped the kidnappers in Broomfield, Colorado. And now it seems odd that Charlie and her husband and Catherine and her husband were together when Glen West was shot, and that the same PI was there that helped in Catherine's rescue. Tells me there's more to this story."

"Almost sounds like someone is still after Charlie and Catherine."

"Yeah, and I'd almost bet that same PI was in Colorado too."

"Maybe we should see if he'd talk to us." Fred leaned back against his door and smiled, a soft, tenuous one. "Like we agreed earlier, we're partners, and now that includes all of this. You can trust me, Sally. Partners also try to take care of each other."

She did not know how to respond, so she waited, accepting

the comfort of his gentle smile.

"Sorry if I'm being too forward, but I'm glad I'm here. I want to help wherever you need me. But right now, I think we should head over to Farmington and see if Monte's home. Maybe he will talk to us and shed some light on what we don't know. Why don't you see if there's a number listed for Lloyd Smithson?"

When Howard started to leave the motel parking lot, he noticed two police patrol cars heading east on 8-Mile Road, and one heading west. He hesitated and looked down, as if he was checking for directions, until he could not see any patrol cars close by. He turned onto 8-Mile Road and then onto Hoover Road. Two miles north, he stopped at another pizza shop on 10-Mile Road. He went in and ordered a grinder and a beer, taking a table near a front window.

The waitress brought him his beer and he took his time, sipping casually like the other patrons. The sudden increase of street patrols worried him, but he guardedly persuaded himself that no one would know him in his new clothes; it was not reasonable that anyone he knew from before would recognize him now. But, he considered, maybe another new look was warranted, just in case.

Then he thought about Mary's car. As he moved about, he was seeing fewer and fewer Lincolns and Chrysler luxury cars, and he knew he could not keep exchanging plates with other similar cars. *No,* he decided, *I need to get a less conspicuous car.* Then, thinking on the puzzle a little more, he decided he needed a more secure place to stay, and his place in Flint came to mind; recorded under his uncle's name, it ought to be secure enough.

When he finished his lunch, and with a buoyed sense of confidence, he went back to his motel room so he could make plans to get a different car.

It took Howard two attempts to get back to his motel, diverted once by a police patrol car on Hoover. But with Mary's car backed into the parking spot in front of his room, he was finally settled with his new laptop connected to the internet.

He wanted to confirm his cash assets before he tried to buy anything of size, like a car. There was one secreted local account, actually one of his mother's accounts he had never closed after she passed, that still worked because he could access it through the ATMs. But he cautioned himself, knowing that if the police had discovered it, they would be watching for any renewed activity. He sighed, knowing it had a balance of a couple hundred thousand and that it was a risk to keep using it. It was a risk he had to take; he needed cash to function.

Removing the second of the three banking cards from the six by nine envelope he had retrieved from his house, he followed the instructions on the sheet of paper folded and wrapped around them. He logged into the associated investment house webpage, and with a few quick verification answers, the links led him to the familiar secured account access page. But when he tried his passcode and password, an *Account Not Accessible* banner flashed before him.

Damn! he thought, almost cursing out loud. *The police did find that card. Damn, damn, damn!*

He paused and poured himself another glass of beer from the growler he had purchased at Earnie's the day before, and tried the second set of instructions. He remembered moving funds around before Sonny had told him he had found the other lookalike in July, but he could not remember how much he had moved where.

After a few steps, he linked with the webpage for his second card, but had the nagging feeling that it was the one he moved his funds from, not to. The login page popped up and he entered his passcode and password for it; an account menu page popped open. He sighed and clicked for a balance: just under twenty-six thousand.

He stared at the screen and forced himself to accept that all was not lost, especially with the two account balances combined. He shut the laptop off and placed it, the envelope, and his second identity papers and cash in the briefcase. Then, with a deep inhale, identification in his alternate name in his pocket, he forced himself to stand erect and once again face the day. He stepped out, got into Mary's car, and cautiously left the parking lot. He drove north through Warren and up to Sterling Heights, looking for a suitable used car lot.

Sixty
Monday, October 9

South of Flint, Howard turned off of Baldwin Road, halfway between Sharp and Hogan, where two long driveways extended north, each on opposite sides of an old, partially intact wire fence. He took the west drive for three-eighths of a mile, past the dogleg to the left, and stopped on the apron nestled in the *L* of the two-story house and the workshop and garage extension. A dense stand of trees rose up behind the house, filling the northwest corner of the acreage, and a thick row of trees ran across the acreage at a distance south of the house, successfully hiding the house from the traffic on Baldwin. He smiled, pleased that he had remembered the arrangement correctly.

He stepped up onto the wide front porch, took the spare key from its hiding spot in the nearest window box, and unlocked the front door. Switching on the living room light, he started a methodical walk-through, reacquainting himself with the house and the forgotten details of a place he had not visited in nearly fifteen years. He had bought the place from his mother's brother five years before that, but had let him live there until he passed.

Satisfied the house was still in livable condition, he went back to his car and unloaded the groceries he had picked up on his way up from Detroit. Then, with the cabinets and refrigerator reasonably well stocked, he sat down at the dining room table and opened the new bottle of Four Roses.

He filled a glass with ice from the bag he had bought at the grocery, poured it half full from the bottle, and thought about the services he had left connected after his uncle's funeral: the water, the electric, the gas, and the internet and cable TV. He had ordered a new internet modem for the cable service and found it waiting in the mailbox at the end of the drive.

He set the shipping box on the table and opened it, retrieving the hookup instructions as he slid everything out. Installation looked easy enough: just connect the cable, the power cord, and plug it in. Then call an 800 number with his mobile phone and enter an authorization code after pressing the initialization button on the modem. The process took three minutes.

Pouring himself a second drink, Howard went to the front upstairs bedroom, the one he was going to be using, and got his laptop. He set it on the dining room table and switched it on. After a suitable boot time, he connected with the internet and began a number of public searches to see what was happening in the world, especially when it came to the manhunt for one Howard Collingsworth.

Thursday, October 12

Woody stopped beside the C model restoration project and looked around the plane, desks, and carts of parts. "Have you seen Mel?"

"Hmm, let's see," Bump said as he put his hand to his forehead and thought. "I think Ratchet sent her down to stores for a new gear unlock cable. One of the two we have is pretty worn."

"Okay," Woody said as he turned to leave. "I'll call her cell phone."

"Wait. Helen gave her a phone?"

"Yup." He smiled at Bump. "Since she's taken the lead on the fence details and is out and about so much on errands, Charlie told Helen to issue her and Mike their own ranch phones."

"Well, that's nice." Bump poked his head back up into the

wheel well and he could not tell if he agreed or disagreed with what Helen did.

Woody continued on his way to hangar three as he punched the numbers into his phone.

"Hey, Mel," he greeted when she answered. "Woody. I need you to put your flight suit on and meet me outside Hangar Three as soon as you finish getting that cable for Ratchet and Bump. Yeah, that's right. I'll be waiting, so don't take too long."

Woody had just finished cleaning the windshield and side glass on the L-19 when Mel scampered up the ramp and hurried to him and the plane. She stopped and waited politely. He smiled at her growing patience and respectful nature before he put the cleaner and rag in the canvas tool case and secured it behind the rear seat.

"Do you remember what I showed you on Tuesday?"

"I remember."

"Good, then you're in front today," he said, glancing at her and gesturing to the open side door. He helped her up the step and in. "The mic and earphone hook up like it does in the back, so get settled, adjust the seat like I showed you so you can get full pedal movement, then belts and shoulder harness."

"Yes sir," she said, pulling her helmet on and securing the belts. He could see she was barely able to contain her excitement.

When she was secure, he leaned in and pointed to the checklist in the plastic holder on the sidewall. "Take a deep breath and get the checklist out. I'll walk you through the steps and be sure you remember where the switches and controls are."

She complied and quickly read each of the steps, placing her hand on the appropriate control, then switching or positioning it as required. When she reached the *Start Engine* section, he had her wait while he slipped into the rear seat, buckled up, and latched the door closed.

"Okay, follow the next step," he said as he buckled himself in.

She pumped the brakes and then held them, set the ignition switch to Both, confirmed the mixture was Full Rich, throttle open just above Idle, and primed the engine. Then she yelled "Clear" to the surrounding ramp and engaged the starter. In two blades, the engine barked and started.

"Twelve hundred RPM," he commented, and she adjusted the engine speed.

"Oil pressure upper green, oil temperature low green, fuel pressure stable, vacuum steady in the green."

"Okay, altimeter and directional gyro."

"Field elevation set, heading set to match the compass."

"Trim set in the green band."

She looked down. "Trim is in the green."

"Okay, young lady, let's taxi straight ahead slowly until I tell you to stop. We'll go northeast for about a quarter of a mile, not too far past the hangars."

"Roger."

"Is the radio set to the ranch frequency?"

He saw her head bob as she checked, then, "Yes, sir. Radio set."

"Very well, call the ranch and tell them *Snoopy* is taxiing out for some local flight time."

He listened as she confidently called. "Ghost Ranch. *Snoopy* and Ghost Six are taxiing northeast for some local flight time."

"*Snoopy*, this is Ghost Ranch," Eddie's soft voice answered. "Winds are two-four-zero at eleven."

"Roger, Ghost Ranch."

When Woody told her to stop, she turned *Snoopy* into the wind and held the brakes. "Engine mag check coming up." She pushed the engine RPM up and held it at the appropriate setting. The engine responded as expected to each mag check, and then she cycled the propeller, pulling it to high pitch and then returning it to low pitch, high RPM. "Mags are good. Prop is good." Then, without prompting, she turned the plane to follow the standard left-hand pattern. When she had completed a full 360 scan of the traffic pattern, she lined up, pointed into the wind.

"Pre-takeoff checks are complete," she advised, and Woody chuckled.

"Then tell them we're taking off."

"Yes, sir!" She thumbed the mic switch. "Ghost Ranch, *Snoopy* is taking off to the southwest."

"Roger, *Snoopy*. Safe flight, Mel," Eddie responded.

Snoopy's prop wash kicked up a small cloud of dust and they began to roll.

"Keep the nose heading straight and let the tail come up on its own. Let *Snoopy* roll until we get to seventy, then ease the nose up and let her fly."

"Got it. I remember."

He felt her work the rudder pedals, quickly correcting the engine and propeller's tendency to pull to the left. The tail came up and she kept the mains on the ground as the speed quickly built. At seventy, she gently eased the nose up, and *Snoopy* instantly stopped bouncing, settling into a smooth climb.

"Four hundred feet above the runway, make your left crosswind turn."

"Turning."

Woody watched closely, pleased that she was transitioning well, accepting the difference between the tricycle gear and conventional gear configurations, and to using a stick and side throttle.

"Okay. Forty-five-degree turnout and then take me down into New Mexico where we can do a little air work."

"Roger."

Charlie and Felix were watching from the observation room in Helen's topside office as Snoopy taxied away from the hangars. They heard Mel's conversation over the speaker in the adjacent room.

"Are you okay with this?" Charlie asked Felix as Mel stopped *Snoopy* northeast of the hangars and turned into the wind.

"Yeah. She's in good hands. I just hope she can keep herself calm enough to do what Woody tells her to do."

"She's shown remarkable self-control these past few weeks," Charlie pointed out. "She should be fine. You were and you've been a wonderful role model for her."

"Maybe. I was just anxious, worried when Woody started my training, but Mel...well, she's a lot different than me. I'm certain that right now she's beyond simply being excited and extremely eager."

"Probably," Charlie chuckled, remembering how Mel had been the last time they flew together in *My Affair*. "She certainly has taken to everything here on the ranch—the horses, the flying, the working on the planes, construction on the houses, everything. And Mike's right there with her, except for the flying." Charlie thought a moment and then decided she would ask Ratchet to help.

Felix smiled and then hugged herself when Mel made her radio call to say they were starting their takeoff run. "There she goes," Felix whispered, her senses flooded with the remembered thrills of her own first time holding the controls and guiding an airplane across the ground and into the air, the rushing sensation of freedom that one has to experience to understand.

Charlie joined Ratchet and Bump in Hangar Two, working on the C model Mustang. She collected her small tool satchel and climbed up on the wing.

"Hey, Ratchet, I was wondering," she started when she stepped over the canopy rail and into the smallish cockpit, "if I could talk you into taking Mike up in *The Lady* a few times. I don't want him to think that he's being ignored when it comes to flying. West tried to take him every couple of days, and now—"

"And now," Ratchet interrupted, "he sees Mel getting all of the attention." He smiled and nodded from where he stood in the empty engine compartment. "I think I can handle that. Maybe this afternoon."

"Was that Woody and Mel I heard takeoff?" Bump asked as he looked up from his task, adjusting the elevator trim tabs.

"It was," Charlie admitted. "He put her up front."

"Wow. Is this her first actual takeoff?" Bump looked back through the access opening. "Or has Woody let her take off in the 172? How old is she now?"

"She'll be twelve Saturday," Charlie said. "And yes, in the 172. This is her first takeoff in a tail-wheeled airplane."

"That's gotta hurt," Bump continued. "Four more years before she can get her student ticket..."

"Yeah, officially," she agreed. "But Woody has a surprise for her that might make the next few years easier. He'll give it to her at her birthday party Saturday night."

"How's Felix doing?" Ratchet asked. "She seems to be getting around all right. I saw her a few minutes ago heading outside. Did she take a jeep back down?"

"Yeah, she said she needed to get something. She's doing really well and her pregnancy is on track, progressing as it should," Charlie explained. "I think Monte being gone has her down a little, but that's going to change soon. When I talked to West yesterday, he said they have a good offer on the house and Monte thinks he'll take it."

"That'll be good. Is he going to live here on the ranch, or back in—?"

"Here." Charlie knelt down to look at the various control rods. "She likes it here, for obvious reasons: security, tranquility, and for what it's done for the children. She told Monte she was going to stay, and West explained what would be expected of him if he stayed with her. Monte agreed, so the plan is for him to bring their stuff to Albuquerque. We may have to drop him at the Springs occasionally to catch an airliner and pick him up, but it won't be long before Felix can do that."

"How much more does she have left?" Bump asked.

"Two cross-countries and a check ride. She's been burning up the sky."

"I'll say." Ratchet chuckled. "Even working down below, she's spent less calendar time than Eddie did."

"She has," Charlie agreed. "She wants to be ticketed before the baby gets too big, and I don't blame her."

Charlie settled into the routine, and the chatter with Ratchet and Bump diminished. After a half an hour, the sounds of an airplane drifted into the hangar. Absently, she had figured it was Woody and Mel stopping at Hangar Four or Five, and did not give it another thought. She was adjusting a turnbuckle and reached into her tool bag only to realize the tool she needed was not there. "Anyone seen my safety-wire pliers?" she asked, and raised up to look around.

"How about these?" Lenny asked, handing her pliers to her.

"Thanks, Lenny." She stared at him for a long moment. "Lenny? What are you—?"

"There's someone here that really, really needs to see you," he interrupted, and moved aside so she could see the area behind the left wing. West stood there beside Helen, smiling hugely at her.

"West!" She uncoiled and hurried over the cockpit rail, jumping off the wing where the flaps would eventually be. His smile filled his face as he reached out to catch her in his arms.

Charlie squeezed him for a long moment in a tight embrace, until she suddenly remembered his injuries. She relaxed and stepped back, worried. "Are you okay? I didn't hurt you, did I?"

West chuckled loudly. "I'm fine, Charlie. Very fine indeed." Helen steadied his crutch as he pulled Charlie back to him. "I feel wonderful, now."

It seemed like only minutes had passed when Charlie heard a jeep stop outside the hangar. June, Jessie, and Felix hurried in from the stairs and the greetings happily repeated, with West hugging each of them, and then Jessie turned and found Lenny as he slid off the wing. Their reunion was as enthusiastic as West's and Charlie's had been.

"Thanks for taking care of him and bringing him home," Charlie whispered to Helen as they hugged each other. "But why didn't you tell me you were coming home today?"

Helen smiled. "West wanted to surprise you. He said he doesn't get to do that very often."

"You must've started early. What, one gas stop—?"

"Yeah, Topeka," Lenny admitted. "The winds were unusually calm and we made good time. Six hours and ten minutes, block time."

"So you were off by...five thirty?"

"About that," Helen agreed. "We were at Monte's place when you talked to West last night. He hoped Lenny and me talking in the background didn't give it away."

Charlie chuckled, watching West as he talked with Ratchet and June. "No, your talking didn't give it away." Then she smiled at Helen. "Looks like your eating schedule is off by a few hours. You must be ready for lunch."

Helen nodded. "It will be good for him to eat and then rest a while."

Charlie smiled and turned to West. "Okay. Ratchet, Bump will grab another jeep and we can resume our conversations down at the house."

Arthur Stanik settled down at a spot at one of the lesser-used octagonal tables in the research section of the Denver Central Library; there was only one other person at the table, mostly hidden behind the bank of monitors positioned at each facet. He set his cup of coffee to the left of the keyboard and his notepad to the right, scooted his chair up to the table, and tapped the Enter key to open the login screen.

On his way in, he had stopped to talk with the woman manning the desk under the 'Ask' sign. He had arrived in Denver just over three weeks past and began his library research after two weeks of aimlessly waiting for something to happen. But eight days ago, he came in to find out how to find the ownership of different airplanes, and asked the woman under the 'Ask' sign for help. She had caught his attention and he had returned the next day with another *question* for her to help him with. On his third visit, he struck up a casual conversation, asking about local attractions, things to see and do around Denver, having decided that he ought to enjoy some of his time while he waited for the Ghost Ranch airplanes to show up.

The woman, named Patty, had been very pleasant and helpful. And this morning, before he had settled at his computer terminal, he had found out that she was single, had an off-and-on relationship—mostly off, she had explained with a bright smile he felt was for him—and was only three years younger than himself.

Buoyed by the morning's continued pleasantries, he logged into the computer and opened an internet link. This day, he began a search for websites that offered airplane flight tracking capabilities. Most he found were for following airlines from their departure to their destinations, but two allowed the user to track any airplane in the FAA's navigation control system.

He read the detailed explanation on both websites and discovered they followed the airplane's transponder information for identification. By selecting different transponder code filters, the websites let the user select airplanes flying under visual flight rules, or VFR, those flying under instrument flight rules, or IFR, those using a narrow selection of special transponder codes, or all of them together. He quickly realized the last option would only be useful in less congested airspace.

He experimented with the websites and quickly noted that each target displayed on the physical map image also posted the given airplane's registration number. He remembered the list he had found on his first day in the library, opened his briefcase, and removed it. Then he entered one of the registration numbers into the website's search window and clicked the Okay button.

The display dimmed while it processed his search request, blinked, and returned to its previous brightness. Nothing appeared and he zoomed in on a portion of the monitor's screen covering Colorado. No target displayed, so he entered a second registration number.

By the time he entered the last number he had, he had reluctantly accepted that the Ghost Ranch's airplanes were either not flying or they were not using a transponder code. With a barely audible sigh, his mind turned to Patty, working at the information desk as he quietly returned his list to his briefcase and wrote down the two websites he had settled on. He would look at them again from his laptop. In his resignation, he missed the Ghost Ranch T206's singular blip and registration number as it came onto the right-hand edge of the monitor's map image, turned south in western Kansas, and winked out.

Arthur switched his monitor off, stood up, and collected his briefcase. As he passed the information station, he stopped and caught Patty's attention. She looked up and smiled.

"I am wondering, Patty," he inquired, trying to sound considerate and proper as he fiddled with a pencil lying on the counter, "whether I might convince you to have lunch with me."

Patty's expression turned to sweet politeness. "Convince me?"

"If you would join me, I would certainly ask that you select the place, as public as you feel necessary." He hesitated and then continued. "Even the library's coffee shop would be satisfactory."

Patty smiled and shook her head. "The coffee shop is nice, but there are better places for quiet meals. Let me think about it and I'll let you know when I see you again. Tomorrow, maybe?"

Arthur nodded. "Until tomorrow then."

Mary sat at the island eating counter between the dining room and the large kitchen in the nine-year-old ranch-style house, studying the adjacent open great room furnished as a casual living room. She had started the house on Catherine and Emli's inherited property north and west of St. Ignace on a trip north when Howard was away on one of his *business* trips. Emli had been gone for over a year and it was during that period of time when Mary had rebelled at Howard's heavy-handedness. Unbeknownst to him, it was during one of his many trips that she had also filed for a quiet divorce. She knew he did not remember agreeing to one—she chuckled, remembering how scared she had been when she had slipped him the document among a stack of other papers he was signing.

He was in one of his moods that night, but he had needed to finish some year-end paperwork and had not yet resorted to blaming her for his difficulties. As dangerous as it was for her, she had helped to *grease the skids*, so to speak, with a heavy meal, suitable libations—he did so love his bourbon—and herself, pleasantly supporting him in light conversation to hold his temper at bay and to make the bookkeeping tasks easier to digest. She chuckled again—after he had finished the stack of papers and before he had had a chance to read through them again, he had fallen asleep at the table—she had spiked his bourbon with a small amount of the sedative she kept in that small jar marked *"sweetener."*

The next morning, after Howard had gone to work, she had delivered the signed papers to her mother's attorney, Oscar Delany, in Detroit and he had filed the decree. She had watched the mail each day until the official decrees had arrived ten days later, and she had quickly placed them in her new safe deposit box before Howard had a chance to see them.

That had been the start of a new beginning for her, with the one exception: she still had to play the part of the obedient wife until she could move a sufficient amount of funds out of Howard's secreted off-shore accounts. When she had accomplished that, she fought with the idea of moving out, realizing it would be moving out of Catherine's life as well if she was to keep Howard from finding her. But Howard's kidnapping of Catherine and his capture had marked an end to her indecision. Unfortunately, the arrest had delayed her ability to act.

Now, using her mother's maiden name, she found herself free of Howard, at least for the time being. She knew there would be consequences for escaping and for Howard's disappearance from the hospital, but she hoped her emails and his video confession of her innocence would be enough to exonerate her and her actions.

Mary noted the day was getting dimmer and checked the time. She should be fixing something for her dinner, but the sudden seclusion and loneliness stifled her desires to eat. Instead, she opened her mobile phone, selected the text messaging app, and began typing a note to Bobby.

> *Arrived safe Friday evening. Refrigerator*
> *and cupboards are now stocked and*
> *everything seems to be working fine. Take*
> *care of yourself and do not worry. I should*

195

*be fine, for a while anyway. Keeping my
fingers crossed. Love you, son. Remember
to delete this message.*

She pressed the Send icon and then deleted the message, once from the message display page and then from the history page.

With Helen assisting on his right side and Charlie on his left, West lowered himself into his chair at the head of the dining room table. He watched Charlie as she straightened and stood beside her chair, waiting for everyone to settle into their places like he had always done. His pride in Charlie shone on his face as she greeted each one as they came in and sat down. When everyone had seated themselves, she took her place, covering West's hand with hers as Gracie and Camilla began setting platters and bowls on the table.

"Would you care to say anything?" Charlie asked, smiling at West.

"Certainly. Especially to you, Charlie, for coming home and helping to take care of things here. I know it wasn't easy for you, but I speak for everyone when I say thank you." Then West looked around the table and focused on Monte's empty chair.

"You probably already know, Felix, but Monte wanted me to tell you that you have a solid offer on your house and he's thinking you should take it. He'll have to fly back for the closing, but he will be here as soon as he can, maybe Sunday or Monday." He gestured for everyone to start eating.

"Thanks, West," Felix said with a nod. "We talked last night and I agreed we should take the offer. He also hoped he could leave our SUV in the Springs and that maybe someone could pick him up."

"I think Woody and you ought to take the 206 or *Box Car* and do just that." He looked at Woody. "I assume Felix has transitioned into taildraggers." When Woody nodded, West looked back at Felix and then smiled at Mel and Mike. "I think Monte would like that, and you"—he glanced at Felix—"can fly him home, show him a little of what you've been learning."

"Can we go?" Mike asked, then looked at West.

West smiled and looked at Woody. "What do you think?"

He smiled and nodded. "We'll have to see, Mike. We might have a full plane, depending on which day we pick your dad up." He looked at West. "Felix has transitioned into the L-19. She flew us on our spotter missions during the roundup."

Mel smiled and glanced at Ratchet, and then at Woody. "We can get everything done and be ready to go if there's room."

"Good." West smiled. He looked a little sideways at Woody. "Is Felix up to tackling *Box Car*?"

"Yup," Woody confirmed without looking at Felix. "We'll make that happen this afternoon, unless she has something she'd rather be doing." He turned and looked at her.

She shook her head. "Nothing I can think of at the moment."

Dani and Eddie tried to hide their laughter and Charlie snickered.

"I see the enthusiasm is still alive and well." West nodded, chuckling softly to himself.

"And," Woody added, "Mel had her second flight in the L-19 this morning."

"Really?" West asked, but was not actually surprised. He looked at her and continued. "I also hear you've been a big help with the cattle and fence maintenance."

Mel blushed and looked at her mom. "Mike and I both try to help as much as we can." She looked at West. "Is that okay? I mean everyone says it is, but..."

"Of course it's okay," he encouraged. "I'm glad you want to and am very pleased that you do. Like you said, I think everyone is happy for your help. And, I've had nothing but good reports, so please don't worry. You're as much a part of the ranch as anyone here." Then he glanced at Mike. "Are you getting to fly as much as your sister?"

"No...no sir," Mike stammered, then smiled. "But Ratchet says I can go with him this afternoon. *The Lady* hasn't been exercised since Sunday." Then his expression saddened. "I get to ride a lot, but...but my feet still don't reach the rudder pedals." Then he brightened again. "But Mel has been flying a lot too, and we're so happy you think that's okay. And we both rode in the roundup, gathering the strays, the ones that were reluctant to follow the others, and—"

"Mike," Felix said softly. "Don't ramble on so. We're glad you like it so much, but please let someone else talk."

He stared at his mom and slowly let a smile grow across his face. He looked at West and added, "Sorry. I didn't mean to be doing all of the talking."

"That's okay, Mike. Tell you what, you come around this evening, after dinner, and you can tell me everything that's been happening, everything you've been doing. And you can even invite your sister to come if you'd like."

Mike nodded, his wide grin still filling his face.

West added a serving of meat from the platter Charlie held for him and asked, "Can anyone tell me how Robert is doing?"

When lunch was finished and everyone began to disperse, heading out to fill their afternoon with the tasks needing to be done, Charlie and Helen helped West up onto his crutches. They slowly led him out of the dining room as Mike, Mel, Ratchet, and Woody exited through the side door and the waiting jeep outside. Dani and Eddie slipped out through the kitchen and West assumed they were going out to see their parents.

As Charlie and Helen turned him toward the stairs, he noticed Lenny and Jess, hand in hand as they stepped out through the front doors and turned toward the veranda chairs and love seats.

"Is there something new between those two?" he asked, and smiled at Charlie.

She nodded. "His absence has bothered Jess more than she lets on, but now...I think they just need a little time together. Now watch your step. Mom and I will keep you from falling backwards, so slowly hop up one step at a time."

He smiled and slowly followed Charlie's instructions.

By the time they had him in his and Charlie's bedroom, West felt exhausted. He had never been more pleased than he was now at the fact that he had had the foresight to make the staircase wide and the risers short. It meant more steps, but they were easier to hop up onto than normal risers would have been.

"Okay, dear," Helen said as she placed two small medicine bottles on the nightstand on West's side of the bed. "Give him one of each of these and make him rest. I'll see you when you come down."

"I think...I'm going to rest a little while myself before I come down." Charlie smiled at Helen.

"Very well, dear." Helen nodded. "I think you might need it too." She turned to leave. "I'm going out to check on Robert, but when you get up, come and find me."

"Okay." Charlie nodded as West turned and slowly set himself on the edge of the bed.

Helen closed the door behind her and Charlie took West's crutches and leaned them against the wall, close enough that he could reach them if he needed to.

"Now, let's get you settled," she absently remarked. "Scoot back so I can lift your legs and get you turned."

He pushed himself farther from the edge and Charlie quickly swung his legs up onto the bed. He automatically fell back, his head landing on his pillow.

"Thanks," he said as he caught her hand and pulled her to

him. His free hand cradled the back of her head and he stole a gentle but lengthy kiss. He slowly released her lips and smiled. "I've thought about doing that so many times..."

She pushed herself up without a word, went to the foot of the bed, and picked up a soft blanket. With a deft toss, it opened and drifted gently down on top of him, his cast and bent knee poking up like a low mountain.

Charlie settled on the wide chest that spanned the foot of the bed, unlaced her boots and dropped them onto the floor, and slipped out of her jeans. She hung them on the bed's low corner post.

He watched her, enjoying seeing her every movement and smiling hugely when she turned and slipped under the blanket to snuggle close beside him. Then, with a bright smile, she kissed him again, long, gentle, making everything manly in him take notice.

She lifted her head and smiled. "I've been beside myself, worrying about you, missing you—"

"I felt the same way," he interrupted. "I am so very glad you weren't hurt when—"

She quickly kissed him again. "I wasn't. Thanks to you. I can't show you how very much I appreciate what you did and that you're now back home, but you won't be in a cast forever and—"

He kissed her and pulled her down beside him. "Hold me, woman. Help me remember how wonderful I feel when I can snuggle and hold you tight."

Charlie complied and pulled herself as close as she could, her arm wrapped across his chest and her head resting on his shoulder. "I need you to hold me too. I need you every day, all the time."

"I'm here, Charlotte. I think about you all the time and I'm here. Always here for you." He closed his eyes and smiled, feeling her tighten her arm across his chest. "But when this cast is off—"

She slapped his chest playfully, then squeezed him. "I'll be ready. More than ready."

West, wrapped in a *sarape*, was quietly watching the southern evening sky from the love seat on the front veranda. He had talked with Mike and Mel after dinner, and Mike had explained what they had been doing during his absence. Mel was quiet, yet smiling encouragingly at her brother's enthusiastic portrayals. When their mom, with June and Dani in tow, joined the group, they made their greetings and said they wanted to talk to Camila and her brother. They left, and the conversations continued between the adults.

"She's still sleeping soundly," Helen greeted softly as she stepped out onto the veranda and joined them. She sat down beside West, nodding to Dani, June, and Felix in the chairs pulled up in a half circle in front of West.

"That's not normal, Mom."

"I don't think," Felix interrupted quickly as she leaned toward him, "she slept much after we came home." She glanced at June and Dani. "And I know she didn't sleep much while we were in Farmington and you were in the hospital."

"I thought she slept in the recliner at the hospital."

"West," Helen interjected, "she's been so worried about you, she can't relax. I think this was worse for her than her life was before you got her to come to the ranch."

"I could hear it in her voice," he admitted, "when we talked on the phone. It got worse each day, and I prayed she could let the demons go."

"Like when she tried to twist the wings off her *Other Man*?" Mel asked as she returned, stepping out onto the porch, seeking Felix's lap.

West smiled, took her hand, and guided her between the arms of the love seat and Felix's chair. "I understand that was quite a flight."

"Yeah, it was." Mel smiled, but it was only a half-smile. "She was angry with me for making her take me with her. But when we reached ten thousand feet, out over New Mexico, she began to relax." She hesitated. "I enjoyed the flight. It was exciting, especially after she started showing me how to do what she'd done, but..."—she held his eyes for a long moment—"but I was really worried. I thought she might just leave us and head for Farmington alone without thinking..."

"Thanks, Mel. Has anyone told you that you have really grown up in the last few weeks?"

She blushed and looked down at her hands. "I...I think Mike and I both like the beauty and have seen the dangers of the ranch. We have a lot of fun here, learned a bunch of new things, but we know we still have to pay attention to what's going on. When we remember what happened to Charlie, Dani, and to...Mom, we know we have to."

"I can see that you've paid more attention to what's been happening than I thought," West admitted, "and I hope you can still enjoy the opportunities the ranch has to offer."

"Will Charlie be all right?" Mel asked, her expression drawn with worry and concern.

"Yes, dear," Helen answered quickly. "She's still adjusting to her life here on the ranch and hasn't quite accepted that she's home."

"She never had a real home," West said. "Not like you and Mike have had—one where you know you are safe and loved. Charlie has that now, and it is hard for her to accept that she does."

"*K'ébidishní.*" Dani smiled. "To be our friend. Friends, I think, Charlie has never had, not real ones, until she came here."

"That would be scary," Mel whispered, and they all nodded

with her.

"Yeah," June said in a loud whisper. "This place makes very special friends."

Sixty-One
Friday, October 13

West bent over Charlie's side of the bed and gently kissed her cheek. After his second kiss, she slowly stirred and turned her head to catch his lips.

"Good morning, sleepyhead. We need to get cleaned up for breakfast."

"Mmm, what? Morning? Breakfast?" she muttered, and slowly forced her eyes open. Seeing the still dark room, she rolled over to look up at him, hovering over her. "It's morning?"

"Yes, love. You slept through dinner and the night." He kissed her again. "But now we should get you showered and me washed so we can both make an appearance at breakfast and get the day started."

Charlie helped West down the stairs and into the dining room, where everyone was standing around the table and those along the credenza were sipping coffee.

"Morning, Charlie," Helen greeted. "Feeling better now?"

Charlie smiled and realized they all knew how worked up and tense she had been. "Much better now that West is home."

She took her place as Helen and the others moved to their chairs and settled. West handed Charlie his crutches as he lowered himself onto his chair, pleased that he could accomplish the feat without assistance. Gracie, Camilla, and Becky

205

immediately started placing platters and bowls on the table.

"Good morning to you ladies," West greeted as they hurried in.

"*Yáʼátʼééh*," Gracie greeted in return. "Good to see you home. And looking well."

"We're very happy you are going to be all right," Camilla added softly. "We were so worried when we heard you were hurt."

"I was in good hands. Thank you," he said, glancing at Charlie, Helen, and Lenny. "And before long, I will not need the crutches and will be back, nosing into everyone's business like I used to do."

Camilla chuckled and Becky shook a finger at him.

West turned his attention to June. "Tell me, how're the plans for the Tempest inventory visit coming along?"

"Pretty much completed," June replied. "We've been waiting for you to get home so we can arrange a suitable time to meet with Mr. Miles."

"Very good. See when Hubert's ready and I think you and Bump should accompany Ratchet on the trip." He looked at Jess and continued. "I've taken Lenny away for the better part of the last two weeks, so I'd like for him to have some time at the ranch before I send him out again." He looked at Ratchet. "Will that work for you?"

Ratchet nodded and smiled.

"Good, then plan on using the 206 for the trip."

"I'll get on that this morning," June commented, and West saw her squeeze Ratchet's hand.

"Who's going to be away this weekend?" West asked as Charlie spooned a helping of scrambled eggs and two slices of bacon onto his plate.

"Madra asked Celina to change weekends with her and Robert, feeling it was too soon for Robert and her to take a weekend in town," Woody explained. "So Celina and Cappie will go today."

West nodded absently as he listened.

"And with Dani just back, Eddie asked to fly them and to pick up the supplies in Pueblo. She'll be taking *Box Car*."

"Speaking of *Box Car*," Charlie said, changing the subject, "how did Felix do yesterday? I guess I was sleeping and didn't hear."

Woody chuckled and continued. "Felix did just fine. She flew for one point one hours and managed three respectable takeoffs and landings. This morning she will fly her last cross-country in the L-19."

"Watch the weather, Woody," Helen added. "The forecast is for some rain with possible snow following. Should arrive early evening, most likely just after sunset."

"That's why she's going right after breakfast." Woody smiled. "We saw the forecast yesterday afternoon and checked again this morning. Looks like we have a wide enough window. Should blow out of here sometime Sunday."

"Going south again?" West asked, smiling at Felix.

"Yes. Raton, Las Vegas, Clayton, and home," Felix answered. "About 325 miles. I should be back for lunch."

"Might be best to plan on picking Monte up on Monday, after the weather clears," West added.

"Probably best," Felix agreed.

"If you talk to Monte, you might see if that works for him," Woody said.

"Sure." Felix nodded.

"Is there any other business that I should know about?" West asked as he spread Becky's homemade prickly pear jam on a slice of toast.

Mike raised his hand and looked at Felix. "Mom?" he asked softly. "Eddie asked if I could ride with her in *Box Car* today. Is it all right?"

Felix smiled. "Have you done everything else you're

207

supposed to do?"

"Yes. Both Ratchet and Robert said it's okay if I'm not here."

"Then I think you should accept and enjoy the pretty day before the bad weather gets here."

Mike was up and around the table, hugging Felix as quickly as he could. "Thanks, Mom."

Arthur Stanik settled at one of the facets of an octagonal table in the Denver Library for his morning research session. He smiled, first for becoming so predictable with his morning routine, and second for the reason he'd let himself become so predictable.

Glancing up, beyond the adjacent monitors, he saw Patty as she pushed a cart full of neatly arranged books from behind the information desk under the 'Ask' sign, and down an aisle between the shelves in the geographical reference section. He watched her until she disappeared into the canyons of books, and then turned to his monitor. Thinking about her as he slid the keyboard to one side and opened his laptop in the space, he absently switched it on.

Patty had definitely caught his attention. But he wondered what it was that he found so attractive, besides everything from her pleasant manner, her perpetual smile and bright brown eyes, her fresh appearance (whether she wore a simple dress or the stylish slacks and over-blouse like she wore today, showing off her pleasant, healthy figure), to the intelligence and wittiness he encountered each time they spoke.

Arthur pulled himself back to the computers, selecting the internet browser on each. Then he opened the two flight-following programs he had chosen, one on the library computer and the other on his laptop. Then, consulting his list, he entered the first registration number into the search filter of both programs and clicked the Enter keys.

When the map image did not change, did not zoom to a new location centered on a responding blip, and did not flash a new icon, he resolutely entered the second registration number from his list.

It was his fourth entry, the de Havilland Beaver, that caused the imaged to zoom in and center over a transponder target heading southeast from Woodland Park, following the highway through the canyon toward Colorado Springs. The plane's registration number moved beside the blip.

He stared at his luck and fought to control the sudden thrill that washed over him as he flipped his small notebook open and made note of his first positive lead in his search. He inhaled and forced his hand to write slowly and legibly as he watched the blip turn eastward across the northern fringes of the city.

"Is that one of those planes you were asking about?" a soft feminine voice whispered in his ear.

Startled, he twitched and turned to the voice, seeing Patty's pleased face inches from his.

"Sorry." Her smile told him she was not, but rather pleased that she had surprised him. "You looked much too serious, so I thought I'd say hey."

"Don't be sorry, but you did surprise me," he responded, still trying to catch the breath she had stolen from him. "Yes. It is one of the planes I was researching." He quickly glanced around to see if anyone else had sat down at the table while he was not paying attention.

"Where's it going?" She was still all smiles, her face still beside his, looking over his shoulder at the monitors.

He adjusted the image and studied it for another minute. "I think it might be going to Falcon, the little airport there...aah, Meadow Lake."

"Someone you know?"

He slowly shook his head. "No. Not really."

She raised one eyebrow at him. "Then why—"

"I'd love to explain more over dinner..." He turned his head and held her eyes, waiting to say more, watching her expression as it turned from more questions to that of a woman who had made a decision.

"I get off at five. I'll meet you at Sam's Number 3, Curtis and Fifteenth, at six."

Officer Fred Mitchell swung his Mustang into the Third Precinct's parking lot. He'd been out near Saline most of the day and had just returned to the inner city. At the curb near the exit he normally used, he stopped and sent Sally a text. A few minutes later, she slipped out the door and, cowering against the strong norther, hurried to Fred's car and got in.

"Ooh, thanks for the text," she greeted, and shook as if the effort would dispel the chill of the wind. "Your car is nice and warm. I was afraid I'd made you angry."

"No, nothing like that," he replied with a warm smile. "Just busy."

"Yeah, like what's going on with you and Kilman? Last week he treated you like a leper and this week he's had you running all over the place."

Fred chuckled. "Since I figured out where Howard Collingsworth's wife took him, he's had me investigate each of the other seven places they seem to own."

"All of them?"

"Yup. Monday was down in Flat Rock and Dundee, Tuesday was in Livonia, Wednesday was up in Kimball outside of Port Huron, yesterday was Dexter and Southfield, and today was Saline. That completes the list, unless you've discovered more places registered to Mary Collingsworth, Rothman, Madison,

Hancock, or Fitzpatrick."

Sally giggled. "Nothing new yet, but there has to be someplace we're not seeing. I take it you haven't had any luck talking with Williamson."

"Nope. I was sure hoping to and maybe get some leads on family names on Howard's side."

"Yeah, last Saturday was weird. Is Williamson up to something?"

"How so?"

"I'm not sure, but he and his wife and the West couple show up at their house on Saturday, two weeks ago, after being gone for how long? And that fellow, Schmidt, shows up the same night, joins them, and then shoots Mr. West. There are two PIs there, and one of them kills Schmidt. Then Mr. West is rushed to the hospital..."

"Go on, we know that much from the reports."

"Well, in the report, the PI Smithson said Schmidt was not alone. There was another fellow waiting in a car on the street near Williamson's house. I know we were rushed, but when we checked the hospital, they did not have anyone named West admitted.

"While you were running Kilman's errands this week, I checked on Mr. Schmidt. He worked for the government of South Africa, and according to the morgue records, his body was released last Saturday—while we were looking for Williamson—to another South African representative, a Hermidt Ernst. I wondered if he was the other one, the one that had been waiting on Schmidt in the car the night he was killed, but the immigration records indicate he arrived on Friday, the day before he picked up the body."

"South Africa again? So that means there is probably still another agent from there running around, maybe following Williamson."

"I can't tell if he's following Williamson or if they have something going on together. But it really doesn't make any

sense that he would be working with a guy that shot his friend.
"

"Makes one wonder, doesn't it? I drove by Williamson's house late yesterday on my way back to the office, and it appears Williamson has moved—"

"What?"

"The For Sale sign says Sold and the house looks like it's locked up, and according to a neighbor, a moving company boxed everything up on Wednesday and loaded the furniture and boxes yesterday."

"Did they kno—"

"No, they didn't know where Williamson was moving to."

Sally pulled her phone from her hip pocket and tapped the screen a number of times. "He can't have closed this quickly, so let's see what the listing says." In a matter of minutes, she had the public details of the sale on her screen. "Looks like he got a very nice price for the place and...closing is set for Wednesday, November first." She turned her phone to show him the details and where the closing would be held. "I think we should talk to the real estate agent and the title company. Maybe we can find out something about Williamson's intentions, and we should be able to talk to him when he comes back to close."

"I think I agree with you. And I also think we need to visit the hospital again. Someone there has to know something about Mr. West's admittance." He gave her a mischievous grin. "Do you have any plans for tomorrow?"

She giggled again. "I do now."

"Great." He smiled hugely as he drove closer to where her car was parked. "How about celebrating with our Friday night pizza at Earnie's?"

"Sounds wonderful. Give me forty-five minutes to get cleaned up and meet you there?"

"I'll see you there," he agreed as Sally slid out of his car and hurried to open her car door and get in.

Arthur sat at the table in the front corner of Sam's Number 3, overlooking the city foot and vehicle traffic on Curtis Street and on 15th. The diner was a reincarnation of the vintage 1920s diner and bar, now located just a few doors down from where the original Coney Island diner had been built. It was the third in the original chain of five comfort food diners in the Denver area. He had arrived early in hopes of securing a suitable booth where he and Patty could talk and enjoy their time without eavesdroppers or distractions.

He wasn't sure how meeting Patty or his wish to continue seeing her was going to work, considering the demands his work usually had on his time, but something about her had him hoping he could figure out a way. At six sharp, Patty walked past the wide-windowed corner and he waved, catching her eye. He quickly stood and turned to greet her as she entered the front door.

"You're early," she greeted as he helped her with her coat. He gestured to a chair near the corner as he hung her coat on the coatrack standing near the adjacent wall.

"Had to be sure I had the right place," he admitted as he took the seat across from her, noticing she was wearing a different, warmer over-blouse than she had been wearing in the library. "I didn't want you to arrive and wonder if I was coming."

A young waiter quickly stopped beside the table, inquiring if they had a drink preference.

"Can I get you a cocktail, or wine maybe?" Arthur asked, and saw the glint in Patty's eye.

"The house white would be nice."

He looked up at the waiter. "One house white and one merlot."

The waiter nodded, wrote something on his order pad and

then asked if he had a preference in labels as he pointed to the wine list. Arthur selected one and the waiter left to fill their requests.

He smiled at Patty and continued. "Now that that is taken care of, how was your afternoon?"

Smiling, Patty recalled her usual afternoon of sorting and restacking the books in the research sections, conversations with people that asked this question or that one, finally concluding, "...It was more or less usual except for this guy that keeps coming in every morning, and today, when he wasn't visiting with me, keeping me from getting my work done, he was concentrating on his computer program." She raised an eyebrow.

Arthur chuckled. "I see he must have piqued your interest. But I'd like to hear more about you before I explain the mundane activities of my days."

"Well, let's see. What can I tell you?" She thought for a moment. "I was born and raised in Laramie. My dad worked for the Northern Pacific until he retired five years ago. He and Mom still live there." She hesitated and smiled sheepishly at him. "As I've already told you, I'm thirty-nine, married once for three years, no kids. I live with a roommate about three miles from here on the fringes of Lakewood."

She stopped when the waiter returned with their wines and asked if they were ready to order.

Arthur caught the hesitation in Patty's eyes and suggested he give them a little more time. "We've been chatting and haven't had time to look at the menu. We'll need a little more time before we're ready."

The waiter nodded and went on his way.

Patty smiled and sipped her white. "How about some specifics on you?"

He nodded. "Certainly. Born and raised in Cincinnati and I followed in my dad's footsteps, joining the local police force after high school. Eight years in, I was severely wounded

214

responding to a domestic violence situation, ending my police career. Out of a job with little prospects, my girlfriend at the time decided to leave me for my best friend and a life with a better life expectancy." He smiled and reached for her hand, seeing the concern in her eyes. "I'm fine. I recovered from my wounds, maybe better than I was before, but my life was different. Two years later, I took some additional training and became a private investigator. The job is much less threatening." He took his hand back with a gentle pat to assure her everything was all right. "I'm forty-two, dated some but never married, just focusing on work. A little over ten years ago, I decided I needed a place to call home and I bought a beautiful acreage a ways north of Ashville, North Carolina, set in the southern hills of the Appalachian Mountains." With his ballpoint pen, he drew a crude map for her on his paper napkin.

"Is that why you're here? Investigating something?"

He nodded. "Yeah. I have a client that wants to find some secluded airport and two people that seem to live there."

Her eyes grew. "Why does your client want to know about them?"

"Yeah, that's a tough one. The client's intentions are not very clear." He had his suspicions, but decided to keep those to himself—at least for the time being, until he understood more and maybe knew Patty better. "I was hired because they think I have some kind of knack at finding things—missing people, stolen goods, things like that."

"Wow. Do you? Have a knack?"

"Maybe, a little. So far I've had good luck, but this is the first time I've been asked to search for a place—especially a place that does not seem to have a proper name. Some place known to the locals as *The Ghost Ranch.*"

"Maybe you should be a prospector," she teased, and picked up her menu.

"Hmm. I wonder if I'd be any good at that?" He chuckled and began reading his menu. "Does prospecting pay very good?"

She laughed softly and he changed the subject.

"Since you seem to be familiar with this place. What's good here?"

They discussed dinner choices and he waved at the waiter when they had decided. Then, after giving him their choices and requesting another glass of wine for the both of them, Arthur picked up his glass in a gesture of a toast. "To the best company I've had in many, many months. Maybe years."

She blushed and raised her glass to his. "Maybe for me as well." She sipped again and set her glass down. She took her phone out of her purse and quickly entered a search. "There's a webpage and it says *West's Ghost Ranch* is situated in the beautiful Colorado Mountains, and says to contact the ranch at the information url listed. Nothing else listed on the page and I'm not finding any hidden selection windows." She looked up and stared at him. "So, how does the airplane you're following fit into your investigation?"

"I met some of my client's representatives in Reno last month, at the close of the air races, and saw some of the planes that were there from this unnamed airport. I was told the place has the nickname, *The Ghost Ranch*. So I did some checking on the nickname and, of course, came up empty-handed, nothing more than you just found. After I got here, and killed two weeks of idle waiting, I figured there had to be something more proactive that I could do, so I went to the library and—"

"And asked me how to find out who owned certain airplanes." She giggled. "So now you know…what?"

"In searching the FAA records, I remembered that someone in Reno said the planes were owned by a man named West. With that, I was able to get a list of the airplanes he owned—at least the ones that are registered to his business. He has some kind of a restoration business, which is most likely why his airport is secluded. A way to keep gawkers or opportunists at bay."

"I take it then, you're looking for one of his airplanes to show up on that program of yours, and from that you hope to see where it goes."

"Yes, that is my hope." He raised his glass to her again and then took a sip, emptying his glass just as the waiter appeared and served their second glasses of wine.

"The one you saw today, did it help you find the airport?" she asked as the waiter turned to another table.

"Not really. It came down the canyon from Winter Park, flew across the northern edge of Colorado Springs, and landed at that Meadow Lake Airport. About fifteen minutes later, it took off and flew down to Pueblo. It landed again and was on the ground for nearly two hours. I checked after I had left the library and caught it after it took off and headed west. Just east of Cañon City, its icon and information disappeared. Like the transponder was turned off so the plane could not be followed."

"Transponder?"

He smiled and explained what a transponder was and how airplanes used them. He hoped he was not being too technical and apologized if he was.

"No, you're not being too technical," Patty said when he had finished. "But my roommate writes code for the city traffic and transportation department. Maybe she can figure out a way to have your computer signal you when one of those planes shows up, so you won't have to stare at an empty screen for hours on end, waiting for something to pop up."

"That is a marvelous suggestion."

"I'll ask her when I get home, if she's in or up. No telling what she might be doing on a Friday night. If not, I can check with her in the morning."

"Thanks. If she can, that would certainly help a lot." Then he smiled as the waiter brought their salads. "And it might free up more of my time for more dinners or maybe some sightseeing. If, of course, I could find someone willing to accompany me."

Saturday, October 14

The sudden crack and loud bang jolted Sally awake. The room was dark and she instinctively rolled over and reached for her nightstand, but before she could reach the pistol she kept there, a dark, shadowy silhouette swept in through her bedroom door and caught a fistful of her hair.

Jerked across the bed, away from the nightstand, she floundered on the floor. The attacker tried to grab her arms but she pulled her legs up under her and shoved herself into his gut. He fell back, colliding with a chair and then the wall.

He lost his grip on her hair and she pulled away from him, clasped her hands together, and swung as hard as she could, landing a hit squarely across his face; he fell sideways off the upturned chair. She continued her spin, catching him again as he tried to get back on his feet. Her heel slammed into his face, and the lamp and table beside the chair tumbled under his weight as a second shadow entered the room.

She instantly turned her attention to the newcomer and swung again. Her fists grazed off a rock-hard shoulder as the silhouette dropped and grabbed the attacker on the floor. As he lifted the first, she landed a jab with her foot squarely in his middle, driving the second against the doorjamb—

"Stop it, Sally! I'm trying to help!"

Hearing Fred's sharp voice, she was suddenly confused. Halfway to him, intending to land repeated jabs with her fists, she faltered. "Fred?"

"Yeah. Who'd you expect to come to your rescue?" He remained crouched over the attacker until she heard the distinctive sounds of his cuffs. "Catch a light in the living room."

How? You're blocking the door? she questioned, until she heard the sounds of someone else in her apartment; a light snapped on at the end of the hall.

"We're secure here," Fred added to the other someone as he stood and turned to her.

He stepped close and adjusted the gaping neck of her long-sleeved, button-front pajama top. She barely noticed as he smiled down at her. "Damn! I hope you didn't break a rib." He grimaced, holding his side. "Good to see you haven't forgotten your training."

"Sorry. I didn't know it was you. I thought—"

"I know." He nodded and squeezed her shoulders between his strong hands, but to her surprise, he did not pull her to him in an embrace.

"What are you doing here?" she asked when he released his gentle grip.

"I was waiting to see if he'd come back, the one you said tried to pick your lock. If he did try, I wanted to be here to get him."

"You were waiting? All night?"

He chuckled. "That's what partners are for. Besides, I've worked a lot of nights, remember?"

She did and was smiling herself.

"I called for backup when I saw this one nosing around your stairs. I worked my way close and followed him when he kicked your door open." He looked at the man on the floor. "We'll process him and then I'll keep watch until the office opens and we can get your door repaired and your apartment secure again. Maybe he will tell us who he's working for." He nodded to her disheveled bed. "You can go back to sleep if you want."

"Back to sleep? You think I can go back to sleep after this?"

He smiled and shook his head. "Then get dressed while we take care of this one. I'll wait with you and we can go to Farmington after we get your door taken care of."

"Okay." She nodded and watched as he picked the man up off the floor and half-dragged him down the hall. She could hear two other officers taking the man from Fred.

"I'll be back in a few minutes. Make yourself presentable."

Presentable? She shook her head at his tease and what the other officers might be thinking. Then, with clean clothes and her gun, she stepped into the master bath, locked the door, and began getting ready, wondering what the rest of her day was going to be like.

Fred led Sally up the walk from the multilevel parking garage and through the Bradmont Hospital's front doors. She followed him as he stepped to the admissions waiting area and stopped at the counter in the wall opening. The woman behind it smiled and asked if she could help them.

"Good morning. I'm Officer Fred Mitchell and this is Officer Sally Ableman from Detroit's Third Precinct. We need to talk to someone concerning a patient that was admitted around midnight on this past September thirtieth." He flipped his badge wallet open for her to verify his identity.

The woman tapped a phone console and spoke a few soft words into the headset mic she was wearing. "Our Admissions Administrator will be out to talk with you in just a moment," the woman informed him with her continued smile.

He thanked her and then gestured Sally aside, away from the counter and closer to the only obvious door leading into the administration offices. Moments later, another woman opened the door and invited them in, leading them to an office off a short hall.

"Officer Mitchell, Ableman, I'm Mrs. Beale. How may I help you?"

Fred gestured Sally to a chair and took the one beside her as Mrs. Beale sat down.

"Do you mind if I record our conversation?" Sally asked, and pulled a palm-sized recorder from her pocket. "It makes it so much easier when I have to transcribe everything."

"No, that's perfectly all right," Mrs. Beale agreed.

Fred nodded thanks and began. "We're looking for information concerning a Mr. West that was brought here late on the night of September thirtieth with multiple gunshot wounds. Possibly just after midnight. Our records do not show the exact time."

Mrs. Beale turned to her computer and began entering information. "And what sort of information are you looking for?"

"We need to speak to Mr. West and also with a Mr. Williamson. The ambulance driver reported that Mr. Williamson was the man that called for their assistance."

Mrs. Beale frowned at the screen. "A Mr. West, you say?"

"Yes, ma'am. He was visiting the Williamsons' home when the shooting occurred. We tried to speak with Mr. West while he was here, but the woman on duty said no one by that name had been admitted. We're assuming he has been released, but we still need to speak with him. Mr. Williamson has sold his home and has moved, and we hope Mr. West might know where."

"Well, Officer Mitchell"—she looked up from her screen and shook her head—"I don't find anything about a Mr. West in our admission records."

"Could *West* have been a nickname?" Sally asked. "I just realized our records of the incident only call him West, not Mr. West."

Mrs. Beale shook her head and pursed her lips. "We don't admit people under nicknames...unless..." She picked up her phone and made a call. "Stacy? Can you tell me who had the night shift on your floor the night of September thirtieth? Uh huh, Dean, you say? Is she still on the floor? Okay, I'll page her."

She looked up at Fred and Sally and held up crossed fingers as she pushed a button on her phone console. "Nurse Dean,

Claire Dean. Please call extension 7201. Please call extension 7201." They could hear the echo of her request from the public address system in the hallways and rooms beyond the office door.

As she hung up, Mrs. Beale explained. "Stacy on the severe trauma floor said Nurse Claire Dean was the night nurse that night. She signed out and has just gone off duty and left the floor. Maybe"—the phone chimed—"she's still in the building." She answered the call. "Mrs. Beale. Good morning, Claire. Can you come to admissions, please? Before you leave for the day? Yes, thank you."

Mrs. Beale smiled. "We caught her at the front doors."

A minute passed, then another, before a woman in scrubs stepped into Mrs. Beale's office.

"Good morning, Claire," Mrs. Beale greeted, quickly standing and gesturing to Fred and Sally. "These are Officers Mitchell and Ableman. They have some questions that maybe you can help us answer." Mrs. Beale pulled a third chair from the corner of the room by her desk and positioned it closer to Sally's chair.

"Okay," Claire said as she settled in the chair. "What can I help you with?"

Fred repeated the explanation he had given Mrs. Beale and added Sally's comment about nicknames.

"Yes, I remember the night, and the name *West* is a nickname. Mrs. Montgomery—Charlie—explained everyone close called her husband West, and he went by the name of Glen West in their daily lives. It was something about their business and their need for personal privacy."

Sally was smiling, pleased that her hunch was correct.

"Montgomery?" Mrs. Beale asked as she keyed her computer.

"Yes. G. W. Montgomery. Charlie had me change his initials on the whiteboard to *West*. I remember the night mainly because his wife, Charlie, and Mrs. Williamson—Cathy—

looked so much like twin sisters. Mrs. Williamson said they were just friends and not sisters, but the resemblance was uncanny—"

"The report said Mrs. West was a lookalike for the *missing* daughter, not Catherine." Sally stared at Fred. "And we saw the beat photos from the night of the shooting. They certainly do look a lot alike."

Startled, Nurse Dean asked, "A missing daughter? There are *three* of them?"

"Apparently," Fred admitted softly, and inhaled. "I can't tell you much, but we are searching the small details concerning a much larger case, and though some of our questions may seem odd or insignificant, we are trying to piece together a much larger whole. But yes, part of this case involves a missing daughter, and a kidnapping that happened in Denver this last July involving Mrs. West and another woman. They were rescued within minutes and the perpetrators captured. Everyone at the Denver Police that we talked to assumed Mrs. West's kidnapping was because of her and her husband's wealth, but it may have more to do with Mrs. West and Catherine Williamson's likenesses. That is one part of the puzzle we're trying to piece together."

Claire and Mrs. Beale waited, watching as Fred thought about what he was going to say next, but instead of explaining further, he asked another question. "Did you get a home address for Mr. Montgomery?"

Mrs. Beale turned back to her computer, slowly shaking her head. "Mrs. Montgomery gave a P.O. Box in Trinidad, Colorado, as their address. No phone number. Nothing more specific."

"Thanks," Fred said, and took the slip of paper she slid to him. "Do you know if he's gone back to his home?"

"Yes, I believe they have. His surgeon had him in for a final checkup on Wednesday."

"They had a plane waiting," Claire added. "Charlie had West's mother, another woman, and a man come. There was some reason that she and Cathy could not stay, so she said she had West's mother and the other man fly here to stay with West and that the man would bring him and his mother home when the doctor said West could fly. Charlie said she had brought two planes when they came, and the other woman came to fly one back. She and Cathy flew the other."

"We think there was a second man besides the gunman," Sally added softly, "a partner, so it's likely they may have felt unsafe with him still at large."

"That's possible," Claire agreed. "Charlie said West jumped between the gunman and her and Cathy when he shot at them. West took the hits, saving them from injury."

"That's what the responding officers' report says." Sally smiled weakly at Fred.

Fred smiled in return and then looked at Claire. "Is there anything else you can tell us about Mr. or Mrs. West, or Montgomery?"

Claire shook her head. "I think that's about it. Everything was business as usual after Charlie left. Occasionally West and the other man would discuss rebuilding something or another—I think a plane, by their descriptions—but nothing of significance while I was on duty. I'm a night nurse and my patients are usually sleeping. I can check with our day nurses and see if they remember anything we haven't mentioned."

"That would be nice," Fred agreed, and stood up. "If you find out anything new, please call me or Officer Ableman at these numbers." They each handed their cards to Claire and to Mrs. Beale. "We thank you for your time," Fred continued as Sally picked up her recorder, "and we'll let you get back to your day. Thank you again."

He extended his hand to each of them and Sally followed his example. Then they turned and left.

As they stepped out through the hospital's front doors, Fred pondered out loud, "I wonder how hard it would be to get an audience with Mr. West-slash-Montgomery if we were in Colorado?"

Sally hip-checked him and looked up. "Our job is to find the Collingsworths, and that's right here." She pointed to the ground. "Besides, I'm not sure I'm ready to let you lead me off to another state, especially one half a country away."

He shoved her shoulder playfully. "A guy can hope, can't he?"

"Oh, he can, can he?" She laughed at him as they crossed the street to the parking garage. She thought about him having spent his nights outside her apartment, waiting for her intruder to come back, and when he had, he was there moments after the man broke in. She studied his profile as they pulled out onto the main drive and onto Grand River Drive. "I need to transcribe that interview, and since I have copies of the various reports, we should take the time to look at everything again. Do you have anything to make breakfast with?"

He smiled, watching the road and carefully glancing at her when he got a chance. "I...do, some things, but usually I just zap a frozen egg and sausage sandwich and eat on my way to work."

"Do you have coffee?"

"Yeah. A nice dark roast."

"Okay. Take me to your place and show me how a quiet, keeps-to-himself bachelor lives. You can feed me and we'll discuss what we've learned." She smiled politely. "You dragged me out of my apartment before I got a chance to eat."

"I believe you said you were 'too wound up' to eat anything," he teased, glancing briefly at her, "when we left your apartment."

She punched his arm again. "I'm not 'too wound up' now, and I'm hungry. Feed me."

Sixty-Two

Karl deVon stepped out of his office and into the main hallway down the state security offices wing. He saw Elrich Voster walking away, toward the wide doors to the central colonnade, and he hurried to catch up, calling for him to stop and waving a sheet of paper as he went.

Elrich heard him and stopped at the staircase leading either up to the next level or down a flight to the kitchens, dining rooms, conference rooms, and to the main entrance and exits. It was late in the day and Karl knew Elrich was heading home.

"What has you so excited, Karl?"

Puffing lightly, Karl stopped and held the paper out to Elrich. "An email from Agent Brown. I did not know if you would be in tomorrow, so I was just going to your office to give it to you." He inhaled deeply, finally catching his breath. "He has little to report, no signs of Collingsworth or his wife, but I thought you would want to know what he said."

"Thank you." Elrich nodded and took the sheet of paper. "I will review his message in the car. And you are correct. I am out of the office tomorrow."

"Did everything go well with Ernst's trip? You had not said."

"If by going well, you mean did Hermidt bring Schmidt's body back, then, yes, it did." Elrich glanced at the lighted colonnade beyond the glass doors, then added, "But if you mean everything, then no, it did not. The authorities there have many questions—mostly the same ones we have and have no answers for. Schmidt's actions were unbecoming of what the public expects of a diplomatic agent, and more so, from one visiting from another country." Elrich sighed. "Schmidt has entangled us with a tremendous burden of paperwork, and in his moment of indiscretion has weakened our standing in the eyes of the American government."

"Does that mean we should abandon our search for Collingsworth?"

"No. But it does mean we must be more careful and our movements in their country will be closely monitored. They have reminded our president of a standard reporting clause in our visitation agreement. It is rarely enforced, but in light of Schmidt's actions and that we are present in their country *on official, governmental business*, we must now report *where* and *why*, when we away from our embassies."

"That will make our task much more difficult."

"Like I said, the burden of paperwork. It is a burden both ways, and if we are careful, we might be able to find Collingsworth before anyone notices."

"And the woman?"

"Her also. This is why I hired Stanik to work for us. He is an American and not inhibited by our *visitor* status, and why I decided to keep him in Colorado for the time being."

"I see."

"One thing you can do for me. Find another investigator that we can couple with Agent Brown." Elrich smiled and nodded as he turned and started walking toward the stairs. "Find someone, preferably another American, to help Brown search for Collingsworth."

Sally sat curled up on Fred's sofa, her folder of notes in her lap and her laptop balanced on the arm and end table. They had spent the remaining hours of the morning at Fred's place after returning from the hospital, reviewing the details in the police reports and the information they had put together the previous weekend, hoping to get more pieces to fit together.

Fred stopped, poured her another cup of coffee, then picked his cup up from the end table and refilled it.

"I've searched and re-searched the Howard Collingsworth name," Sally said as he returned the pot to the coffee maker in the kitchen, "and I don't see any other places."

"What do we know about his side of the family? His mother's maiden name? Grandmothers' maiden names?"

"Not much." She shook her head. "That's the blank spot in our data." She took another sip of her coffee. "I looked him and his company up, but there is not much on his family background. I'm checking for marriage records now."

"Marriage records could help," he jested. "His wife's maiden name was…" He checked his notes. "Rothman, Mary Carole Rothman."

"Got it." She smiled and read the date on the record out loud. "Looks like a first marriage for both of them. Hmm, nothing here that we don't already know."

"Who were the witnesses?"

"Both of the fathers signed as witnesses. Warren Collingsworth and Hamilton Rothman."

"That's odd."

"Yes, it is, now that you mention it. The witnesses are usually the best man and the bridesmaid or maid of honor. Not the parents."

He set his cup on the end table. "Church wedding or Justice of the Peace?"

"JP in Flint."

"Hmm. A JP wedding and the fathers as witnesses. Sounds like an old-fashioned shotgun marriage, doesn't it?"

She chuckled. "Might be. My notes indicate that his parents

also lived somewhere near Flint before they passed."

He hesitated and watched her for a long moment. "I wonder where his mother's family lived."

"Howard's mother? No information." She focused on her laptop screen as she entered another search. "Nope. No marriage data on Warren Collingsworth. So we don't even have a name."

Fred sighed and took a sip, frowning at his now tepid coffee. "Can I get you more coffee? Mine's cold."

She shook her head and set her laptop aside. "No. I've had enough." She laid her folder aside and slowly stood. "Point me to the bathroom?"

He smiled. "Of course. Hallway"—he gestured to the hall leading to the two bedrooms—"first door on the left."

He picked up her cup and hesitated, watching her as she walked away from him. She made him smile, and he had to admit there was just something about her trim, five foot two, fit feminine stature with the right curves in the right places, all topped with her shoulder length auburn hair pulled back into her usual ponytail. Couple that with her good hearted sincerity, her decisiveness, dedication to her work and her intuition and keen intelligence and he knew he was hooked. He was falling hard.

He shook his head, inhaled deeply, and turned to the kitchen where he washed the cups, dried them and placed them back in the cupboard. She was playful and friendly enough, but he could not tell if she had feelings for him or if she just saw him as someone from work helping her with her assignment. Back in the living room, he settled into his overstuffed chair with a sigh as she stepped out of the hallway.

"I like your place," she announced as she came into the room and slowly looked around the living room again. "You seem to take care of it."

"Thanks. I try to keep it picked up, but I only vacuum and dust about once a week."

She smiled and stopped to look out into the back yard. "When do you find the time to keep up with the leaves?"

"That"—he leaned back in his chair and crossed one leg over the other—"I have to hire out. I hire a neighbor's two sons for my yardwork. They're dedicated and do a very nice job. Their dad even lets them use his pickup to haul the leaves and trimmings away. Nice family, and great boys."

"Dad always hired ours too." She smiled at the scene she remembered. "But I was the brat that kept jumping into the piles of leaves when the help raked them up. Man, did I get scolded, over and over again." She turned and smiled at him. "I don't think I outgrew doing that until I graduated from high school."

"Oh, I'm not sure you really did outgrow it." He chuckled at her mischievous, playful smile, remembering the hip-check she had given him that very morning. He suddenly remembered other instances where he had seen glimpses of her tomboyishness. "The opportunity may have just been removed from your grasp."

She stuck her tongue out at him, then sat down on the sofa and curled her legs up beside her. Taking her phone out of her pocket, she started tapping the screen. "Since we cannot find anyone to talk to about Howard's background, I think...aah, yes." She tapped again and he heard the phone on the other end ringing. She had put her phone on speaker.

The connection made. "Williamson Tech. One moment please."

They listened to a short message explaining that Williamson Tech had moved and the new number would be posted shortly. Before he could comment that they already knew that, the phone rang again, another connection was made, and a live person answered.

"Monte Williamson. How may I help you?" There was background noise but the voice was clear.

"Mr. Williamson. You don't know me," Sally began. "I am

Officer Ableman from the Detroit Police Department, Third Precinct, and I am hoping you will talk to me concerning the shooting at your home and maybe answer some questions about your father-in-law, Howard Collingsworth."

Monte hesitated before answering. "Officer Ableman, I gave my report to the officers that night. I doubt I have anything else to add."

"Please, are you where we can talk for a couple of minutes? As you know, we are desperately trying to locate Howard and I am hoping you might be able to answer a couple of questions for me."

Monte hesitated again, then, "Give me a minute. I need to pull over. I'm driving and I need to find a good place to stop." A moment passed. "Okay, I've got a good place."

They heard the background noise diminish.

"All right, Officer Ableman. What can I do for you?"

"Thank you so much, Mr. Williamson—"

"Monte, please."

"Thank you, Monte. I have my phone on speaker so my partner"—she glanced sideways and smiled at Fred—"Officer Mitchell, can listen in."

"Hello, Officer Mitchell."

"Hello. Thank you for speaking with us."

"Monte." Sally began quickly, not wanting to waste any of their time. "We are trying to locate places that Howard might be hiding. We have noted that he and his wife have a number of properties listed in the names of relatives, like the house in Gratiot, and we think he's likely to be hiding in such a place. But what we can't find are records of Howard's relatives. Do you know anything about his mother's side of the family—any adoptions or anything else from her side of the family?"

"Well..." Monte paused in thought. "His mother was Agatha. Agatha...umm, Wilson. Agatha Wilson. Warren supposedly met Agatha in Saginaw, Bay City area. I believe she was the daughter of Henry and Estel Wilson, of the Lake Huron Shipping Wilsons. I'll have to ask my wife for better details."

"Did Agatha have any siblings?"

"Agatha was one of four children, if I remember right. Two brothers, Bill and Stan, I believe. And a sister, Becky. I met her at a family gathering just after my wife and I got married. She was the last living, related Wilson."

"Are there others then?" Fred queried.

"Agatha's father had two brothers, but I have no idea how their lineage has grown. I don't even remember if I ever heard their names."

"What kind of a family gathering was it?" Fred asked. "Was there some special reason for the gathering?"

Monte chuckled. "Mostly I think for the still living relatives to see each other once more. But I do remember my wife's great-grandfather, Carl, gave my wife and her sister a parcel of land, to be completely theirs on their twenty-first birthday. He passed a couple of years later."

"Carl who?" Sally asked.

"Oh, Carl Madison. His wife had passed a number of years before then, and his daughter, Carol, came with him. She was my wife's grandmother on her mother's side."

Fred nodded to Sally, thinking that was what he had discovered earlier.

"Do you know where the land was located?" Sally queried.

"No, sorry. I'll have to ask my wife when I see her."

"Thank you. Please let us know if you find out."

"That's about all I know concerning Howard," Monte explained. "Is there anything else I can do for you?"

"Yes, please, a couple more things. First, can you tell me why Mr. and Mrs. West were at your home the night of the shooting, and why the two private investigators that helped in your wife's rescue were there?"

"I thought that was in the reports," Monte admitted softly.

"Well, basically, the Wests flew us back to Farmington so my wife could pick out things she wanted me to be sure to move. It was supposed to be a quick trip, and she would go back and I would stay and get the house sold."

"Back? Where is back?"

"Where she's at now," Monte evaded. "I really can't say more about that."

"Okay, But what about the private investigators? Did they just happen to be there?"

"Sort of. After all that has happened, especially to Charlie and to my wife, Lloyd watched our neighborhood to see if anyone was snooping around or waiting for us to show up again."

"So you were still concerned for your wife's safety?"

"I'm more concerned than I used to be." Monte exhaled audibly. "Ever since the kidnappings, I watch our surroundings a lot."

"And the man that shot Mr. West? Our report says he was asking for information and then drew a gun and started shooting."

"That's about the size of it."

"What information was he looking for?"

"He was looking for information on where he could find Howard, my wife's father. I told him we did not know where he was and that we did not want to know where he was. Then I told him he would have to leave. He turned to leave and saw Charlie and my wife, and before I knew what was happening, he drew a gun and shot at them. West stepped in front of them, taking the shots."

"Can you tell me why he wanted to find your father-in-law? There's no reward—"

"I do not know for sure. All I know is that he saw us at the air races in Reno and then showed up at our house the night we got there. That's what I know. I have no idea how he figured out that we would be there or when. We had not planned a date until a day or two before we came."

"Thank you, Monte. I know this is a lot of questions, and I thank you for your help and patience with us. But I'd like to change the subject, if you don't mind." Sally continued before Monte could comment. "May I ask about the uncanny resemblance of your wife and Charlie, Mrs. West? Is there a relationship there?"

Monte chuckled. "Everyone thinks there is, but as far as we know, there is not. Charlie is a Bassett from Jackson, Wyoming. Her parents died when she was in high school, leaving her with a small amount of money—I don't know how much—and their home. An elderly aunt moved in with Charlie so she could keep their family home, and helped her finish school. Charlie's history is filled with hard-won opportunities, and I understand that her inheritance from her aunt gave her the one she needed to learn to fly and start her life in aviation."

"A self-made woman," Sally muttered on a deep exhale. "Wow."

"Literally. West saw her working in Pueblo—she was a mechanic there—and he watched her about a year, so I'm told, before he had her boss have her fly a client of West's to the ranch. Now, remember, I may have a few facts not quite right, since I've only heard this from my wife and a couple of things from one of the other mechanics."

She laughed. "Okay. We won't quote you too much."

"I can't say very much about what happened between then and now, but obviously she and West hit it off. They were married this last April."

"So, there's no explanation of why they look so much alike?" Fred asked.

"None that I know of."

"Does their resemblance have anything to do with Charlie's kidnapping, or your wife's kidnapping?" Fred continued.

"My wife and her sister looked very much alike, even though

235

Emli was two years younger. That also means Charlie looks a lot like Emli, the missing daughter." Monte paused. "I guess it's no secret that Howard was very abusive to the girls and to his wife, thus the charges my wife filed against him. When Emli disappeared, he launched a huge, ongoing manhunt for her. To no avail. But when Charlie's picture showed up in the Alamosa newspaper this spring, Howard saw it. I tried to convince him that it was not his daughter, and finally told him I was going to prove it. So I hired two private investigators to check out everything we could find about Charlie.

"But he sent two men anyway—a Tony and a Tom—to find her, and they waited for her at the Fourth of July fly-in in Broomfield Colorado. Two others Howard sent joined them to ensure they could catch her." He paused again. "They knew she flew. They knew she was married to Glen West, and they knew that if he brought airplanes to the fly-in, she would be there. Between my investigators and Norman Kent, Celia...aah, Gibbings, that's it, Gibbings' fiancé, we knew they were there, but they struck before we thought they might. We weren't ready for them, but luckily we were able to stop them.

"The man Charlie shot when he grabbed her confessed before he died that evening. He named Howard as the money behind the hunt. You should contact the Broomfield Police and get the full details from their combined reports."

"Thanks," Sally said. "We'll certainly do that."

"As for my wife's kidnapping, it was just her resemblance to Emli that caused that." He sighed. "The strange thing about that was that Cathy had talked Charlie into taking care of the children. I was away at the time, and she knew something was wrong. She knew she had to protect the children, so she called Charlie. And thankfully, Charlie finally agreed. Howard thought I had the children, and thought he could threaten them and keep me in check. But I didn't have them and didn't know where the children were until West contacted me after she had been kidnapped. He told me they were safe and Howard could not get to them."

"West knew something was happening?" Sally asked, surprised.

"Only because Cathy talked to them when she took the children to them. But somehow, West did know when Cathy disappeared, and between him and Charlie and the children, they figured out where he had taken her: the Gratiot house. West emailed me and then called so I could arrange for police support. I called a friend of mine in Livonia and he arranged police backup."

"We have the report on that rescue," Sally commented. "I understand you were shot that night. Are you okay now?"

"Yes to both. I tried to help that night, but I didn't think about not having a gun. I am very ignorant of guns—my wife, not so much. She's an expert compared to me. She knows how to handle them. I don't."

"I see." She chuckled. "But I'm glad you're doing okay. We saw you have sold your house. Are you relocating?"

"I am. I am opening my practice in Colorado Springs. I can service my existing customers from there and I have leads on some new customers in that area."

"Will your wife be joining you there?"

"I don't know how I should answer that." He hesitated again. "With Howard still at large and a number of his, shall I call them *acquisition contracts,* still active, we both feel she and the children should stay where they are. This way, neither Howard nor his hired cronies can find them. I expect to see them more often than if I were still in Farmington and a two-and-a-half-hour airline flight away, but no, they will not be joining me. Probably not until sometime after Howard is captured and her memories of what he did to her have faded."

"I can only imagine," Sally consoled. "I presume she's with Charlie and West at his ranch."

"I can only say she isn't and won't be with me. Now, if that's all you need, I do need to get back on the road. I still have a long way to go today."

"Of course," Sally agreed. "Thank you for your time and answers. It helps us a lot."

"You're welcome, Officer Ableman and Officer Mitchell. But please, do me one big favor."

"Yes?"

"Get Howard before he shows up again and I do something to him I shouldn't do."

"We'll do our best, Monte. Call us anytime, if you need to. You have my number now."

"Thank you. Bye."

"Goodbye, Monte. Safe travels." Sally tapped her phone and disconnected. "Wow." She looked at Fred in disbelief. "Talk about intertwined and complicated."

"Wow is right. I knew there was more to this lookalike issue. But to not be related and looking so much alike..."

"I know. Doesn't seem natural. I sure am glad I thought to put my phone in record mode."

"I recorded it with my phone, just in case." He smiled and stood up. "And now, after that brilliant decision to just call his old business, I think I owe you lunch. Your choice. Wherever you would like to go."

"You need to be careful with offers like that. I can think of some pretty expensive places." She got up and collected her coat from the back of the sofa.

He helped her put it on. "I can too, and if that's what you want, we'll go."

Sally stared at him a long, puzzled moment, then smiled. "I won't make you suffer, but it's nice to know you aren't against going to a nice place sometime."

"You're welcome." He put his coat on as she picked up her purse. Then he followed her to the front door. "When did you start carrying a purse?"

"It's just a prop with a few dollars in it so I'll look like a normal woman," she said, and batted her eyelashes at him. "My stuff is in my pockets, just like you."

"I would never be so demeaning as to call my partner a *normal* woman. I was just curious." He closed the door behind them, ensured it was locked and latched, and then led her to his Mustang, thinking they needed to start looking for clues around Flint, Saginaw, and Bay City.

Mel's Birthday

Just after midnight, the front blew in from the northwest and low clouds skimmed over the Colorado mesa lands and the ranch. Through the night and early morning hours, the ceilings dropped, obscuring all of the ranch and the mesa above six thousand feet in thick clouds; the airfield lingered half-visible in ghostly fog and drizzle. By noon, the overriding moisture carried on the southwesterly winds aloft had turned the drizzle into another round of steadily falling rains.

With everyone using the tunnels to get to the hangars and store rooms, the day's activities unfolded normally, in spite of the weather's gloominess. But the dreariness did not penetrate into the ranch world, for a spirit of happiness was alive and well, especially for Mel.

From the moment she woke and her mom had wished her the best for her birthday and the many years to come, Mel felt the warmth and love of her extended family. She had been greeted by each and every person on the ranch with similar blessings and gestures. Breakfast had been filled with pleasant conversation, plans and expectations for the day, and as they left the main house to head for the tunnels, each of those not at breakfast had made a special effort to wish her the best of days. Even Robert, hobbling on his crutches, had made it a point to come and greet her before she went up top.

The morning had progressed quietly, yet not quite routinely, for the air had been filled with pleasant overtones. Not that the days were ever unpleasant, Mel reminded herself, but this day felt different for many reasons: obviously because it was her special day, but also because her mom and dad had sold their house in Farmington and her dad was now on his way to Colorado, West was home, and Charlie was feeling much better. This was finally, and definitely, home for her—maybe more than Farmington had ever been.

Mel helped Mike, Bump, Dani, and Lenny on the C model, while June chased more airplane parts on her phone from her topside office or at Charlie's desk beside them. Bump showed her how to look up the specs and taught her how to use a torque wrench, with and without extensions, for the brackets she was installing. Then he set her to installing the ailerons and the inner landing gear doors.

Charlie, Eddie, and Woody were somewhere in the warehouse caverns, and West and Ratchet worked from his office in the main house. Jess and Felix worked on new security ideas, wrote software code, and discussed new camera ideas for the two main ground entrances to the ranch.

The afternoon was lost in work until, at sixteen hundred sharp, each mobile phone chimed. Mel looked down at hers and saw Helen's text.

"Quitting time has arrived! Everyone take 30 minutes to freshen up, change clothes or whatever you need to do, and then gather in the main house living room. Don't be late."

At 1625, Mel and Mike hurried down the stairs and into the living room. They snuggled up to their mom, one on each side, and both wrapped an arm around her. They stood in front of the fireplace as the others slowly entered. Madra helped Robert to a chair to one side of the archway from the dining room and hall, and she, Dani, and Eddie stood beside him. Camilla, Patrick, Billy, and George, along with their parents, Gracie and Henry, entered and stopped beside Robert. George slipped behind them and stood beside Eddie. Ratchet and June followed them in.

Lenny and Jess entered and stopped at one of the love seats. Bump and Woody stopped beside the wet bar in the corner, but Bump quickly moved to stand beside Dani.

Then, as if on some unspoken cue, idle conversations fell quiet and everyone turned to see Charlie escort West into the room, followed by Helen, carrying a small folding table. Becky entered next, carrying a large, decorated sheet cake.

Helen set up the table, threw a cloth over it, and Becky set the cake down. She looked up, smiled at Mel, and then looked at West. He nodded and also smiled at Mel.

"Mel, would you please stand by your cake?" he asked as Helen took pictures of the cake and then waited for Mel to take her place. When she was in position, Helen snapped a few more, capturing Mel and the cake together.

"Oh my. This is beautiful," Mel exclaimed softly, and studied the cake. "It has every airplane I've flown in...no...just the ones I've actually flown." She looked up and smiled hugely at everyone. Then to Becky, she said, "Thank you so much. This is truly beautiful. And thank you to everyone that helped. I know Lenny must have helped with the planes, because the coloring looks so very real."

He chuckled and nodded.

"You're very welcome," Becky replied, and lit the twelve candles as everyone began singing a reasonably in-tune rendition of "Happy Birthday."

When they stopped, Mel closed her eyes for a few seconds and then blew the candles out.

Becky and Helen quickly began cutting the cake into appropriate squares as Mel stepped to one side.

From a table that Mel had not seen when she came in,

Charlie picked up a tray of goblets and stemless wine glasses. She carried the tray and made sure everyone had something to drink: champagne for the adults and sparkling cider for those that were not. When she stopped beside West, he raised his glass.

"Here's to you, Mel. We are very proud to be able to share this special day with you and to have you here on the ranch. We thank you for coming and being such a big part of our family. We all love you." Then he gestured for everyone to take a sip. "Now, I invite anyone that would like to say a few words to Mel, to please do so."

Before anyone could say anything, Robert began squirming, trying to stand up. Madra and Dani quickly assisted and steadied him on his one crutch. He raised his glass to Mel.

"From one father that has seen your inner and personal beauty and strength, you soar with *atsá*, the eagle. You have courage of a dozen *maicohs* and inner seeing of *nééshjaa'*, the owl. I am proud you are *atsi'*, daughter, and have come to our *diné*." He raised his glass and then sipped.

Mel stood transfixed, tears suddenly running down her cheeks. Everyone was toasting her and Robert's words and she did not know what to say, until she finally just said, "Thank you. That's maybe the nicest thing anyone has ever said to me." She wiped her eyes with the napkin she had picked up with her cider. "I am very happy to be here and to be part of *our diné. This is home.*"

After a moment, Henry added his thanks and expressed Cappie's appreciation for the help she and Mike had given with the construction projects.

"Thank you, all of you," Mel said in gratitude when Henry paused and stepped back. "I am so very happy to have such great friends and teachers. I have learned sooo much, and I really don't know how to say what I feel. Just thank you, most of all, for being my friends." She wiped her eyes again. "But I...I'm keeping you all from eating the cake. I know Becky worked very hard to make it so pretty." She turned and gestured.

"Please take a piece."

She stepped over to Charlie and West and hugged them both as tight as she could. "Thank you both for letting us stay." Then she released them and gently pushed them toward the cake. "You better get in there before it's all gone."

She hugged her mom again as Mike came back with a plate and two squares of cake, one half-eaten.

"Man, this is really good," he said through a chocolatey smile. "And the airplanes look so real!" He showed her a portion of one on his piece.

As Camilla collected the empty plates and forks, Bump asked, "When do we do presents?"

West chuckled as Dani punched Bump's arm for his outrageous impatience.

"I think it's about time," West agreed, and three large sacks were quickly brought from around the room and placed in front of Mel. "Just a few things to help you remember this day."

"Oh, my," Mel muttered as she knelt down and peeked into the sacks.

"They won't bite," Lenny encouraged. "But it's a good thing they won't melt either."

Mel took the gifts from the sacks, one at a time, savoring the time she took opening each one and proudly showing each to the gathering, huddled close enough to see. She gave her thanks for each and quickly took another until the three sacks were finally empty. She looked up and smiled, about to say a final thank you, when Ratchet stepped forward with a larger-than-normal card.

"We all chipped in for this one and the next one," he said, and handed the card to her.

She opened the flap and pulled out a card with a P-51 on the front, a birthday phrase inside, and a picture of a roll-around tool chest. She looked up at Ratchet, questioning what she was seeing.

"It's up top with your name on it. You're learning how to be a mechanic, so we figured you'd like somewhere to put your tools."

Mel jumped up and hugged him, reaching with one hand for Lenny, Bump, and Woody. "Thank you. All of you."

Ratchet gently separated himself from her and glanced at Woody. "We have one last thing for you." Then he stepped aside as Woody moved closer.

He handed her another gaily wrapped package.

Mel looked up at him, a questioning expression still on her face as she started tearing the wrapping. Suddenly she was holding a large format logbook in her hands. "A logbook! My very own logbook. With my name embossed on the cover." Then she looked at Woody. "But I'm not old enough—"

"Look inside," he said, and patted the book.

Slowly she opened the front cover and saw her name printed neatly, along with *Ghost Ranch* listed as her address. Then she turned the page and her knees went weak, dropping her slowly to the floor. Kneeling, she stared at the page filled with entries, each dated and signed as dual instruction with the specific maneuvers taught or simply as a familiarization flight. She looked up at him, and then at Charlie and then Ratchet.

"Each flight," Charlie explained, "that you flew has been recorded. Where you were actually on the controls, the times are listed as dual, noting what you were flying and what you were being taught. We each went through our logbooks so we could put the correct hours in your book."

"But this says…" She quickly thumbed to the fifth and last page of entries, added the last page time to the previous page's total. "I have over thirty hours?"

"Thirty-six point seven, I believe," Charlie agreed. "This time can't be used toward your FAA ratings, like your private or commercial or instrument, but all of your time after you get your student ticket will be official. These hours, before that time, will show your experience, and you will always have them for the memories. Happy birthday, Mel."

Mel sprang up and hugged Charlie again, and then she turned and hugged Woody. After she had hugged Ratchet, Lenny, and Bump, she turned to West again. "I don't know how to thank you enough. This is the best day I've ever had, except maybe for those when I'm flying."

West laughed and hugged Mel. "I can appreciate that."

"Mel," Felix interrupted. "There is one more thing." She handed Mel her phone. "Someone else wants to wish you a happy birthday."

Woody stopped beside West as Felix and Charlie talked. Felix kept glancing at Mel's animated conversation on the phone with her father.

He leaned in close to West and whispered louder than normal, "I think we'll need to schedule another party Tuesday evening."

West glanced at his smile as Charlie and Felix turned to listen.

"Do we?"

Woody nodded and gestured to Felix. "Yes, sir. This one has a check ride with Paul Clark Tuesday morning at 0800. I think she ought to take the 172. Weather should be cool but clear with light winds."

Felix stared at Woody.

"Paul got back with me just before Mel's party. Sorry I couldn't say anythin' sooner."

Felix smiled and nodded. "I understand. What do I need to do? Do I need to brush up on anything?"

Woody chuckled and shook his head.

"You know what to do, Felix. Just take your sectionals, logbook, the manuals on the plane, and your flight computer. You're ready and you'll be fine. We can talk more after a while, but I just wanted you to know."

"Thanks."

Sixty-Three
Sunday, October 15

Arthur stopped and leaned against Patty's counter in the Denver Library. "What is a pretty woman like you doing working on a Sunday?"

Patty looked up, surprised that she had not heard him come up. "A little filing and restocking."

"I thought you said you had the weekends off." He smiled. "I'm glad you're here, because you haven't given me your number, and if you're not here, I wouldn't know how to find you."

She stared at him a minute.

"It's okay, Patty. I understand that we haven't known each other very long, and you have to have reservations. I'm okay with that, but I was hoping I would find you today."

"And why is that, Mr. Stanik from North Carolina?" she teased.

"I have this urgent desire to take you out again," he explained with a wide smile, "and if I could not find you, I could not ask you."

"Urgent, huh?" She set the stack of books she was sorting on the counter and looked at him.

He nodded. "What can I say? I like your company, and dinner Friday night was such a wonderful change for me. And after being cooped up all day yesterday with the rain and wind and all, I wanted to see and talk with you again."

"You are certainly glib of tongue, Mr. Stanik." She smiled and leaned against the counter, closing the distance between them. "Where did you have in mind?"

"Do you like a good steak?"

"Why, being raised in this part of the world, I love a *good* steak. But most good steakhouses are either busy or swamped with diners or just downright expensive."

"How about Shanahan's? I made reservations just in case."

"Shanahan's?" She was impressed. "I've never been there, but I've heard a lot about it."

"Good, I hope." He cocked his head and smiled. "Will you go with me? I'll look very silly if I show up alone."

She hesitated, then smiled sheepishly. "Sure. Should I meet you there?"

"Patty, you know I would love to pick you up, but if you feel more comfortable driving yourself, I will meet you there."

"It's not that...well, some, I guess. I never used to worry about it, but I...I've had a few dates go wrong and I'm still—"

"It's okay. I understand." He took a notepad out of his pocket and wrote on a blank page, then tore it out and handed it to her. "This is me. Please check me out on the internet by name, my office website, my address, and that's my mother's name, address, and phone number. You can even call her and hear what she says about me."

"Your mother? You'd let me call your mother?"

"Sure. I truly want you to be comfortable, Patty. I would like to get to know you better, and for you to know me as well. You can ask me anything—except maybe about my clients. Call and talk to my secretary. She probably knows me better than my mother."

"Can I have your phone number? Is that too much to ask?"

"Not at all," he said, and wrote his number on the same slip of paper. "Call me from a payphone if you don't want me to have yours." He smiled and cocked his head again. "I'm trusting that you aren't an agent trying to get information on my clients."

"Oh," she said suddenly, her eyes wide and round. "That reminds me."

"What?"

"This morning, early. A man in a lightweight navy jacket, much too light weight for our climate and weather, stopped and asked me for information on the Ghost Ranch. I was surprised, but I think I hid it well enough. He had two pictures for me to look at, but they looked like the same woman with different colored hair."

Arthur shook his head. "Did he say who they were of?"

"Yes." She leaned close and continued softly. "One was Glen West's wife, Charlie—I've seen her picture before—and a darker-haired woman he said was Cathy or Catherine..."

"Williamson?"

"Yeah. Aren't those the ones you mentioned?"

"Yes. Yes, they are." He studied her face and settled on her concerned eyes.

"Have you thought to just call and ask this Cathy's husband? He has a number listed down in Widefield. He probably won't tell you where she is, if she's actually hiding from someone, like that guy this morning, but it's a residential address, so maybe he's setting up a home office."

He shook his head and chuckled. "Or someone like me. You have a good idea, but I think I have to think about this a little."

She watched him as he retreated into his thoughts a moment. "Does this change your plans? Are you still wanting to pick me up tonight?"

He smiled and squeezed her hand. "It does not. And yes, ma'am, I certainly would like to do that. How about six thirty? Gives me a little time to get us there and some for a drink before our table is ready."

"That will be wonderful," she replied, and wrote her address and phone number on the back of a library business card. "I'll be ready at six thirty sharp."

Monday, October 16

Sally was placing her open files in her lap drawer and looked up when Fred stopped in front of her desk.

"Hey. Hungry?"

She smiled and locked her desk. Fred's imposing figure in his uniform always caught her off guard. Actually, if she was honest with herself, it took her breath away. At first, she recalled how his sheer presence had intimidated her, making her nervous, until she understood that was just how he was; he was not doing anything on purpose to intimidate anyone. He was polite, unassuming, and certainly not arrogant or overbearing like she had first assumed. Now, his presence was comforting, knowing him for what he was: sincere, dedicated, pleasant, and that he obviously liked her more than she first realized. She was even getting to like that as well.

"Sure. Been a busy morning."

She locked her desk and stood up as he stepped aside to let her lead the way to the cafeteria.

"I've been going over the names we got from Monte on Saturday," he commented softly as they reached the line to the serving counter.

"Good. Oh great. Salisbury steaks and boiled cabbage again." She shook her head. "Sorry, find anything out?"

"Maybe," he said, and grabbed two trays and handed her one. "Get the toasted cheese and soup special. They added ham to the sandwich and the soup is jazzed up a bit from regular tomato."

She smiled but followed his lead, ordering the soup and sandwich. "And you know this how?"

"I was passing by this morning and talked to 'Londa while

she was preparing the soup." He smiled at her and ordered the same. Then he took a glass of iced tea and she took a canned pop.

He let her lead them to a corner table where the crowd was not too thick, and he sat down opposite her.

"Thanks for Saturday," she said. "I think that turned out to be the nicest working day I've ever had." She turned her tray to give him room at the small table. "And thanks for..." She hesitated, the words stuck in her throat. "...well, everything."

"You're very welcome. Saturday was a good day for me also. And you don't need to thank me for Saturday morning. You nearly had the guy when I got there. You took your self-defense classes to heart. I'm proud of you." He sipped his tea and took a bite of his sandwich, savoring the hot ham and cheese flavors. "Hmm, not the usual cheddar either."

She agreed after taking a bite herself. "I still can't believe you staked out my apartment."

"Like I said, that's what partners do for each other—watch each other's backs. Would you mind," he asked, and hesitated between bites, "if I had a copy of that email your father gave you?"

"No. Why?" she asked through a mouthful, and stopped chewing to stare at him.

"Do you know if he still has the original email on his computer?"

She finished her bite. "No, I don't. What's up?"

"I'm trying to figure out how we can locate Howard's server and track his email traffic." He set his sandwich down and leaned closer. "We're missing important information and I'm trying to find a way to get it. If your father has the original message, we should be able to expose the headers and see where it came from and where it went to get to your father. The trail should be there. I talked with our IT guy this morning also, and noted things we would need to do to uncover that routing information."

"I'll ask Dad." She smiled and caught his hand. "If he does, I'll see if he'll let our IT guy do the searching. I'd hate for one of us to mess it up."

He smiled. "When can we ask?"

"We?"

"I'd like to go with you. You know, moral support and all."

She thought about it a long moment and then decided. "That might actually help. I'll call and see if we can go by their place tonight."

"Okay. On our way to dinner?" He cocked his head and smiled. "Or after?"

She cocked her head and returned his smile. "On the way. That way we'll keep our visit short." Then she tapped an icon on her phone and listened. After a short conversation, she put her phone away and looked at him, her smile not as bright. "Dad's still at work, working late for an out-of-town client. And he leaves early tomorrow and won't be back until Friday night late. Next Saturday is the soonest we can talk to him."

Fred nodded and then tapped the table lightly. "So, what time should I pick you up?"

Felix walked along the right side of *Box Car* and back to the tail. They had waited until after lunch to let the field dry out as much as they could, but she privately hoped the northerly winds would dissipate so they could use the hard surface runway. She had made arrangements with Monte so he'd meet them when they landed, and Woody had called Cappie to let him know the plans. With the change in who went off for the weekend—Celina and Cappie and their two boys instead of Madra and Robert—the children had accepted, though maybe not as cheerfully as she wished, that there weren't enough seats for them on this trip.

She had completed her walk-around inspection of the engine cowling and the right wing, looking at each detail and hinge. She remembered Dani talking about the strangely missing cotter pin in the elevator trim tab linkage on one of her walk-arounds, and increased her attention as she carefully looked at each hinge and bolted joint as she went.

Satisfied the tail was as it should be, she started out the left wing, visually checking everything she could see, including the tip fuel tank drain with the cup on the long wand. She checked it for water and then continued to the fuselage and then rechecked the fuel filler caps and left main gear, wheels for cuts or abrasions, and the brakes for wear and leaks.

When she was finished, she climbed the left footholds on the left strut and slipped into the cockpit. Woody was belted into the right seat with his right-side door closed. She scanned the cargo compartment and noted the cargo door was closed and locked and that the two aft-facing seats and the forward-facing, three-abreast couch were installed as expected.

Woody patiently watched as she stepped through the prestart checklist, then, with a nod to Woody, she set the engine controls and primed for a cold engine, shouted "Clear" through the pilot's side window, and engaged the starter.

With the engine's first cough and swirl of gray smoke, Felix set the mixture to *Full Rich*. With a few additional coughs the engine accelerated, the puffs of smoke dissipated, and the speed settled into a fast idle. She adjusted the engine's speed and began the next steps in the checklist.

"Ghost Ranch," Felix called on the ranch's radio. "*Box Car* is taxiing for departure. How're the winds?"

"Winds are three forty degrees at twenty." Then Eddie gave her the barometric pressure and temperature.

"Roger, three forty at twenty." She looked at Woody. "Twenty-mile-an-hour crosswind with a slight tailwind component if I use the hard surface. Not what I'd like. Did anyone drive out onto the field this morning?"

Woody smiled. "Ratchet and Bump checked after breakfast and they think it's okay for a light airplane."

"All right then, we'll use the grass." Felix pushed the throttle forward and turned downwind, taxiing to the southeast. She watched the wheel on her side, looking for any signs that the grass might be too soft; she did not want to sink a tire into a soft spot or rut the field. Neither of those outcomes would be good.

After taxiing a half mile with no discernable rutting and no soft spots, she made a wide turn to point *Box Car* into the wind and conducted the run-up, magneto checks, and cycled the propeller to high pitch and back to low. She set the fuel to feed from the rear tank, then scanned the engine and flight instruments. With the directional gyro set to match her compass, she smiled at Woody.

"Ready?"

He smiled and nodded.

Felix turned *Box Car* to the left in a wide, full circle, checking the area around the airfield for any unannounced traffic. Then she stopped with the nose pointed at Hangar Eight, a little to the right of the headwind.

"Ghost Ranch, *Box Car,* with Ghost Nine and Ghost Six, is departing to the northwest."

"Safe flight, Ghost Nine. Ghost Ranch on standby."

Felix checked the field ahead and to her left, reached up and double-checked the elevator and rudder trim settings, and then pushed the throttle forward once more, holding the plane's track steady as it gathered speed and was quickly airborne. She held a gentle climb, and when the row of hangars slipped beneath them, she turned to the west to pick up their normal, devious route to Colorado Springs and their first pickup.

Monte was waiting beside the hangar at Custer Aviation on the west side of Colorado Springs Municipal Airport when

Felix taxied *Box Car* onto the ramp. With the Beaver turned, right wing pointing at the hangar, engine idling, Woody opened his door and stepped down to greet Monte.

He opened the cargo door and Monte climbed in, quickly catching Felix's shoulders and kissing her while she sat, still at the controls in the left seat.

"So you really do fly these things," he chuckled, and settled into the seat Woody suggested and put the proffered headphones on.

"Yes, I really do." She shook her head and grinned at him.

"Where are the kids?" he asked as he buckled the seat belt and Woody secured his luggage behind the aft bench seat. "I thought they might come along."

"We have a full plane going home," she explained. "We're going up to pick up Cappie and Celina and their two boys. This was their weekend away." She began noting items on her checklist as she spoke through the hot mic. "It's a short flight up to Meadow Lake, but once we're airborne, you can stand between the seats and watch what's going on."

Woody closed the cargo door and climbed back into his seat. Felix smiled at Monte once more and then turned her attention to the airplane and the flight ahead; she keyed the mic.

"Colorado Springs Ground, Beaver Two-Niner George Whiskey departing Custer Aviation with Hotel for Three-Five Left."

Felix taxied up and stopped in front of Central Colorado Aviation's hangar and Will Little escorted Cappie and his family out onto the ramp. They waited patiently as Felix went through the checklist steps and cut the fuel and ignition to the R-985; the propeller quickly spun to a stop.

Both Felix and Woody were out of the airplane to greet and get Cappie and everyone loaded. She noted the extra sacks and teased Celina about her shopping until she replied, "They are for *atsi' Mel's hoʼdizhchínéejí anáyíítká.*" She saw Monte and clarified: "Her birthday."

"That's very nice of you. I know she'll love whatever you bought her," Felix chuckled as she stepped back and went around the nose of the plane.

As Felix climbed back into the pilot's seat, she glanced back and saw they remembered Monte; he was shaking everyone's hands and remarking how nice it was to see them again. She looked around the plane, checking for anyone too close, then yelled "Clear" through the pilot's window.

When Felix started the engine, Monte noticed a man in light slacks and a navy jacket leaning against the corner of the hangar. He was not wearing a hat, but was smoking a cigarette and glancing at a folded paper in his hand as he watched them start and taxi out. Monte tried to convince himself it was someone taking a break and simply plane watching, but the events of the summer were still too vivid for him to completely shake the foreboding he felt.

Felix taxied out and headed south. "Everyone buckled up and ready?" she asked as she turned onto Runway 33. When they confirmed they were, she announced her intentions over the radio, lined up on the runway, and advanced the throttle.

Arthur again sat at the octagonal reference table in the Denver Central Library. It had quickly become his favorite 'office space' after he arrived and discovered it, and the pretty woman that manned the information desk each morning.

He had been studying a map of the central Colorado area when his laptop beeped, and he saw the icon and airplane information for the Ghost Ranch's Beaver. It had appeared as it approached Colorado Springs, coming down the valley from Woodland Park. The icon tracked south along the front range, then turned and landed to the north on the west-most runway at Colorado Springs Municipal Airport.

Everything seemed routine, except that the icon remained and the airplane taxied out and took off again within ten minutes of landing. It proceeded northeast to Meadow Lake Airport.

"My, but you are being so serious this morning," Patty's sweet voice whispered close to his right ear, and she leaned over his shoulder to see what he was watching.

"Hey." He smiled as he turned his head to look at her. "The Beaver again." He pointed to where the icon had disappeared. "Made two stops and now I am waiting for it to leave again."

"My roommate says she'll work up a routine to watch for you—probably have something to try by the end of the week."

"Thanks. That will be wonderful. Tell her I really appreciate it."

"I will. And thank you again for a very, very nice dinner last night. You really shouldn't have spent so much on me. It was great, but entirely too expensive. Sam's Number 3 is more my speed."

"I understand, but a guy has to go all out once in a while." He grinned crookedly. "I won't spoil you every time, but I wanted to go all out last night."

"I thank you, but there are many good steakhouses that are much less expensive." She held his eyes for a moment. "But I'll let you choose where some of the time. You make nice choices."

"Thank you. How about lunch? Are you free today?"

She chuckled and shook her head. "Yes, about eleven thirty."

"Okay then. Eleven thirty." The movement on his laptop's screen caught his attention. "Aah, it's moving again."

"I'll leave you alone and get back to my sorting and filing," she said. "Until eleven thirty."

He smiled and watched her walk back to the information desk under the 'Ask' sign, then turned and followed the Beaver's icon as it departed Meadow Lake Airport.

The icon followed the same route he'd seen it fly before, only this time it turned south at Florissant, staying illuminated for another minute before it disappeared. He leaned back in his chair and pondered what he had seen. He wondered if the turn to the south might mean the elusive Ghost Ranch was somewhere south or southwest of Colorado Springs, as opposed to just west. He studied his map again and noted the long valley stretching south from Florissant, and that it led to the southern end of the high, grassy plain and possibly on toward Cañon City and the plains to the east. *Of course,* he chided himself, *it could have skirted south of Saddle Mountain and continued west into the Arkansas River Valley. Or,* he supposed, *they could have another stop to make before going back to the ranch.*

He shook his head and waited patiently. It could have gone almost anywhere, except his growing feeling was more certain it was not to the northern half of the state.

Charlie and West were waiting in front of Hangar Five when *Box Car* taxied up and Felix cleared the engine and shut it down. Mel and Mike were waving enthusiastically, standing together beside Charlie. As the propeller spun to a stop, they moved closer and stopped under the right wing, where Lenny and Bump joined them, parking a second jeep beside the plane.

Woody climbed down and opened the cargo door while Felix remained in the cockpit filling out the flight's log sheets. Celina was the first to step down, followed by Peter, then Philip and Cappie next. Monte was last, and the children were across the distance and hugging him before he had taken more than two steps.

Lenny loaded Celina and Cappie's bags into the closest jeep while Cappie and Celina visited with West and Charlie, thanking them again for the weekend transportation. When the pleasantries were complete, Cappie ushered Celina and the boys to the jeep and started driving toward the oasis below the lip.

Charlie gave Monte a quick hug and stepped back as Felix ducked under *Box Car*'s engine and stepped up to him. She smiled, and she quickly lost herself in greeting him back to the ranch with a tight, lingering hug of her own. Charlie nodded to West and they stepped back and turned to the jeep they had driven and parked by Hangar Five's people door. She helped West into the passenger's seat and stood beside him to wait on Felix, Monte, and the children.

Bump drove a third jeep up out of the hangar and parked beside West and Charlie.

"I figured they might want to drive down together." He smiled as he stepped out of the jeep and glanced at Monte, Felix, and the two children, still embracing under *Box Car*'s wing. "And this way you don't have to wait if you don't want to."

"Thanks, but I think we'll wait anyway." Charlie smiled at the huddled family. "I need to talk to Felix."

"Okay by me," Bump commented as he moved Monte's bags from their jeep to the third jeep. "I'm off to get the tug. *Box Car* needs to be fed and put back in his stall."

"Thanks, Bump." Charlie patted his shoulder as he turned and started back into the hangar.

It was only a few minutes before Felix led Monte and the children to the jeep. She helped Mike and Mel into the back seats and turned to Charlie. She glanced nervously at West and then back to Charlie.

"What is it?" Charlie asked, realizing something was bothering her.

"It's probably nothing," Felix began, "but when we landed in Meadow Lake, there was a guy hanging around Will's hangar. By the time we shut down to start loading Cappie and his family, he had taken a spot at the corner of the hangar to watch us and the plane. "

"He could be just someone—"

"I know. It could be innocent enough, but it bugged me the way he kept watchin us and glancing at what looked like a folded map."

"I noticed him too," Monte added in support. "I couldn't tell what he was looking at, but he was referring to something—a map, a small notebook, something like that. Lightweight navy jacket and light-colored khaki slacks and regular shoes, not boots. Definitely—"

"Someone that is not from around here," Felix interrupted. "I kept watch of him as we loaded Cappie and his family and while I got *Box Car* started. He didn't move and kept watching. Woody said he was still in the same place, watching, when we flew past Will's on takeoff." She hesitated and studied Charlie's concerned expression. "After the emails Jess found a week ago Friday about Howard sending someone new, I guess I'm just overly cautious."

"Thanks. It's probably the best way for us to be." Charlie gave her a quick hug and a thin smile. "You need to get your family down and settled. We can talk more about this later."

"Thanks, Charlie. See you down below for lunch."

Tuesday, October 17

Felix, dressed in her Ghost Ranch flight suit, chocked the 172's left main tire and then closed the pilot side door. It was ten till eight as she turned and walked to the Perry Stokes Airport Terminal building, east northeast of Trinidad along Highway 350. A middle-aged man met her at the terminal door and opened it for her.

"Mrs. Williamson, I presume," he greeted politely.

"Felix, please." She stepped inside and he closed the door.

"Thank you, Felix. One of West's nicknames?"

She nodded.

"I'm Paul," he said softly, "Paul Clark. I was surprised when Woody called and said he had another pilot needing a ride."

"I'm an unexpected addition, I'm afraid." She followed Paul's gesture to the conference room off the pilots' lounge. "I'm the fourth woman to fly for the ranch, if you count Charlie. I'm here because Woody said I needed to finish up before the baby"—she rubbed her abdomen—"gets too large and interferes with the controls."

He grinned. "Well, I see you have some time before that's a problem." He gestured to a chair on the long side of the table, next to the end. Then he sat down at the end of the table. "May I have a look at your logbook?"

He studied the pages, reading slowly, nodding as he read. "My, my. 172N, T206, L-19E , the one with a constant speed propeller, AT-6, and—is this right?—the TF-51?" He looked up and saw her nod.

"Backseat time in Charlie's *My Affair*, cross-country, navigation, limited aerobatic maneuvers. I haven't made any takeoffs or landings yet."

"I see. And Woody noted here that you're flying *Box Car*."

"Yes, sir. Woody expects me to help with the weekly supply runs."

"Is there any two-place airplane at the ranch that you haven't flown?"

"Yes, Charlie's Legacy. My daughter has gotten to fly it twice, but I haven't."

"Your daughter?"

"Yes. She turned twelve on Saturday and has thirty-six point seven hours total—she *has* flown everything there that has two seats or more."

Paul smiled and shook his head as he closed the logbook. "Interesting family. Did Charlie do your ground schooling, like she did for Rosita and Bell?"

"Yes, she did. By the way, Rosita now goes by Dani and Bell goes by Eddie. They got their nicknames after they got their tickets."

"Charlie, Dani, Eddie? *C*, *D*, and *E*, and now *F*, Felix? Is the alphabetical progression on purpose?"

She nodded. "Dani—er, Rosita—wanted to start a trend for the women pilots, each having a boyish-sounding nickname like Charlie, and each in sequence based on the order of us getting our tickets."

Paul shook his head. "I might have known." He inhaled. "Okay, Felix. Now it is time for you to show me how well you've absorbed what Woody and Charlie have taught you." He gestured at her tote bag. "To begin, get out your charts and manuals. I'm a hundred and ninety-seven pounds today, and I want you to plan a cross-country from here to Pueblo and then to Durango."

Arthur was up early and eating his breakfast like he usually did at the Denny's near his motel. He had a restless night, woken numerous times thinking about Pat's questions of why his client was so interested in the two women—people, instead of just things.

He had reminded her that many times people hire private investigators to follow a spouse suspected of cheating or having any number of kinds of secret affairs, someone that was suspected of wrongdoing or having a relationship with a competing company. The reasons were unbelievably varied.

But, when his client contacted him, he ran a character search on the two women and discovered that they had each experienced a kidnapping. That was shocking enough, but it was just this very week that he had uncovered the police reports on those kidnappings, and realized that both were alleged to have been arranged by Cathy Williamson's father.

What he could not figure out, at least not yet, was why the South African government was looking for them. Why would they be searching for two seemingly normal women? What made them targets? And for what end?

He did not like where his mind was leading him, but he agreed with Pat: something was certainly wrong with his client's intentions.

When he finished eating and had returned to his room, he considered her other comment—the one when she said he should call Monte Williamson and ask his questions. He wondered if it could be that simple, but quickly decided it could not. It had never been that simple before, but then...

He tapped the screen on his phone, unlocked it, and entered the number Pat had given him.

Sixty-Four
Felix's Celebration

"I am so proud of you," Monte said again as he and the children hugged Felix. They had gathered in front of the fireplace, where its low flames licked the new log he'd added. The welcoming warmth dispelled the evening chill. It had gotten cold in Farmington before he left, but he had been remembering the warmer days in Colorado Springs and on the ranch when he started west, and was not ready for fall in the mountains. "I still can't believe you fly airplanes. And now you actually have a pilot's license."

"Me either," she admitted, and glanced at Mel, still hugging her waist. "All because our darling daughter suggested—well, sort of *challenged* me—to give it a try,"

"I'm gonna be a pilot, too," Mike added. "Mel first, then me."

Monte chuckled and squeezed the children. "I don't doubt that for a second."

"Looks like the cake was a hit," Charlie commented as she stopped beside their group. "Did you get enough pictures of it?"

"I think so," Monte said as Felix nodded vigorously. "I got the cake, and the pictures of the airplanes from a few different angles, and then a few with Cat behind it. I think they look great."

"Thank you." Felix caught Charlie's shoulders and hugged her. "This was a very nice party. You really didn't have to do all of th—"

"Of course, we did!" Charlie smiled, squeezed Felix once quickly, then pushed herself away. "This is your night. You've earned the opportunity to enjoy and celebrate the results of your efforts."

"Thank you, again." She smiled and turned to Monte. "How about a little more punch before these two turn in for the night?"

Monte caught Mike's hand and Felix caught Mel's, and together they went to see Celina, where she manned the punchbowl.

"Monte told Cat their furniture should be in Amarillo next week," Charlie remarked as she sat down on her dressing table bench and slipped her boots off. The party had ended on happy notes and Monte and Cat ushered the children off to bed, but she knew Cat really wanted her time with Monte. "And Jess's house is finished and Lenny is back, so she asked if they could go and pick her stuff up on Thursday or Friday."

"Looks like this and next week are going to be busy," West agreed as he dropped his shirt into the clothes hamper. Leaving one crutch beside the bed, he hopped into the bathroom and, with Charlie's help, got ready for bed.

When he was settled, Charlie got herself ready for bed, turned the lights off, and snuggled beside him, pulling the covers tight around them.

"I'm so very glad you're back home." She raised up and kissed him, then resumed her position beside him, his arm holding her snug against his side.

"I am too. When you slept for eighteen hours straight, I realized how tense and worried you must have been. We both do better when we're together, and we're the best when we're here on the ranch."

"I know. I feel the same way, but I have something to confess, and it might make you angry."

"Angry? What?"

"My promise. Well, part of it."

"I'm not angry, but you know you have to do it."

"Yeah, I know. But I haven't been able to bring myself to tell her. She's so comfortable here and I'm afraid...I'm afraid of what she'll think...of what she might do." She buried her face against his neck. "It'll be painful, and I don't want to drive her away. I don't want her to feel anything that would make her want to leave."

"I know it isn't going to be easy, but you have to let the chips fall where they may. She needs to know—especially now. knowing that Howard is active again and—"

"Yes, I know. I need to tell her, but I can't. She'll despise me for what I've done." Her voice dropped to a whisper. "I'm afraid. Afraid for her more than anything."

"I can see that, but you know she has to know. And the truth has to come from you."

"I keep thinking there's something else that I can do. Somehow, I have to find Howard and help the authorities get him. Then, maybe, I can relax a little. Then maybe I can tell—"

"You have to tell her. And I'm betting she'll understand. But if I'm wrong, she'll know the truth. And if, heaven forbid, something should happen to us, you can't leave her in the dark, without knowing the truth."

Charlie wilted beside him and tears began to wet her eyes. "I know you're right, but—"

"You have to be strong, love, like you were the day you met her in Broomfield. You have—"

"I know," she whispered. "I know."

He pulled her tighter against his side. "I'm sorry to be so insistent," he said, his kiss soft, gentle, and she knew he was with her, knowing how hard this was for her. He released her lips and continued softly. "Right now I have more important things to *discuss* with you tonight. We'll talk more about your promise tomorrow, or maybe later..."

She clung to him, slowly responding to his gentle caresses and touches.

Friday, October 20

It was 0909 and Felix was finishing the Before Engine Start checklist when Eddie swung the co-pilot's door open, climbed *Box Car*'s right landing gear strut, and settled into the right cockpit seat. They were both assigned to make the usual Friday run to pick up groceries and supplies, this time from Ryan's Air Service in Pueblo.

"Walkaround complete," Eddie announced as she fastened her seat belt and shoulder harness and closed the door.

Felix glanced around the left side of the plane, and when Eddie nodded, gesturing that there was no one on her side, she waved to Bump standing beside the large fire extinguisher mounted on equally large spoked iron wheels, then shouted "Clear" through the pilot's side window. She set the throttle and engaged the starter. On the third blade, the engine popped and gray smoke swirled around the cockpit, each cylinder quickly adding their staccato pulses. The engine accelerated and settled at a fast idle.

She adjusted the throttle and waved to Bump. He quickly withdrew the fire extinguisher and Felix pushed the throttle forward.

"Ghost Ranch, Ghost Nine and Ghost Eight are taxiing *Box Car* for departure," Eddie announced into the mic.

"Winds are two six zero at eighteen," Helen's calm voice answered. "No reported traffic."

About a quarter mile past Hangar Eight, Felix turned into the wind and accomplished the requisite run-up, magneto, and propeller checks.

"Ready?" she asked, and Eddie nodded.

"Ghost Ranch, *Box Car* is departing." Eddie smiled.

"Safe flight, Ghost Eight and Nine."

Felix pushed the throttle forward, holding the nose into the wind as *Box Car* accelerated. The tail came up on its own, and at seventy the roughness of the grassy field fell away; they were airborne, and Felix climbed to four hundred feet above the field and turned west-northwest as they slipped over the lip of the mesa.

"I got the APS-13 installed in the C model last night," Eddie commented, making small talk. "Has Woody shown you how that works?"

Felix shook her head. "We've talked about it, but only the fighters have them installed. Charlie once said West was going to put them on all of the other planes, but I don't think he has. *Box Car* doesn't have one yet."

"Ratchet flew *Bad Luck* back from Broomfield last Fourth of July and said he about had a heart attack when a business jet passed across his path, behind him. The APS went off and he said he suddenly thought he was back in his F-14, with the missile warning blaring." Eddie giggled. "You hadn't come to the ranch yet, but you knew he flew Tomcats in the navy, didn't you?"

"He mentioned it once after I got here."

"Felix"—Eddie changed the subject—"can I ask you a personal question?"

"Sure. I guess." Felix smiled, but felt a bit uncomfortable, wondering what Eddie wanted to know.

"You and Charlie. Were you surprised at Broomfield when you met her? I mean, because you and her look so much alike. I know Dani and I were when we saw you."

Felix smiled and shook her head. "I thought you knew that I had seen a picture of her before we came. That was a big part of why we came, and as it turned out, I'm so very glad we did. Monte was there and able to help after you started screaming."

Eddie blushed. "That wasn't what I was meaning to talk about. I just wondered how you felt, seeing someone that looked so much like yourself. I know you're used to it now, like we all are, but I keep thinking about how strange that must have felt."

"Well, Eddie. It wasn't all that strange. I had a sister that I saw every day until I was married. Then, when she went off to college, I saw even less of her." She paused a long moment. "But you see, I know what it's like to see someone regularly that looks like me."

"Yeah. I still think that would feel strange."

Their conversation dwindled until they were twenty miles out and Eddie called the Pueblo tower. She turned the transponder on, entered the four-digit VFR identification code, and pushed the squawk button.

"We're cleared downwind for Runway Two Six Left," she informed Felix, even though she knew Felix could hear everything through her headphones. "Now cleared to land with an immediate left one eighty and taxi to Ryan's. Elevation 4677 at the threshold. Information Delta, winds 230 at 15."

Arthur was preparing to leave his motel room and head for the library when the program on his laptop beeped. With his jacket half on, he leaned over the computer and saw the highlighted icon and the Beaver's registration number southeast of Pueblo. As he watched, he slowly realized it was *southwest* of Pueblo and on a path straight for the airport. It was inbound and *not* coming directly from the mountains to the west.

He immediately wondered where it was coming from, and a confident feeling slowly came over him—maybe wishful thinking and maybe he was seeing something important. He zoomed the image and watched as the icon slowed and lined up parallel with the Pueblo runways and, after a minute or two, turned and stopped midfield. It began moving back to the east and he knew it had landed.

He knew he was letting his emotions push him to a quick decision as he quickly closed the laptop and finished putting his jacket on. He would study his maps when he got to the library and thought maybe Pat could help him with his deductions. She seemed to have a very logical mind, and he knew she would have helpful ideas.

Arthur saw Pat at her information desk, concentrating on something on her counter. He had decided to call her "Pat" instead of "Patty" after their second dinner together. He liked the more proper, mature sound of it, and she seemed to like it also.

Today was his turn to surprise her and he quietly slipped through the counter opening to her left and leaned close to her ear, careful to not make any noise. "Hey, beautiful. What're you so interested in?"

Startled, she jumped and snapped her head to look at who had spoken. Seeing him, her expression broke into a wide grin.

"My turn to surprise you." He smiled and stood up, slowly returning to the customer side of the counter. "I saw something this morning just before I came here, and I thought I might run my ideas past you to see if you agree with my deductions."

"I'd love to help."

"I'll get set up at a regular table and show you what I've found out. Can you take a break?"

She looked at the clock over the counter and smiled. "Seems it *is* my break time. I'll join you after I go to the powder room. Would you like a coffee?"

"Sure."

He smiled, watching her as she left and turned down a short hallway to the restrooms, and then he set his laptop out and switched it on. In the center of the table was a power and internet outlet, so he connected the computer to both. When Pat returned, with an insulated cup of coffee in each hand, coming from the direction of the cafeteria, he was unfolding his state map and a few printouts he had made from a public satellite mapping program.

"Looks like you've been doing a lot of studying," she commented, and took the seat beside him. She set a cup in front of him.

"Thanks. Some," he agreed, and then explained about the flight of the Beaver he had seen on Monday and how it had turned south at Florissant before the transponder icon disappeared. Then he explained what he had seen that morning. "If I consider both flights as going and coming from the same place, then it points to the *south* part of the state. But if I consider them separately, then I have to assume today's flight came from an airport south of Pueblo, like Trinidad or Raton."

"But you said your gut says the Monday flight was most likely heading back to their home, their ranch."

"That was my first thought, since it left Colorado Springs, flew up the canyon to Woodland Park, and made a specific turn south at Florissant. And if you look at the maps"—he swept his hand across the section below Florissant—"the valley south of Florissant opens up into the valley west of Pueblo. Without a transponder response, the software I'm using can't tell where it might go, but it could have gone this way, out of the higher mountains and southeast."

"But you also said the previous flights that left Pueblo went straight west. So the one that turned south at Florissant might have gone south to pick up the same route heading west. Besides, there are no mountains out southeast. Not real mountains."

"It's actually the mesa lands, which, according to the state, are still considered 'mountains,' just not in a usual sense."

"And you think the flight this morning somehow confirms the ranch is somewhere out this way?" She gestured to the lower right corner of the map. "Instead of coming from another stop on its way to Pueblo or a route farther south from the west?"

"I know, I know. Could be either, but consider, where better to hide an airport than on top of a mesa? You can't see it from the ground." He smiled and nodded.

"You could also hide an airport anywhere in the mountains. And there are mesas in the western part of the state as well."

"Okay, okay. You're right." He sighed. "And if I look at my notes, there seems to be a loosely repeating schedule on Fridays and Mondays, where all the flights, except for this morning's flight, come from the west and return to the west."

Pat nodded. "I think it makes the best sense to look at all of the data and use it to make a decision, not just the part of the data you want to look at."

"I guess I should plan a drive out around Cañon City on Monday and next Friday and see which way they go. But in the meantime, what are you doing tomorrow? Interested in taking a drive down around Trinidad and back?"

She smiled. "I could pack us a lunch and some snacks. They say it's supposed to be sunny, though only in the high fifties or low sixties."

Saturday, October 21

"The El Moro exit is coming up," Pat announced as she studied the map in her lap. "There's a rest area there and I could use a break."

"Okay. Probably a good idea for both of us," Arthur agreed, noticing the exit sign as it approached.

He followed the signs, pulled into the rest area, and parked in front of the modern-looking stone and glass building behind stone planters and surrounded by a wide paved terrace. Numerous metal pedestal tables with attached benches dotted the area around the building.

They got out and he locked the car as they walked around the array of planters.

He was waiting, casually studying the vast expanse to the east, when Pat stepped out and saw him.

"It's a wonderful view, don't you think?" he asked when she stopped beside him.

"It sure is. I see so many pictures from around the state, but it always takes my breath away when I get out and actually see it."

They got back into his car and started back to the interstate.

"Didn't you say you wanted to go east on Highway 160?"

"I did." He nodded.

"If you stay on El Moro Road, we can jog down, cross the river, and connect with 160, bypassing all of the Trinidad traffic."

"Is there a park or a suitable place to pull off and have lunch along 160?"

"No parks that I can see," she admitted, studying the map as he followed El Moro Road. "But it looks like it's wide open country, rolling prairie, so we could just pull over and enjoy the view."

He glanced at her and smiled; he enjoyed the view anytime she was with him, no matter where they were. He also enjoyed the fact that she was not pretentious and liked the more normal things in life. "That'll work," he responded before his conscience reminded him that he was there on a job, which meant that once he found the ranch, his purpose was over. Even if he did not tell his client when he found it, he'd be done, and then where would his romantic thinking leave him? "Point me in the right direction," he said to Pat, and quickly realized he was telling himself the same thing. Finding the ranch had become something personal. Then he smiled to himself and wondered, *Am I thinking about canceling my contract?*

"Okay. There should be a place between where we pick up 160 and where 160 turns to the right—a stretch of about three miles."

When they stopped at the intersection of 350 and 160, where 160 branched off to take a more easterly direction, he stopped just off the highway and they broke out the lunch rations. He stood beside the front of the car and Pat sat up on the fender, eating a sandwich she had brought.

Arthur looked to the east and pointed. "You can just barely see the tops of the mesas, but that is the one I think we're looking for."

"Why that one?" She took a sip from her soda can.

"I'm not completely giving up on the idea that the ranch might be out here, so I looked at the mesas along the state line and there are basically only two suitable mesas. The Fisher Mesa south of Trinidad extends down into New Mexico, but the part that is in Colorado doesn't seem to have any ground access. The other one, the east one, is much larger, extending southeast into New Mexico and the Oklahoma panhandle. There are two or three roads leading in from the south."

"You think they need ground access because they rebuild and restore airplanes and would have to have a way to bring them to the ranch. Right?"

"That's a big part of my thinking. But obviously there are people living on the ranch and there are a lot of things they would have to bring to the ranch that wouldn't fit in an airplane."

"Building supplies," she continued, thinking out loud, "and things like that?"

He nodded and took another bite of his sandwich.

"It's a ranch, so they would have horses and cattle, needing hay and fencing materials and things like that..."

"Most likely." He took a sip of his drink, wadded up the

wrapper from his sandwich, and dropped it in a trash sack he kept in the car. "And I'm hoping we can find someone on some ranch out there that will talk to us."

Pat wasn't finished, so he leaned back against the car and continued studying the seemingly empty rolling landscape. "This country is captivating..."

"I'll be finished in just a minute, then we can try to find one of those someones."

"I'm in no hurry. Please take your time."

Forty-five minutes later, they crossed the New Mexico border just south of Branson, and Colorado Highway 389 turned into New Mexico Highway 551. Seven miles farther, they turned east on New Mexico 456 and followed the Dry Cimarron River. The mesas rose up on either side, immersing them in the solitude and striking beauty of the mesa lands.

"My, oh my," Pat whispered. "If someone wanted to get away from the hustle and bustle of today's life, this would certainly be high on the list of places to go."

Twenty-five minutes after they turned east, he slowed the car as they neared the crest in the road just before the place where the map indicated it made a sweeping curve to the southeast around an unnamed small mesa that rose up nearly six hundred feet on their right. Pat noted the markings he had made on the map, and they watched for the dirt road heading north.

He turned north on the second of two roads marked as Long Canyon Road. The map identified each with a different number.

"This looks like the right one," he said, pointing to the small peak to their northeast. "That should be the one marked as 'Baldy Hill.'"

"And, if you're right, there should be a ranch up here somewhere."

Jess hurried, nearly ran, into the main house and turned down the long hallway to the security offices. It was just after 1320 when the alert summoned her on her mobile phone and then, hearing the "GROUND ACCESS ALERT" coming from the office speakers, she swung around the doorjamb and quickly dropped into her desk chair, keying for the status screen.

Felix was right behind her, coming as quickly as she could from her room on the second floor, and palmed the alert mute as she crossed the room to look over Jess's shoulder.

"What have we got?" Felix asked as Jess identified where the alert had come from and keyed for a visual.

"South entrance. Two miles out." They both studied the array of monitors on the office wall. "A car, coming slowly."

"We aren't expecting anyone. You and Lenny got back from Amarillo before lunch, and you were the only ones scheduled."

Jess tapped the phone console as Charlie, Dani, and Eddie squeezed through the office door. Others filled the hallway.

"Ratchet?" she asked as the connection made.

"Yes. I see the alert."

"A single car is coming slowly up the south road. Can you and one of the other men meet me on the road to the south gate? I'm taking a jeep from here."

"We're on our way."

Jess opened the bottom desk drawer and retrieved a western-style gun belt and wrapped it around her slender hips. She glanced up at Felix's surprised intake as she buckled it. "Gotta look the part. Watch the store and answer them if they ask any questions. You know the drill." She grabbed a weatherworn western hat from the drawer and kicked it closed. Everyone made way for her as she turned to the door and hurried through.

The desk phone rang and Felix quickly answered it.

"She just left, Woody. Ratchet and either Lenny or Bump will meet her on the road to the south gate. Is Mel okay?"

Mel was flying her second circle around a watering pond 11.2 miles west-northwest of Clayton, New Mexico, when Woody asked her to reverse direction and do two turns to the right.

Woody had tapped her shoulder after lunch and said he had a few hours of free time. He asked her if she was also free and she had said she was. The next thing she knew, she was sitting in the front seat of *Snoopy* and starting the engine. Woody was in the back. When she pointed *Snoopy* into the wind, Woody told her to take him to Clayton for some air work. She happily complied.

He had her fly visually below the tops of the mesas to practice her dead reckoning: navigation by terrain and not with the aid of navigational fixes. Like checking fences, sometimes it was necessary to fly low and know where you were. He had once told her the same thing, only at that time he ha stressed that she needed to know, on sight, every detail of the land around her home, so she would always have her bearings.

"Those were very good," Woody commented from the back seat. "Take us up a thousand and show me your slow flying. Two three-sixties, one left and one right, with the horn blowing."

Mel had done this twice before and knew he was talking about the stall warning horn. To comply with his instructions, she had to fly the two circles while keeping the plane's speed within a three- to five-mile-per-hour speed band above the plane's stall speed. If she flew too slow, the plane would no longer support itself; if she flew too fast, the horn would stop blowing.

She continued her slow flight, heading northwest when the

second circle was completed and Woody had not said anything. She leveled the wings and flew straight and level with the horn still blaring in their headsets. "All right, Mel. Take us home. We'll do some landings."

"Okay. Heading home." She smiled and held her speed and altitude, turning northward toward the mesas.

"You can speed up to cruise and drop down to about four hundred feet, AGL."

"Roger." She gently lowered the nose and added power; the horn quit blaring. "Three-fifty degrees should take us pretty close, maybe between the house and the airstrip."

Woody chuckled and settled back to enjoy the ride. When they entered the wide Dry Cimarron River Canyon, he began to look around at landmarks, but the car slowly driving up Long Canyon Road caught his attention.

"Hey, Mel, there's a car coming up the ranch road."

Mel jerked her head to see what Woody was talking about.

"Drop down over the river and let's check it out while I call the ranch. Lenny brought Jess and her things back this morning, so there shouldn't be anyone else coming up that road today, and certainly no one in a car. Watch your terrain and fly slow circles around it."

"Got it."

Arthur saw what looked like a gate from about a mile out on Long Canyon Road, but lost sight of it as the road dropped down into another wide depression caused by years of water runoff. They crossed another "low water" bridge, nothing more than a paved section of the road where the water sometimes ran, and started another gentle climb.

"That's one big gate," he remarked, and glanced at Pat.

She was happily taking in the natural beauty and solitude of the wide river valley. She lowered her window to better feel the landscape; the soft engine sounds of an airplane caught their attention. He looked up through the windshield and his side window, but did not see the plane.

A few minutes later, he stopped in front of the twenty-foot-wide, five-rail gate made of steel pipes welded together and painted white. It was a swing-up design, anchored on both sides by heavy concrete buttresses. A similar, white three-rail pipe fence extended west a couple of miles until it and the adjacent mesa intersected, and east about the same distance to the place where it disappeared over a crest at the foot of another mesa.

"I guess we should get out and look around." He opened his door and Pat followed his example.

He walked up to the gate and began reading the engraved sign on the right-hand buttress to himself as Pat joined him.

Maria Felipa Montoya Jefferson Ranch

Private Property – No Trespassing

Admittance by prior arrangement only

"Well, this certainly isn't the Ghost Ranch or West's Restorations," Pat said softly. Then she pointed to a 3 x 3-inch perforated brass square with a push button beside it. "That looks like a speaker."

Arthur squared his shoulders and pressed the button. A female voice responded.

"This is the Maria Jefferson Ranch. May I help you?"

"Yes, please. I am Arthur Stanik and I am looking for Glen West's Restorations."

"I'm sorry, but you have arrived at the Maria Jefferson Ranch."

"Can you tell me where I can find Glen West's Restorations?"

"I'm sorry, but I cannot. If you do not have a previously arranged visitation, I cannot help you. Good day."

"No, but I need to find Glen West's Restorations."

The speaker did not respond, and he was about to press the

button again when Pat tapped his shoulder and pointed up the road beyond the gate. There, where the road disappeared over the crest of the next hill a half mile away on the sloping base of the western mesa, three vehicles had parked side by side. He looked closer and studied the vehicles.

"Looks like trucks...no...jeeps," he muttered softly, and slowly looked closer at the fence and the terrain on the other side. There were numerous poles with obvious camera pods atop them, set fifteen to twenty feet back and periodically spaced across the space between the flanking mesas. And there was the plane slowly circling above them. "It looks like we are being watched, probably recorded."

He turned quickly and went to the car and retrieved a pair of binoculars from the floorboard behind the driver's seat. When he returned and stopped beside Pat, he was looking at the vehicles.

"Yup, they're jeeps all right. The two on each side have a driver and a man standing up with...carbines. The one in the middle...is standing on the hood of the jeep and...is...a woman, in jeans, vest and...wearing a cowboy hat, a gun belt, and holding a carbine cradled in her arm. She...looks like she's the one that's in charge."

He handed her the binoculars.

"Sure looks like they're waiting to see if we're going to try to go in. I think they want us to leave," Pat added. "And maybe we should. We didn't come to cause anyone any trouble."

She lowered the binoculars and he smiled at her, wondering why a ranch in Colorado would need armed security people, or even an airplane. "I agree. Let's take the rest of the day and see what you can show me while we wander back to Denver."

He slipped his arm around her shoulders, turned, and led her back to the car.

Felix sat back and stared at the array of monitors, watching the man and woman as they walked back to their car. She was absently fingering the paper she had been reading from.

"Looks like they're going to leave." Then she turned to Helen. "Why did West name the ranch"—she glanced down at the paper—"the Maria Filipa Montoya Jefferson Ranch? No one's ever said why."

Helen smiled. "That was my grandmother. Her family was from Spain—Seville, actually—a well-known horse family. She married my grandfather when they were both nineteen. And from everything I was told as a child, she lived up to her name, having a wild, rebellious, obstinate side, and extremely passionate about her horses."

"Sounds like there's a good story in there somewhere."

"There is, but that is a topic for another time," Helen remarked as the phone rang.

Felix answered it. "Hey...Okay. Woody's still watching? Okay. See ya when you get back." She looked up as she cradled the phone, and announced, "That was Jess—she's started back."

"This guy Stanik—Arthur Stanik," Charlie added, looking at her phone and standing just inside the doorway, "is a P I out of Weaverville, North Carolina." She looked straight at Felix, her expression rigid. "I think you, me, and Jess need to talk to West and Ratchet when everyone is back."

"Damn! If what you're thinking is true," Felix said, her expression matching Charlie's, "I think you're right."

Charlie's story continues in West's Ghost Ranch Series, Book 6: *When the Past and Present Collide*

Phonetic Alphabet

World War II   Current usage

A	Able	Alpha
B	Baker	Bravo
C	Charlie	Charlie
D	Dog	Delta
E	Easy	Echo
F	Fox	Foxtrot
G	George	Golf
H	How	Hotel
I	Item	India
J	Jig	Juliet
K	King	Kilo
L	Love	Lima
M	Mike	Mike
N	Nan	November
O	Oboe	Oscar
P	Peter	Papa
Q	Queen	Quebec
R	Roger	Romeo
S	Sugar	Sierra
T	Tear	Tango
U	Uncle	Uniform
V	Victor	Victor
W	Whiskey	Whiskey
X	X-Ray	X-Ray
Y	Yoke	Yankee
Z	Zebra	Zulu

Glossary

Characters:

-A-

Ableman, Sally – Officer with the Detroit Police Department, Third Precinct.

Alice – Monte Williamson's secretary.

-B-

Baron, Richard – Owner of Jet Services in Broomfield, CO, located on Rocky Mountain Metropolitan Airport. Member of West Restorations, LLC board of directors.

Basset, Charlie – See West, Charlie.

Bellini, Antonio (Tony) – One of Howard Collingsworth's "investigators" tasked with finding and capturing Emli Collingsworth or her lookalike. Partnered with Tommy Laker.

Bingham, Lucky – Owner and pilot of P-51, *Trust Me*. Lives in Oregon.

Brown, Cecil – South African agent sent by Deputy Minister of State Security Elrich Voster and Deputy Minister Vincent deVon to watch Cathy Williamson and Charlie West. Partnered with Claude Schmidt.

-C-

Celia – See Gibbings, Celia.

Collingsworth, Catherine – Older of two daughters of Howard and Mary Collingsworth (34). Birthday July 20. Sister Emli.

Collingsworth, Emli – Missing younger of two daughters of Howard and Mary Collingsworth (32). Birthday June 12. Sister Catherine.

Collingsworth, Howard - Owner and founder of International

Opportunities, a multinational commercial land development and construction firm. Married to Mary and has two daughters, Emli and Catherine.

-D-

Delany, Oscar – Attorney in Detroit; Mary's mother's attorney when she was alive.

deVon, Karl – Deputy Minister of Rural Development - Assistant to South Africa's Minister of Rural Development.

-E-

Eight – West's nickname when he flies pace, chase, and safety for various racing classes. Named for the eight o'clock formation position he flies.

Emli's college friends

Celia Gibbings (domestic and family law)

Norman Kent (business, domestic, and family law)

Marty Logan (archaeological law and ethics)

Ben Scroles (banking law)

Nancy Gomez (business law)

-G-

Ghost Ranch Hands

John "Ratchet" Powers – Lead mechanic, pilot, Ghost Three (40)

Lester "Lenny" James – Mechanic, pilot, Ghost Four (31)

Jimmy "Bump" Ashward – Mechanic, pilot, Ghost Five (28)

Norm "Woody" Stold – Mechanic, pilot, Ghost Six (50+)

Rosita "Dani" Ventura – Pilot, Ghost Seven (20)

Bell "Eddie" Ventura – Pilot, Ghost Eight (18)

Jessie Miller – Security (30)

Cathy "Felix" Williamson – Pilot, Ghost Nine, Security (34)

Ghost Ranch, LLC Board

Board of Directors (voting):

Glen West (Griff Montgomery) – Chairman

Charlie West (Montgomery family)

Helen West (Montgomery family)

Richard Baron (Jet Services, Broomfield, CO)

Carl Henry (Henry & Sons Refining, Cactus, TX)

Bill Strong (NW New Mexico Ranching Supplies, Clayton, NM)

Investment and Legal Support (non-voting):

Thomas Grant (LLC Investment Manager)

Norman Kent (Legal Counsel, Colorado Springs, CO)

Ghost Ranch staff

Cappie Montez and wife, Celina, and sons Philip (21) and Peter (17).

Henry Astera and wife Gracie, Celina's cousin, sons George (18), Patrick (16), Billy (14) and daughter Camilla (15) help on big weekends and holidays. Moved to the ranch when Rosita started flying.

Robert Ventura and wife Madra and daughters Rosita (20) and Belle (18).

Becky (35), the Senior Ranch Cook.

Gibbings, Celia – See Kent, Celia.

Gibbings, June – Celia's sister (34).

Gibbings, Walter – Owner and co-owner of multiple stone quarries in New Hampshire, Maine, South Dakota, South Carolina, Texas, Italy, and Brazil. Widowed father of two daughters, June and Celia.

-J-

Jessie – See Miller, Jessie.

-K-

Kent, Celia – Wife of Norman Kent and one of Emli's college friends at Yale Law College (33). One sister, June. Father Walter. Mother deceased.

Kent, Norman – One of Emli's college friends from Yale Law College (35). Norman introduced Emli to the world of flying. Also a friend and husband of Celia Gibbings. Parents, Steve and Margaret. Younger sister Ronnie.

Kent, Ronnie – Norman's sister (20).

Kent, Steve – Norman's father. Wife Martha. Living in Shelbyville, outside of Louisville, KY. Daughter Ronnie.

Kullet, Curt – Owner and operator of High Plains Aviation on Meadow Lake Airport in Falcon, northeast of Colorado Springs.

-L-

Laker, Tommy – One of Howard Collingsworth's "investigators" tasked with finding and capturing Emli Collingsworth or her lookalike. Partnered with Tony Bellini.

Larry – Teamed with Benny, Larry is one of two additional investigators Howard hired to kidnap Charlie at the Broomfield fly-in.

Lawrence – Howard Collingsworth's lead negotiator in Paris.

Little, Will – Owner and operator of Central Colorado Aviation at Meadow Lake Airport in Falcon, northeast of Colorado Springs.

Lloyd – See Smithson, Lloyd.

-M-

Miller, Jessie – Software Coder (30). Originally hired by Griff Montgomery when she was seventeen. Stayed with his company when it sold and Griff left.

Mitchell, Fred – Officer with the Detroit Police Department, Third Precinct.

Montgomery, Grifford Westfield – Internet and Software Entrepreneur (38). Founder of an internet security company. Aka, Griff in family and business circles. Birthday March 19.

Montgomery, Helen – Widowed mother of Grifford Sr. (56). Aka Helen West. Trained and worked as a registered nurse, maintained her currency and credentials after moving to the Ranch.

Morgan, Matt – Private investigator working for Lloyd Smithson.

-N-
Norman – See Kent, Norman.
-P-
Peuler, Sam – Private investigator. One of Monte Williamson's "investigators" tasked with verifying public information on Charlie Bassett. Partnered with Lloyd Smithson.

Powers, John "Ratchet" – Ghost Ranch lead mechanic and shop foreman (41). Mechanic and pilot. Longtime friend of West's.

-S-
Sam – See Peuler, Sam

Schmidt, Claude – South African agent sent by Deputy Minister of State Security Elrich Voster and Deputy Minister Vincent deVon to watch Cathy Williamson and Charlie West. Partnered with Cecil Brown.

Setters, John – Owner and pilot of C model P-51 Mustang, Oh Seven Zulu (07Z), named *Malevolent Greetings*.

Smithson, Lloyd – Private investigator. One of Monte

Williamson's "investigators" tasked with verifying public information on Charlie Bassett. Partnered with Sam Peuler.

Smyth, Lydia – Charlie Bassett's aunt. Sister of Arthur Bassett. Buried in the family cemetery in Jackson, WY.

Stanik, Arthur – Private investigator hired as a South African agent to Deputy Minister of State Security Elrich Voster to watch Cathy Williamson and Charlie West when agents Schmidt and Brown are reassigned to look for Howard Collingsworth.

Strong, Bill – Owner of NW New Mexico Ranching Supplies, Clayton, NM. Bill is on the board of directors of West Restorations, LLC.

-T-

Tommy – See Laker, Tommy.

Tony – See Bellini, Antonio (Tony).

Troy, Buck – Runs a business supplying airplane restorers with hard-to-find aircraft parts. Longtime friend of Glen West.

-V-

Voster, Elrich – Deputy Minister of State Security - Assistant to South Africa's Minister of State Security.

-W-

Warren, Doc – "Adopted" uncle to Grifford. A family friend, Doc knew Grifford's father and mother when Grifford was a child. Doc was an air force mechanic.

West, Glen – Pilot, Ghost One. Mechanic and owner of West's Ghost Ranch and airplane restoration business, Glen West's Restorations. In the race circuit: works in the pits and flies some competition. Nicknames: West and Eight. Grifford Montgomery's alias. Father deceased. Mother, Helen, living with Glen on the Ghost Ranch.

West, Charlie – Glen West's wife. Pilot, Ghost Two, and mechanic. Birth certificate shows parents as Arthur and Sarah Bassett, deceased. Resided in Jackson, WY. Birthdate on her birth certificate is 4 July.

Williamson, Ralph – CEO and president of an East Coast multinational banking firm, Openlands Financials.

Williamson, Melony (Mel) – Daughter of Monte and Catherine (Felix). Birthday October 14 (11).

Williamson, Michael (Mike) – Son of Monte and Catherine (Felix). Birthday November 7 (10)

Williamson, Monte – Son of Ralph Williamson. Husband of Catherine (Cat) (Collingsworth) and father of son, Michael (Mike) (10), and daughter Melony (Mel) (11).

Williamson, Catherine – Wife of Monte Williamson by an arranged marriage when she was 17. Called "Cat" by her family and friends.

Places and Things:
-A-
AGL – <u>A</u>bove <u>G</u>round <u>L</u>evel. The term used when altitude is measured from the local terrain level.

Asti' – Navajo for "daughter."
-B-
'bilagáana' – Navajo expression meaning "white man."

-C-
Charlie's Airplanes –

Cessna 180, work airplane she restored until it was destroyed in a ground accident in Denver.

Legacy, a rebuild project to replace the 180.

North American TF-51 *My Affair*, a wedding gift from West.
-D-
Diné – Navajo for "tribe" or "clan."

-E-

'¿Estás listo para esto?' – Spanish expression for "Are you ready for this?"

-F-

FBO – <u>F</u>ixed <u>B</u>ase <u>O</u>perator. A business located on an airport.

-G-

Ghost Ranch, West's – Private ranch of Glenn West and his airplane restoration business. Structures consist of multiple, semi-buried hangars and a refueling ramp.

Airstrip:

> Flying field concept with the hangars in the middle of the usable surface area, approx. 1.5 miles in radius.

Mean elevation 5,840 ft.

Ghost Ranch LLC Airplanes –

Flying Utility:

> Cessna T206
>
> De Havilland Beaver – "Box Car" (29GW)

Flying Fighters:

> TF-51 Mustang * – *The Beautiful Lady* (07GW)
>
> P-40 Kittyhawk – *Anxious Delivery*
>
> P-51D Mustang – *Lucky Shot*
>
> P-51D Mustang – *Hell Raiser*
>
> SBD-5 Dauntless – *Deep Six*
>
> F6F-5 Hellcat – *Steppin' Out*
>
> Spitfire Mk XIVe – (Unnamed) (Griffon powered)
>
> Spitfire Mk IIIB – (Unnamed) (Merlin powered)
>
> F4U-5 Corsair** – *Your Bad Luck*

Flying, Personal: (Separately Owned)

Lancair Legacy – Charlie's personal airplane

TF-51 Mustang * – *My Affair,* subtitled *"Charlie's Other Man."* Charlie's personal airplane.

Airplanes in Restoration:

P-51C Mustang – (Unnamed)

AT-6B Texan – *Pistol Packin' Mama*

Customer Rebuild Projects:

Hawker Tempest – (Unnamed) Hubert Miles' rebuild project that West agrees to complete.

Available in Stores for Rebuild:

P-51D Mustang – (Unnamed)

P-51A Mustang – (Unnamed)

F4F-x Wildcat – (Unnamed)

P-38L Lightning – (Unnamed)

Typhoon Mk IB – (Unnamed)

Hurricane Mk IIA – (Unnamed)

Mosquito – (Unnamed)

Fw. 190 – (Unnamed)

SNJ-3 – (Unnamed)

Fw. 190A-3 – (Unnamed)

Bf. 109K-4 – (Unnamed)

A6M5 Reisen – Mitsubishi (Unnamed)

Fw. 190D-9 – (Unnamed)

* No Fuselage Fuel Tank; 2 ea. 85-gal. wing & 2 ea. 110-gal. drop tanks; equals 390-gal. total.

** 233-gal. fuselage fuel tank & 2 ea. 170-gal. drop tanks; equals 573-gal. total.

-H-

Halgai – Navajo for "prairie."

-K-

K'ébidishní – Navajo for "friend."

Kleshes – Navajo for "snakes."

-L-

Llanura – Spanish for "plain" as in a grassy plain.

-M-

Maicohs – Navajo for "wolves."

MSL – Mean Sea Level. A term used when altitude is measured from the mean elevation of sea level, worldwide.

-N-

Né'éshjaa' – Navajo for "owl."

Nítch'i – Navajo for "wind."

-V-

Vámonos – Spanish for "Let's go."

-Y-

Yá'át'ééh – Navajo for "good morning," "hello," or literally, "it is good, the morning."

Preview

An excerpt from When the Past and Present Collide,
Charlie's Promise Part 3
Ghost Ranch Series, Book 6

"Well, the website indicates the Maria Jefferson Ranch," Pat was saying, reading from her phone as Arthur Stanik pulled off the highway at the El Moro exit north of Trinidad and stopped at the same rest area they had stopped at that morning, "is named for Maria Felipa Montoya, the daughter of Rafael Montoya, a noted horse breeder near Seville Spain. She and her husband established Jefferson Farms in Kentucky. Rafael passed back in the Eighties."

"So, who's been running things since then?" Arthur asked as they walked up to the rest area's stone and glass building.

"Don't know yet," she answered and left him to find the Men's room on his own.

He was waiting when she rejoined him and they resumed their discussion as they walked back to the car. "It seems, the Seville operation is under a trust that Rafael set up and still raises horses under the original ranch's name."

"So what about the ranch here?" he asked as he opened the car door for Pat.

He hurried around the front of the car, slid in the driver's side and started the engine.

"Maria Felipa Montoya was nineteen when she married Robert Thomas Jefferson of Kentucky. She came to the states with him and the two of them continued the legacy of raising horses. Thoroughbreds and specialty breeds."

"So, I presume this ranch has something to do with the

Kentucky horse business." He headed north on I-25.

"Yes. It appears this ranch was established to continue and rehabilitate the wild Mustang breeds. The website says the horses are raised on the various ranches in the Montoya Farms Corporation but it doesn't say where the corporation is headquartered. Oh, there is a url for *serious inquiries only.*"

He laughed softly. "I take it Maria has passed and the corporation runs the ranches under various Montoya ancestral names." He glanced at Pat and smiled at her focus.

"Yes, there are six counting the Maria. They are the Consuela, the Gabriela, the Lucinda, the Rafaela, and the Trini ranches listed, but the website does not show where they are. Not even the Maria."

"Well, horses can be expensive assets." He chuckled. "And as we've seen, they are a bit protective of their investments."

"And I suppose," she continued, "the airplanes are used to help keep track of the herds?"

"And probably fences and anything else they need to keep track of." He chuckled again. "Even unannounced visitors."

"Yeah. We know all about that." She chuckled with him.

"I guess the part that worries me the most," Charlie explained from where she sat beside West on the front veranda love seat, "is that he's a PI, and that means he's looking for something—"

"Or someone," Felix added.

June sat beside Ratchet, Lenny stood behind Jess and Monte sat beside Felix, listening. Helen sat in the chair at West's end of the love seat.

"We have no way of knowing what he's looking for," Ratchet countered, "anything other than the Glen West Restorations, like he said."

West nodded and held Charlie's eyes for a long moment. "I know this worries you, but you know that we have had people looking for the mysterious Ghost Ranch and the place where our restorations are kept for many years. I agree we should continue to keep watch and we can check with Will and others to see if he's been asking a lot of questions around the smaller airports."

"As for Security," Jess interjected, "we have very good pictures of him and the woman with him. We'll know them if they come around again."

"I don't think they'll just come snooping around," Helen added. "I don't know what you, Ratchet and Lenny did, but the expression on their faces when he saw you three and then went for his binoculars, was priceless."

"We couldn't see what they saw," Felix added. "What did you do?"

Jess smiled and looked away for a second. "Well, I've never had to *greet* anyone that way before, so we just parked side-by-side about a half mile up the road, on the last rise before the gate. And then Ratchet and Lenny stood up with a rifle cradled in their arms. I'm too short to just stand up and look intimidating, so I climbed up on the tallest thing I could find, the hood of my jeep, and then I cradled my rifle in my arms."

"And wearing a gun belt and side arm and that weathered hat must've helped a lot." Charlie chuckled, concocting a mental image of her. "Once he got a look at you through the binoculars—I imagine something like a cross between *Hannie Caulder,* and *Sarita* from *100 Rifles*—it sure didn't take him long to get the message."

Jess snickered behind her open hand then looked at Felix. "Thanks for the help rewriting that alert program and for delivering the greeting."

"You're welcome," Felix responded. "I was a bit apprehensive to have to read it, but I just envisioned myself as a recorded message."

Charlie turned to look at West. "That makes me wonder. I've been here for just over a year now, not to mention a few visits before that, but this is the first time anyone mentioned an official name for the ranch. Why haven't I heard this before?" She looked at Helen. "And all you said was that it was named after your grandmother."

"Well, first," West added in an effort to help Charlie understand, "once we're *on* the ranch and coming and going by air, the *official* name is somewhat unimportant. I never thought to mention it. Sorry."

Charlie shook her head and turned back to Helen. "So what's the story?"

"Not too much of a story, really. Maria Felipa Montoya was my grandmother. Her family is from Spain, Seville actually, a well-known horse family. How they chose Maria's name, I don't know, but it fit her perfectly. She was spirited, rebellious when she didn't like what was going on or when she was told what to do. She was obstinate and what one might call a wild-child today. She married Robert Thomas Jefferson from Danville, deep in the heart of horse country. They are my grandparents. He told me once that her fire and deep love of her horses, why she was named Felipa, was one of the things that drew him to her, besides being a fair beauty in her own right. He was visiting Montoya Farms in Spain with his father and met Maria there. He said it was love at first sight and they were married two years later when they were both nineteen.

"When Glen decided to buy the Ghost Ranch, he knew he had to give it a public name and being here in cattle country, horses would not be too big of a stretch to believe. We talked and he chose to name it after Maria. He even built a website that touts it as a place that raises, rehabilitates and breeds wild Mustangs"—Helen's eyes twinkled.

"But we don't—" Jess' response was cut short by Lenny's laugh. "What?"

"Mustangs. Get it?" he tried to explain through his chuckles. "Only ours are actually made of sheet metal and powered by Merlin engines."

Jess' eyes widened and she slowly smiled. "Okay, okay. I get it! I maybe slow, but I get it."

"Need to get away from your software occasionally," Lenny continued and slipped his arms around her shoulders in a tight, affectionate hug.

Books by Aidan Red:

West's Ghost Ranch Series
Eight's Warning
(A tale in the world of high octane aviation fuel and restored warbirds)
Book 1: *The Past Hunts*
Book 2: *The Past Attacks*
Book 3: *The Price of Escape*
Charlie's Promise
Book 4: *A Most Uncertain Present*
Book 5: *The Present Conspires*
Book 6: *When the Past and Present Collide*

Paladin Shadows Series
Terran Assignment
Book 1: *Things Are Not As They Seem*
Book 2: *When Luck Is Not Enough*
Book 3: *Fate Has A Different Idea*
Terran Recruits
Book 4: *In the Wake of Chaos*
Book 5: *Terran Talents Join Forces*
Book 6: *New Rules of Engagement*
Operation Retribution
Book 7: *The Training Phase*
Book 8: *Taking the Fight Off-World*
Book 9: *Luring the Prince Into the Open*

More Books by Aidan Red
Paladin Shadows Series (Continued)
Garda Nua
Book 10: *The Proliferation of Talent*
Book 11: *When A Planet Is Stolen*
Book 12: *Right Does Not Ask Permission*

Assignment: Casha-Six
Book 13: *No Warning*
Book 14: *The Best Laid Plans*
Book 15: *A change of Heart?*

Keeper and His Tiger Series
(After living homeless to find his parents murderer...)
Book 1: *An Unexpected Complication*
Book 2: *Deadly Undercurrents*
Book 3: *The Trap*

Fearin' the Banshee

About the Author

Aidan Red's passion for aviation and aircraft design, engineering, and a deep interest in space and space travel go back many years. An avid reader from an early age, Aidan, with great trepidation, ventured into the world of writing during college. With real world experience in business aviation, Aidan's creative side led him to create an alternate world where the beautiful Riggs Valley was born and Shara's life became chronicled in his epic science fiction series, Paladin Shadows.

Paladin Shadows consists of the five triptychs (three-part works), *Terran Assignment, Terran Recruits, Operation Retribution, Garda Nua* and *Assignment: Casha-Six.* In between the Paladin triptychs, Aidan has penned three, three book series, *Keeper and his Tiger Series,* and *Eight's Warning,* and *Charlie's Promise* in West's Ghost Ranch Series and a novel, *Fearin' the Banshee.*

The unpublished books in his various series are scheduled for release on a regular basis in the coming months.

You can visit

www.RedsInkandQuill.com or

www.AdianRedBooks.com

for more information on Aidan Red's books and where to purchase them.

www.ingramcontent.com/pod-product-compliance
Lightning Source LLC
Chambersburg PA
CBHW070808180626
46818CB00001B/157